Stepping into the Light

By
Dan Schmelzer

Cover: The Descent from the Cross is the central panel of a triptych painting by Peter Paul Rubens in 1612–1614. It is still in its original place, the Cathedral of Our Lady, Antwerp, Belgium. This particular work was commissioned on September 7, 1611, by the Confraternity of the Arquebusiers, whose Patron Saint was St. Christopher.

This is a faithful photographic reproduction of a two-dimensional, public domain work of art. The work of art itself is in the public domain for the following reason: This work is in the public domain in the United States because it was published (or registered with the U.S. Copyright Office) before January 1, 1923.

ISBN: 1793169098

TABLE OF CONTENTS

STUDY GUIDE

Chapter One:
Disappointment

They were exhausted: physically, emotionally, and spiritually! That is how Nicodemus and Joseph felt as they sat exhausted, in Joseph's home. The sun had just set and Sabbath had just begun. They had rushed to bury the one they believed to be Messiah! Their flowing robes were stained with blood, with his blood. These robes marked them as members of the powerful Jewish ruling council. "Sanhedrin" as it was called, in Greek *synedrion*. In their tongue — *bet din ha-gadol*. They no longer felt powerful. Anticipation had given way to disillusionment. Hope had been dashed just outside the Shechem gate on the rocky outcropping called Golgotha. There the one they came to believe was the promised King of Israel was nailed to a cross. Their own brothers in the "Council" had rejected him and sentenced him to death. But without the power to execute, they had turned him over to the Roman Procurator Pontius Pilate who earlier that morning sentenced him to the most tortuous death penalty ever devised by human beings. Suspended on a wooden cross by three long nails, Jesus had hung for six long hours as Nicodemus and Joseph watched the King of Kings slowly die the death of the worst criminals.

For a long time they didn't move. Their own sweat, mixed with the blood of Yeshua, dripped from their beards onto the finely tiled floor. They were too tired to weep, too confused. Finally Nicodemus heaved a heavy sigh, turned to Joseph and said, *"The Centurion, he spoke to Caiaphas in Aramaic. Did you hear him?"*

"I did." Joseph replied, *"He spoke with a Galilean accent. And when Yeshua died, he called him 'righteous and the son of God.' I couldn't believe it at first,"*

Nicodemus answered, *"A Centurion confessed while the High Priest mocked!"*

1

Nicodemus wiped his arm with his hand. The blood was no longer liquid; it had become sticky and thick.

"But now, I don't know what to think." Nicodemus continued, *"What I can't figure out is why he allowed it. I mean, it doesn't make any sense to me. We saw him perform so many miracles. Powerful miracles. He healed and even brought his friend Lazarus back from the dead! We were there. We helped bury Lazarus, remember?*

He could defeat any of the brightest minds in the Council. Remember when they tried to trap him with the woman caught in adultery? Remember how that ended? Other times they wanted to stone him! He just slipped away... But not this time!" The two sat for a long time before Nicodemus continued, *"Why? It is almost as if he wanted it to happen!"*

"His mother, Mary, told us why!" Joseph replied, *"For now, let's get out of these bloody clothes and wash. You are welcome to spend Sabbath here. Celebrate Sabbath with us, Nicodemus. Perhaps it will bring us some solace. After all, you know we can't go to the Temple. We are unclean. We touched the .... dead."* With that Joseph wept silently, his voice cracking. His Rabbi, the one they called "Lord" was gone and he still could not quite believe it all.

Just the night before, Nicodemus and Joseph had laughed and rejoiced as they celebrated the Pesach (Passover). The two families had shared a yearling lamb. Although both of their families were more than able to afford a lamb alone, they often shared feast days together. They and Gamaliel the teacher were the only ones in the Sanhedrin of 71 who had concluded privately and spoken openly that Jesus of Nazareth was in fact the promised Messiah, the coming King who would sit on David's throne and restore Israel to its glory again. Others believed but feared speaking out. Still others were sympathetic but were also afraid. They had eaten the Passover and recalled how God miraculously had delivered his people from slavery through Moses. It had been such a joyous evening. They even contemplated that this might perhaps be the day when Jesus would reveal himself publicly as Messiah. They had even dared to consider how Pilate and Herod would lose their thrones to Jesus. But now, those imaginations were just that: dreams, long lost hopes.

Sarah, Joseph's wife of 35 years, interrupted their reminiscing and announced that the simple Sabbath meal was ready. Rachel, Nicodemus' wife, had already gone home with their boys. As they reclined on the plush benches covered with richly ornate patterns and prayed, it struck both of them at the same time: Yesterday there was feasting and anticipation! Tasty food and full hearts. Tonight: nothing, just some bitter herbs and unleavened bread left over from Pesach. *"How fitting!"* they both whispered at the same time! With everything that had happened on this Day of Preparation, they now felt completely unprepared for what the future might bring!

Something inside them seemed to be coming to an end as they sat quietly, reciting the Scriptures from Genesis, Exodus and Deuteronomy. As was tradition, Joseph as the male host began the meal and lifted the bread, *"Blessed are you Lord God, King of the Universe, who bringeth forth bread from the earth!"*

He broke it and handed it to his wife and Nicodemus. This Passover Sabbath was supposed to bring true rest: deliverance, freedom and salvation. But now it seemed like restless, faithless, servitude.

Looking back more than 14 centuries to the Exodus, each man began to reflect on his own life. *"So much change from where I started,"* Nicodemus whispered to himself, *"So much change!"* He raised his head and met Joseph's eyes. Moist with tears he continued, *"He taught me to have a courageous faith, to look at my life honestly, to find peace in the Lord's mercy instead of my own perception of obedience. From my youth I never dreamed such honest peace was even possible!"* Nicodemus looked off into the distance as he gathered his thoughts. *"Joseph, I never told you this: when I was only 10, I believe I met Yeshua!"*

3

Chapter Two:
Ein Karem

(Flashback 33 years to 6BC)

"Tela, let's go! Zechariah will be here any minute!" Nicodemus' father, Benjamin, had called him "Tela" since he was about two because he had such a sensitive spirit. Nicodemus had never felt the cane that other fathers used to reprimand their children. A mere glance from his father when he had misbehaved would send the small boy running and weeping for his mother. He would crawl into his mother's lap sobbing, *"Mama, I'm sorry! Please forgive me"* before she even knew what the offense was. When he was five and ready for Beth Sepher (an elementary school at the synagogue conducted by the Rabbi) his father explained to him the meaning behind the name. "Tela" was a word for a small, wounded, male lamb in their mother tongue: Aramaic. *"Now you are a 'big boy' and no longer a little lamb,"* Benjamin shared with his only son. *"Maybe you would prefer I no longer call you "Tela."*

But Nicodemus just smiled and said, *"No Papa, I love it. It means you love me. Just as we learned at Beth Sepher, the Lord Almighty chastises those he loves! King Solomon wrote that!"* Benjamin was always impressed with Tela's knowledge of the Hebrew Scriptures. And from that day the nickname stuck.

Now that Nicodemus was nearly 10 years old, he would be transferring to a school in Jerusalem where his father served as a priest at the temple. There he would study the oral Torah. He had yet to meet his Rabbi. All week he had been asking his father about the different Rabbis in Jerusalem and what each was like. Benjamin served as a priest at the temple on rotation; his division would serve for one week every six months and then he would come home to Ein Karem. That continued until one of the three major festivals when a larger percentage of the priests came to Jerusalem to serve the worshiping Jewish population. Every male over 21 was required in Jerusalem for these festivals and the city population swelled to many

4

times its normal population size. At Pesach (Passover) there could be as many as 2-3 million families represented in Jerusalem. This was going to be Tela's first visit to Jerusalem with his father for Pesach. He would be staying at the house where his father stayed with other priests and he couldn't wait. They would be traveling there with Zechariah, his father's longtime friend who also lived in Ein Karem. They were on the same rotation and almost always walked the six miles together.

Tela loved Zechariah. He and his wife Elizabeth were almost like second parents to him. They were older than his mother and father and until just a few months ago, had no children. The whole town was still buzzing five months later at the miraculous birth of little John. Nicodemus remembered his father telling him that Zechariah and Elizabeth had taken a vow for the boy and that he would be raised as a Nazarite. *"Why didn't you take a vow for me?"* Nicodemus remembers asking his father. Nicodemus knew that the three to four hours it would take to walk to Jerusalem would be filled with stories recalling Zechariah's "Episode", as he called it. In the Temple he had seen an angel telling him he would have a son. Tela couldn't wait. He loved these kinds of conversations. He had often asked deep questions of his Rabbi at Beth Sepher in Ein Karem. In fact, the Rabbi often mentioned to Benjamin that Nicodemus showed much promise as a student of the Scriptures and could one day sit at the feet of one of the great Rabbi teachers in Jerusalem. The mere mention of his son one day becoming a *Talmidim* (disciple) of someone like Gamaliel, the grandson of the great Hillel, always sent a shiver down Benjamin's spine.

Nicodemus gathered up his clothes along with the dried fish and figs his mother had set out for their journey. He was longing to listen in on the conversation his father would have with Zechariah. He hoped to ask a few questions of his own. *"Meeting an angel! "What an honor from God,"* Nicodemus thought to himself. He had so many questions not only about the angel and what it looked like but his message to Zechariah.

Zechariah never knocked when he entered Benjamin and Rachel's home. He was a tall and burley man, a head taller than anyone Nicodemus knew. He had a graying beard and bushy eyebrows and Nicodemus always thought it made him look wise. He looked like an older version of his own father. Zechariah had such a fondness for little Tela and seemed to show more compassion and gentleness with him than any of the other children in the community. This touched Tela's heart with a deep love for the old man.

"Are we ready for the big journey, Tela?" Zechariah shouted as he entered.

"I can't wait." Nicodemus replied. *"Has father told you who will be my Rabbi at the Temple?"* Nicodemus whispered.

With a wry knowing smile, Zechariah responded, *"Haven't heard a thing, little one but I'm sure your father has arranged the best one for you."*

Benjamin appeared from an inner room as Zechariah and Nicodemus were talking. *"Let's go men!"* Benjamin said, looking right at Tela and smiling. He gave Rachel a big hug and the three headed out the door, ready for the long walk to Jerusalem.

As the three walked along, they began to descend from the hill top village of Ein Karem. The town center had a flowing spring which watered the surrounding vineyards and orchards. It was a small town with only about 200 residents, mostly farmers who grew grapes and olive trees on the terraced slopes of the southern hills surrounding the small village. The road was more of a path that meandered around small olive and grape farms. Zechariah and Benjamin knew the paths well, but this journey was new to Nicodemus. He had never ventured farther than their family vineyard in his 10 short years and he was often distracted by the new vistas as they made their way. He walked behind his father and this made it even more difficult for him to hear the conversation between his Father and the elderly priest. He knew they would have to stop and rest often along the way as climbing a hill left Zechariah winded.

6

But the old priest seemed to have a bounce in his step since the miraculous birth of his son. And sure enough, after climbing the first hill, Benjamin insisted they sit and rest awhile. They had often discussed the events of "the birth" but not with Nicodemus. Benjamin knew just how much his son wanted to hear the details. He had been pestering him for the last five months ever since the birth. His father gave his son a knowing wink and asked, *"Tell me again Zachariah, what was it like to meet an angel face to face?"* Nicodemus turned to Zechariah, intently listening to the old priest's response. This was the very question he wanted answered. Zechariah smiled broadly and said, *"This may not be for every child's ears but Tela is something special, and Rabban Terah has remarked often to me what a brilliant mind and keen knowledge of the Scriptures Tela has. So let me give him a few details about that day: It was my duty to enter the temple, to approach the altar of incense in the Holy Place. You know Tela, that altar stands directly in front of the veil in the Holy Place. That veil is the only thing between you and the Ark of the Covenant inside the Holy of Holies. The altar is overlaid with gold and even though I have never entered the Most Holy Place, I imagine it is the most impressive piece in the Temple except for the Ark."*

Zechariah wanted to continue to speak about the Altar of Incense but could tell that Nicodemus was anxiously waiting to hear about the angel. *"I was about to light the incense which I had just placed on the flat surface of the altar,"* Zechariah continued. *"Just as I began turning to light the flame from one of the candlesticks, there before me standing in brilliant white was the angel Gabriel!"*

"How did you know it was Gabriel?" Nicodemus asked anxiously.

"He told me! He said, 'I am Gabriel'" Zechariah responded beaming!

"Wow, did he have anything in his hand?" Tela asked.

"Why yes, how did you know that Tela?" Zechariah asked. *"Rabban Terah often described Gabriel the Archangel as holding a golden*

scroll. Just last year we read about Gabriel in the <u>Book of Enoch</u>" Tela continued, breathing fast and almost shaking with excitement. *"What did he say?"*

"He told me that the Lord had heard our prayers, mine and Elizabeth's. You know we had been praying for a child for a long, long time. I should be honest and say that it was more of a routine now after all these years. You know, Tela, women cannot give birth after a certain age." Zechariah gave Benjamin a knowing nod.

"I know, I know." Nicodemus answered with a groan, *"Papa talked about all that with me last year. . .what else?"*

"He told me what you already know. We were to have a son and that he would be a special man and be great in the sight of God and a delight to many!"

"What does that mean: 'A delight to many?'" Nicodemus asked.

"Gabriel said he will be a man who will speak in the spirit of Elijah,...and I still have not figured out what this means but he said, 'to make ready a people prepared for the Lord!'"(Luke 1:17)

"That's the coming of Messiah!" Tela blurted out almost shouting, *"Messiah is coming, and your baby will prepare us for that day! When? Did he say when?"*

"Wait, Tela, there's more. You remember I could not talk for a long time last year? I never told anyone why I could not talk for nine months. Everyone just concluded that it was because of the vision, but....it was because of my lack of faith. I...didn't believe Gabriel. I told him I am an old man and old men don't have babies."

"But this was Gabriel the archangel!" Tela interrupted with just a hint of correction in his tone.

"Tela!" his father scolded. *"Don't speak to Zechariah in that tone."*

At that, the wounded lamb for which Tela was named, surfaced. He blushed and apologized, *"I'm so sorry Zechariah, please forgive me. I got excited."*

"My dear boy," Zechariah spoke in a comforting tone. *"I know. But you did speak the truth. I should have trusted Gabriel's words.*

This was the Lord speaking and I doubted. Gabriel told me I would not speak until the baby would be born. I was forced to keep quiet about the event and this taught me a valuable lesson. Faith comes by hearing, not talking! I learned to measure my words more carefully."

"Yes, I remember you shouting when John was circumcised," Nicodemus stood up tall and reenacted the old man's bold statement: ***"His name is John!"*** (Luke 1:63)

"Let's talk more when we reach the crest of that next hill," Benjamin interrupted. Benjamin was overjoyed to watch his son interact with Zechariah. With that the three stood and made their way around the olive grove on the slope of the hill. Along each Olive grove terrace was a narrow trail with steps that had been reinforced with stepping stones. This prevented erosion and made it easier to move up and down the terrace. As they moved along, Tela continued to comment to himself on the scene Zechariah had described. Every few minutes, he would interrupt with *"Amazing!" "The angel Gabriel, unbelievable!"* This brought a chuckle from the men. They too were amazed, but they had discussed this event countless times already.

Nicodemus began singing as they reached the bottom of the hill. It was a melody taught to him by Rabban Terah and it had helped him to memorize words from the Torah. They often sang in school after a lesson had been taught. The lessons were long portions of Scriptures which students would reproduce on long scrolls. Rabban Terah focused mostly on the first five books of Scripture. One of Nicodemus favorites was the Covenant with Abram. Tela had made up his own melody for this Scripture. He loved the image of Abram looking out at the night sky and the verses to the song told the story of the conversation between God and Abram. Nicodemus added a chorus from a verse that repeated every few sentences:

"Abram believed the Lord and he credited it to him as righteousness." (Genesis 15:6) When Nicodemus sang the chorus his voice swelled on the words: "believed" and "righteousness." The last verse was his favorite even though he did not understand the imagery. Nicodemus always sang this verse with a dark and foreboding tone: ***"When the sun had set and darkness had fallen, a smoking firepot with a blazing torch appeared and passed between the pieces."*** (Genesis 15:17) He had asked his father about this image many times, but his father never answered him to his satisfaction.

Then as Nicodemus had finished his last chorus, he remained quiet for a long time. His Rabbi had taught his class of 15 boys that contemplation and quietness was an important element of their studies. Terah had said, *"When God spoke the Law to Moses, he would often pause after a time to let Moses think and contemplate the meaning. We do the same. So keep quiet and focus on the Word of the Lord. Always remember, faith comes from listening!"* This was a discipline Nicodemus learned and practiced. He would often walk the hills around his home alternating between singing long portions of the Torah and then keeping quiet and contemplating the Word of the Lord.

As they reached the top of the hill, Nicodemus was still quiet and swaying as he walked, at times humming the chorus. *"I love that tune,"* Zechariah turned and smiled at Nicodemus as he sat and rested on a large stone. *"That image of the animals cut in two with the blood trail between them, do you know what it means, Tela?"* Zechariah asked.

"I think so." Nicodemus replied. *"A covenant is sealed with blood. It reminds Abram that this is a life and death agreement with God."*

"Correct," Zechariah answered, *"but why blood?"*

"Well, Leviticus tells us that life is in the blood. (Lev. 17:11) And when animals are sacrificed in the Temple, the spilling of blood brings forgiveness," Nicodemus answered.

"You will learn more about this in Bet Midrash when you study Halachot (Rabbinic Law). I've told your father that I think you are ready now, but you can't enter Bet Midrash until you are 13."

10

"Can I ask you one more thing about the angel Gabriel, Zechariah," Nicodemus asked.

"Go ahead," Zechariah responded.

"Gabriel told you that John was not to drink any wine or have his hair cut! That sounds like Samson or Samuel. Is John going to be a prophet or a judge?" Nicodemus asked.

"Good question, Tela, you have an inquisitive mind. He will be someone special. I know that. And I will most likely not see that day since I am already an old man. Maybe Gabriel knew that and didn't think I needed to know all the details. But one day you *will know!"* Zechariah replied with a hint of resignation.

"That will be a great day," Nicodemus replied, *"Surely something special is going to happen in the coming years."*

Benjamin wanted to join in but was so enjoying the conversation between his son and the elderly priest, he just kept quiet. Finally, he said, *"Well, that should be our last rest before Jerusalem; we will see the city just over that next small hill. The easiest path for Zechariah will be to take the road and enter from the north through the Shechem Gate. I think that will also impress Tela. It is such a busy gate."*

Benjamin also knew that Zechariah would be annoyed at the sight of Herod's Palace that dominated the southwest corner of the city. This half Jew and Edomite was an offense to the old man. He had seen Herod come to power. He rose from Governor of the Galilee to King of Judea. While some in the current Council of 71 took a more pragmatic approach to Herod now that he was in his late 60's and was becoming more and more a puppet of Rome, Zechariah would have none of it. Yes, he had rebuilt the Holy Temple and it was almost finished and magnificent; yet Zechariah found the King lacking in humility, arrogant, consumed by lust and just like his father Antipater. Antipater had endeared himself to Caesar and had been made Procurator of all of Judea. Antipater immediately appointed his two sons governors in Judea and Galilee. At just 25, Herod began his power grab by putting down a resistance by a man

11

named Hezekiah and in short order had him executed. Every member of the Sanhedrin back then was united in opposition to this flaunting of Jewish law.

Zechariah remembered well the day that Herod had marched into the meeting of the Sanhedrin in full military regalia, elevating himself above Jewish law. Now Herod was King in place of his father. It had been a bloody transition thirty years earlier when Herod, having been declared "king of the Jews" by the Roman Senate, returned to Judea and three long years of conflict ensued. In Herod's absence a man by the name of Aristobolus took control of Judea with the help of the Parthians. Eventually Herod prevailed, and it was rumored that Herod had drowned Aristobolus in his own bath and declared himself "Basileus", *"King of the Jews."* Thirty years later, Herod was now paranoid and subject to his baser instincts. He had his own sons killed, fearing they might take his throne. Ironically, he still observed Jewish dietary laws and would not eat pork. This convoluted lifestyle led Caesar Augustus to comment, *"I would rather be Herod's pig than his son!"* Rumors of licentious orgies in Herod's palace only increased Zechariah's disdain and he always avoided the gate next to the palace, preferring to walk north to the Shechem gate even though it meant an extra hour on his journey. Benjamin remembered Zechariah commenting that he felt unclean just looking at Herod's palace.

Nicodemus had continued his singing as they approached the road that led to the Shechem gate. As he sang some of his favorite Psalms, Zechariah joined in. Together they sang one of the "Songs of Ascent". He had taught Tela some of these traditional Psalms sung by pilgrims who came to Jerusalem for the festivals. The road they walked had been paved with stones by Roman construction crews years earlier. This made the walking easier and the singing became more energetic. Others who were coming for Pesach joined in a traditional favorite which many Jewish pilgrims sang at the first sight of Jerusalem:

I lift up my eyes to the mountains—where does my help come
from?
My help comes from the Lord, the Maker of heaven and earth. He
will not let your foot slip—he who watches over you will not
slumber;
indeed, he who watches over Israel will neither slumber nor sleep.
The Lord watches over you—the Lord is your shade at your right
hand;
The sun will not harm you by day, nor the moon by night.
The Lord will keep you from all harm—he will watch over your
life;
The Lord will watch over your coming and going both now and
forevermore. (Psalm 121:1-8)

A Jewish boys' first sight of Jerusalem could be overwhelming, and Nicodemus was no different. They approached the city gate called Shechem by Jews (Damascus by Gentiles), for the road led to the city that was the first capital of Israel. Nicodemus began to point with wide eyed amazement as they passed through the market just inside the city gate. It had taken just over four hours to walk from Ein Karem to Jerusalem. They had left home a little late in the morning and it was approaching the time for the evening sacrifice. Benjamin would not be assisting on this day, but they did want to be at the temple for the sacrifice before settling in for the evening. There were also only a few hours left to obtain a few provisions for Shabbat the next day when they would not be able to buy anything. Nicodemus had almost finished the figs and dried fish on the way, so they needed to buy a few things that they would not have to cook that evening after Sabbath began. Nicodemus was easily distracted by all the new sights, and Benjamin had to repeatedly remind him to walk a little faster. But Nicodemus hardly heard his father over the hawkers along the narrow road that meandered through the city. The number of Roman soldiers increased as they neared the Antonio Fortress, another huge eyesore to Zechariah. Herod had made a point of making sure the Roman fortress tower was 75 feet taller than the temple.

Herod seemed to take delight in irritating the Sanhedrin. Their condemnation of him when he was still Governor of Galilee, 35 years earlier, had made the man very bitter. The animosity was mutual. The Fortress was an imposing structure that dominated the city, and from the southern-most tower the temple courtyard could easily be observed. Herod had even constructed a secret underground passageway from the Fortress to the Temple courtyard. This made for quick access by soldiers who could easily put down any uprising in a matter of moments. Nicodemus would soon be exposed to all these political issues, so Zechariah held his tongue as they approached the Fortress on the way to the entrance to the Temple courts.

Benjamin stopped at a stall that sold bread, cheese and figs. He had frequented this business regularly as he knew the family to be honest people. They greeted each other warmly. Just as they stepped back into the street, four Roman soldiers walked passed them. It was the first time Nicodemus had seen a soldier up close. With the approach of Pesach, several additional centuriae (80) had been brought in to keep the peace. Sometimes as many as a cohort (480) or six centuriae would be added to the 600 who stayed permanently on duty at the Fortress. It was common to see soldiers in the market buying a spiced wine mixed with honey called mulsum, bread, and vegetables. They too knew that food supplies would not be available for the next 24 hours. These soldiers were cordial but not too friendly. They knew that with the approaching Shabbat and Pesach, devout Jews like Zechariah and Benjamin would not want to risk becoming unclean from Gentile contact. It did not surprise Nicodemus that both Zechariah and his father took a step back as the soldiers passed. They both looked down at the same time, not wanting to engage the soldiers in any conversation. The soldiers stopped at the next stall; Nicodemus watched as they bought apples and several skins of wine. He caught the eye of one of the men as he picked up the wine. The man gave him a short smile and nodded briefly as they turned together and headed back to the Fortress.

"We have what we need." Benjamin took Nicodemus by the hand. *"Let's get going. We can worship and then retire for the evening at our house. Nicodemus and I still have to purify ourselves at the mikveh before we enter the Temple courts."* Twice a day, the priests sacrificed a lamb in the temple for morning and evening sacrifice. Nicodemus had learned the words from Numbers by heart as preparation for his time at the temple. ***"See that you present to me at the appointed time the food for my offerings made by fire as an aroma pleasing to me. This is the offering made by fire that you are to present to the Lord: two lambs a year old without defect as a regular burnt offering each day. Prepare one lamb in the morning and the other at twilight together with a grain offering of the tenth of an ephah of fine flour mixed with a quarter of a hin of oil from pressed olives."*** (Numbers 28:2-5) Benjamin charged Nicodemus to stay at the base of the Southern Steps while he and Zechariah made their way to the priest's mikveh. After immersing themselves in the mikveh, they changed into clean robes and departed to rejoin Nicodemus. The three climbed the broad, steep steps along with many others and entered the courtyard. The evening sacrifice was to be performed at twilight, but the chief priests had altered the time for their own convenience to the ninth hour (3:00 PM). This annoyed Zechariah and Benjamin, but they chose to focus on the substance of the daily evening sacrifice. They joined the throng in front of the temple. Already the lamb was about to be slaughtered as they approached the altar of burnt offering in front of the temple. The altar itself was larger than Nicodemus imagined. It was more than 50 feet wide at the base and made from stones taken from virgin soil. No tool had been used on any of the stones, and they were fastened together with mortar, pitch and lead. The altar was three levels high, like a step pyramid, 22 feet high. The second level was 40 feet wide and the top level just slightly less where a fire was already burning. The altar had a walkway around it that enabled priests to easily bring

in wood and start multiple fires for sacrifices at different places on the altar.

Nicodemus watched in fascination as priests moved about, each performing a different function. Six priests were pouring water out of gold and silver pitchers over the lamb on the north side of the altar while others gathered around and examined the lamb for any defect. The designated sacrificing priest then came forward and led the lamb to the north-eastern corner of the altar. Zechariah whispered to Nicodemus, *"The morning sacrifice is done at the north-western corner and in the evening on the north-eastern corner so that the lamb always faces the sun as it is killed."* The fore and hind feet were bound together so that the animal could not struggle or run. Nicodemus felt frozen in place as elders to the side shouted, *"Open the gates!"* At that the gates to the temple opened slowly. Just as the last gate opened, Nicodemus heard three long trumpet blasts coming from somewhere inside the temple complex, followed by men in simple linen garments moving out of the temple court shouting: *"The evening sacrifice is offered!"*

People who had been busily moving through the market came to a standstill and faced the temple. Nicodemus pushed his way forward filled with curiosity as he saw the great gates inside the temple open to the Holy Place. As he glanced to his right, he heard the signal for the slaying of the lamb. One priest stepped forward, grabbed the head of the lamb and clenched the windpipe of the young lamb. He made a quick thrust upward with a knife severing the major artery in the lamb's neck. Another priest caught the stream of blood in a golden bowl. Nicodemus swallowed hard. He had never witnessed the sacrifice of an animal before. It touched him deeply. He had tended animals at home and was the one responsible for feeding and changing the straw in their pens. He helped with the shearing with his mother Rachel. But he had never before witnessed the slaughter of one. The priest with the golden bowl filled with blood approached one corner of the altar, moving the bowl in a circular pattern as he walked. This was to keep the blood from congealing. He dipped his

16

forefinger into the blood and used his thumb to sprinkle—almost flit—the blood from his forefinger onto the corner of the altar. A thin red line ran entirely around the base of the altar about four feet off the ground. The priest continued to sprinkle the corner of the altar below this red line until it began to run down the stones. He then moved to the corner farthest away from Nicodemus and did the same. Climbing the stairs to the top of the altar, he poured the remaining blood at the base of the altar. The blood pooled in front of the altar, overflowed and ran down a channel that eventually ran outside the temple and into the Kidron Valley. By this time Nicodemus had tears streaming down his face. He couldn't believe how willingly the lamb had died. It almost seemed to lift its head for the priest's knife to cut its neck. It had not even bleated. This young boy, Tela — the wounded lamb — sobbed quietly as the he watched the lamb bleed and die.

The priests left with the lamb and Zechariah explained to young Nicodemus that they had gone to an inner court of the priests where the lamb was being prepared for the sacrifice. And within a few moments six priests reentered, all carrying pieces of the lamb that had been flayed. As they reached the top of the altar, two priests sprinkled salt on each piece. These pieces were placed on the hot coals and the smell of roasting meat filled the temple court. Other priests carried the grain and drink offerings.

Just as Nicodemus assumed the sacrifice was concluded, Benjamin placed his hand on his son's shoulder to keep him from moving. All the priests had exited to the right. Benjamin bent over and whispered to Nicodemus. *"It is time for the prayer. Stand still!"* Later his father would explain to him that this was the most solemn part of the service. In the distance echoing from another room, all could hear the 2 dozen priests speaking in unison:

"With great love hast Thou loved us, O Lord our God and with much overflowing pity hast Thou pitied us."

At this Zechariah and Benjamin lifted their hands to the heavens. Nicodemus followed suit along with those assembled in the courtyard.

"Our Father and our King, for the sake of our fathers who trusted in Thee, and Thou taughtest them the statutes of life, have mercy upon us and enlighten our eyes."

After this the priests recited the 10 Commandments together. As they finished, the entire assembly raised their arms once more and spoke the "Shema" in unison:

"Hear O Israel: The Lord our God, the Lord is one. Love the Lord your God with all your heart and with all your soul and with all your strength!" (Deuteronomy 6:4,5)

Tela had been standing in front of his Father in order to see everything. As the assembly finished reciting, he turned and wrapped his arms around his father, buried his face in his robe and sobbed! *"The lamb of God!"* He repeated again and again between quiet sobs, *"Why?" How would he ever be able to endure this scene twice a day for the next three years!?*

Chapter Three:
Pesach

Benjamin and Zechariah shared the upper flat of a house, which was just steps from the Temple and enabled them easy access there the next morning. They would rise early for the casting of lots to determine their duty on Shabbat (Sabbath). But for now they wanted to settle into their home away from home. Many years ago they had arranged with several others of the 24 divisions of priests – called "cohanim" – to rent this house together, and it was nicely furnished. Each would stay twice a year for a week when it was their turn. Sometimes as many as 10 priests would stay together in the three-room apartment during the three festivals. Their landlord lived on the floor beneath them. He bought yearling lambs from shepherds in Bethlehem and sold them to the priests for the temple sacrifices. He made a tidy profit, especially during Pesach (Passover) week when every family in Jerusalem needed to buy a perfect male lamb on the Sunday before Pesach. This way he avoided the controversial practice of selling animals in the Gentile court in the Temple. As a result, he had regular clients among the priestly families who detested the intrusion into the court of Gentiles by animal hawkers. The upper flat had enough rooms for Nicodemus to stay here while other cohanim occupied the house, even when Benjamin's one week was finished. It was the perfect arrangement as Nicodemus would easily be able to walk to the room in the Temple where his new Rabbi would teach him for the next three years. He would eat with the friends of Benjamin and Zechariah in the Temple during class hours and then have his evening meal with the cohanim in the house.

Tela had recovered from the emotional experience in the Temple during evening sacrifice and he was now talking nonstop about the magnificence of the Temple, Solomon's Colonnade and the countless priests who practically filled the Jewish court for the sacrifice. All priests were welcome to serve during Pesach, so the court had been filled with thousands of priests. Each division was given a day room where they stayed when they were not officially on duty or involved in worship. Zechariah had used the same room closest to the Temple for a number of years. The rooms were assigned according to years of service and Zechariah was among the most senior. It was here they kept their official priestly garments and took their meals. Zechariah, Tela and his father walked the long Colonnade until they came to Zechariah's room. He hung his robes with care next to the door. The places for each priest were designated by the Hebrew alphabet and each man's place encircled the room along the wall. Zechariah's place was "Beta". The elderly priest Simeon who served full time at the temple had the "Alpha" position. The letters of the Hebrew alphabet were made of polished bronze and affixed to the tall garment wardrobes that encircled the room. Twenty-two priests shared each room and during Passover it was crowded. Many of the priests had not yet arrived.

The three exited the room and walked slowly behind the crowd through the covered porch and down the long Southern Steps into the city streets. They arrived at their house in a matter of moments. Four other priests had already arrived and were engaged in conversation about the upcoming Pesach and the latest political intrigue about King Herod. Benjamin had bought a few more provisions on their way to the house, and he laid them on the long table. Even though fruits and vegetables were not in season yet, one could still buy them from Egyptian traders who sold them to local shop keepers. They were expensive this time of year, and it was a real treat for Nicodemus to have an apple in the month of Nisan.

The sun was just about to set, and Sabbath found the seven of them gathered around the table. Priests could not drink wine during their assigned time at the Temple, so the meal consisted of milk, cheese, bread, figs and the three apples Benjamin had bought. They all waited for the trumpet sound from the Temple signifying the beginning of the Shabbat. Before it sounded, Benjamin lit the Shabbat lamp that was always kept in the center of the table. Zechariah, as the senior in the room, stood and lifted the bread

20

heavenward and recited the blessing: *"Blessed are you Lord our God, King of the Universe who brings forth bread from the ground."* They ate, and the priests in turn recited Scriptures designated for the Shabbat meal. The liturgy encouraged leaders to share personal insights about the meaning of Shabbat. The first priest recited from Genesis and spoke about the cycle of creation, work and rest:

> *By the seventh day God had finished the work he had been doing,*
> *So on the seventh day he rested from all his work. And God blessed the seventh day and made it holy,*
> *Because on it he rested from all the work of creating that he had done.* (Gen. 2:2,3)

The second priest recited from Deuteronomy, mentioning that Sabbath rest was not just pausing in a cycle of work and rest but also entailed remembering that Shabbat was about the redemption of God's people from Egypt.

> *Six days you shall labor and do all your work,*
> *But the seventh day is a Sabbath to the Lord your God.*
> *On it you shall not do any work, neither you, nor your son or daughter,*
> *nor your manservant or maidservant, nor your ox,*
> *your donkey or any of your animals, nor the alien within your gates,*
> *so that your manservant and maidservant may rest, as you do.*
> *Remember that you were slaves in Egypt*
> *And that the Lord your God brought you out of there with a mighty hand*
> *And an outstretched arm.*
> *Therefore the Lord your God has commanded you to observe the Sabbath day.*
> (Deuteronomy 5:13-15)

Nicodemus was touched by the insights of this priest who commented on these verses: *"At the close of our work week, we experience holy rest in the Lord, just as at the end of the sorrow and labor in Egypt, we enjoyed redemption and rest; and we also look forward to a better rest in the Messiah and ultimately the eternal Shabbat of completed work, of completed redemption in glory."*

Benjamin closed the meal with a blessing. They wrapped up the uneaten food. Dawn would come early, and all the priests needed to be at the Temple first thing in the morning. Shabbat duty was light except for the two lamb sacrifices. The priests who were assigned to the Temple as Shabbat commenced would also perform the morning sacrifice. Benjamin and Zechariah, as senior priests, would remain the entire day in the Temple until the close of Shabbat at sunset. Usually senior priests were part of the dawn patrol that would inspect the courts to be sure nothing had been disturbed in the night and that all of the 93 sacred vessels used in the morning sacrifice were in place and ready for use. Since it would still be dark during the patrol, candles were lit that surrounded the courts and illuminated the walkway all along the Colonnade. In this way, no actual work needed to be done, and no torches needed to be lit.

But all priests on duty needed to be at the Temple well before dawn for the purification rites, and with so many men on duty with Pesach approaching, the six priests would need to rise well before dawn and head for the temple. Knowing this, all rose from the table, Zechariah extinguished the Sabbath lamp, and all headed for their rooms to sleep. Nicodemus didn't need any encouragement. He spread his blanket on the floor in their room and was asleep within moments with visions of the lamb sacrifice filling his dreams.

All had departed well before dawn when Nicodemus awoke. He climbed to the roof of the house in the cool of the morning and watched the sunrise in the east over the Mt. of Olives. He recalled his conversation with Zechariah and what Gabriel had told the old priest: ***"to make ready a people prepared for the Lord."*** (Luke 1:17) As he looked to the east and watched the golden sun light up the olive groves with an orange hue, he couldn't help but wonder if he would see, with his own eyes, the Messiah enter Jerusalem from the same direction. Tradition held that just as the glory of the Lord had departed Solomon's Temple to the east, the Messiah would come from the same direction and enter the Temple once again. Nicodemus stood transfixed at this thought and watched the sunrise. *"What a day that will be!"* Nicodemus whispered to himself.

The remainder of Shabbat was uneventful as Nicodemus watched the city streets from his perch on the roof. His father's house was a story taller than most. This allowed him to observe the houses as they came to life that morning. Only a few people were on the streets as there was a strict limitation even on the number of steps one could take on Shabbat, and it was strictly enforced by Pharisees who stood outside their doorways throughout the city and maintained the required rest. All was quiet throughout the day; even the Roman soldiers remained in their barracks. It was as if the city itself had taken a huge breath the night before and exhaled.

Precisely at the third hour of the morning (9:00 AM) Nicodemus heard the three trumpet blasts from the Temple and he knew the morning sacrifice was taking place. In a matter of seconds another lamb was about to die and shed his blood for the people. At this, Tela crawled down from the roof and returned to his room for a morning nap.

Zechariah and Father returned from the Temple just after sunset, having completed their duty for the day. Their lot gave them easy duty after the dawn patrol. They had been assigned to join the Levitical choir that sang Psalm 92 after the morning sacrifice as well as the Song of Moses. (Deuteronomy 32). The remainder of their day they spent in prayer and resting in their day room. Zechariah spent a great deal of time in conversation with the senior most priest, Simeon. The two had much in common beyond their age and experiences. Simeon was very devout and was a permanent priest in the Temple. The two sat in one corner of their room talking for hours about the coming of Messiah. Simeon mentioned to Zechariah that the Spirit of God had convinced him that very soon he would see the Messiah with his own eyes. *"The time is right for the redemption of God's people,"* Simeon told Zechariah. Zechariah shared with Simeon about the birth of John and they discussed in depth the meaning of Gabriel's words, **"to make ready a people prepared for the Lord."** (Luke 1:17) *"Not all will welcome the coming of the Lord,"* Simeon warned Zechariah, *"Many among the Pharisees and the Council are filled with greed and a love for power. Unholy alliances have taken place at the highest levels. Both of us will have received our eternal Sabbath rest when all this comes to fulfillment. Make sure you encourage John to be faithful when he is tested, Zechariah! His ministry will be difficult and opposed by that tyrant in the palace and whoever follows him."*

Nicodemus was glad to see his father and Zechariah. Sunset meant they could cook a hot meal. Shops opened almost immediately after the sound of the trumpets from the Temple signaling the end of Sabbath, and Benjamin had stopped on his way home with a freshly slaughtered chicken, lentils, potatoes and onions. This was Nicodemus favorite meal: meat and vegetable stew. Benjamin had mastered his recipe, cooking it many times while serving in Jerusalem. Nicodemus sat with his father as he added the ingredients to the cooking pot.

"I spoke with your new Rabbi today," Benjamin shared as he added some spices to the pot. *"When can I meet him?"* Nicodemus asked enthusiastically, *"Tomorrow?"*

"Yes, we agreed to meet here tomorrow. He wants to buy his lamb from the flock downstairs and he is coming by at lunchtime. I don't have any duty tomorrow, so we will choose our lamb at the same time," his father added.

Nicodemus was looking forward to celebrating Pesach with his father. Benjamin had always been at the Temple during this week. Nicodemus and his mother had always joined with Elizabeth and another family for the meal. The yearling male lamb was selected by each family on the Sunday before Pesach. It was the traditional duty of the children in the family to care for the lamb for the five days before Pesach. This would be Tela's first time caring for a lamb for Pesach.

Nicodemus' mind was preoccupied with who his new teacher might be and peppered his father with questions.

"When will I start? What is his name? Is he strict? Is he a follower of Hillel or Shammai? How many will be in the class?"

"Slow down, Tela," his father interrupted. *"You will start class on the day after the Passover Sabbath a week from tomorrow. I'll stay a few extra days to make sure you are well settled. After that you will have class every day, even on Sabbath. Your teacher's name is Joshua, and all the Rabbis are very busy this week. Somedays I hear he even takes his class outside the city. He likes to take his class to the very sites you have heard about: Jericho, Bethel, the Valley of Elah, Bethlehem, and Hebron. How does that sound?"*

"Glorious!" Nicodemus was wide-eyed. Of course he would miss his father and mother, but this was an opportunity to learn from some of the keenest minds in Jerusalem. He already had in mind to engage some of the priests like Zechariah's elderly friend Simeon in conversation about Torah and the Messiah.

That evening everyone brought their bowl of stew up on the rooftop and sat in a circle enjoying the sumptuous meal prepared by Benjamin. Some of the other priests had brought home some leeks and cucumbers which made the stew even more hearty and delicious. They watched as the sun set in the west over the city and the stars began to appear.

"Look at that bright star directly overhead" one of the priests remarked, *"It is the strangest sight! I've watched it for the past several months and it never appears to move."*

"May not be strange at all; could be a sign from God," Zechariah responded. *"The stars often signal the arrival of a new ruler."*

25

"A new king? Herod won't like that at all. His sons are disappearing right and left. How many sons are left from his 10 wives?" another of the priests asked sarcastically.

"Be careful how loud you speak of such things," Benjamin added. *"He has spies everywhere looking for plots against his throne."*

"But the star," Nicodemus interrupted, *"what do you think it could mean, really? Could God be about to send a Savior to rescue us ... like Samson?"* Nicodemus turned and looked at Zechariah. They shared a smile in the faint light of the full moon and both nodded.

The next day Joshua the Rabbi arrived around noon. He spent a few minutes inspecting the two dozen male yearling lambs kept on the ground level of the home before climbing the stairs to the second level. Benjamin greeted him warmly as did Zechariah. The other priests had long since left for their temple duties. *"So, this is Nicodemus."* Joshua extended his hand and greeted the boy. *"Shalom! Peace to you, young man!"*

"Thank-you. Shalom," Nicodemus responded warmly. Joshua was in his late forties, just a few years younger than Benjamin. He shared that he had sat under the great Hillel 20 years ago, and this pleased Nicodemus greatly. Hillel had founded a school named for him and he was still living in Jerusalem. He had been born in Babylon and was over 100 years old. He was still widely regarded as a sage and scholar, and his disciples were known as the "School of Hillel!" Hillel was well known for the development of the Mishnah and the Talmud, and his knowledge of the Hebrew Scriptures was vast. Gamaliel, his grandson, was already well regarded as a teacher in the School of Hillel, and Benjamin had expressed a desire that one day Nicodemus would become a Talmidim (disciple) of Gamaliel. But teachers like Gamaliel selected their own disciples from the most promising students.

Joshua put his arm around Nicodemus shoulder and asked him pointedly, *"Are you ready to study very hard, Nicodemus?"*

"I sure am," Nicodemus responded, *"Father was telling me yesterday that sometimes you take your students on journeys to some of the cities of our forefathers, the judges and prophets of old. Is that true?"*

"Yes, we will make one journey every few months as lessons and security determine. I believe it helps to retain the truths of Scripture by connecting it visually with the geography. I hope you don't mind sleeping under the stars?" Joshua asked.

"Mind? I love it!" Nicodemus responded smiling.

"Well, it all starts in just one week, but right now the immediate need is a lamb. My family is expecting me to bring one home today. Shall we?" Joshua motioned to the stairs and the four of them all descended to the ground floor to select their lamb.

In the days that followed, Nicodemus spent the morning tending his yearling lamb, feeding it, bringing it water and changing the bedding. By midweek he had trained it to stay in the corner of their room on the straw he prepared each morning. In the afternoon he would join his father in the temple courtyard and talk with the priests. Zechariah had introduced him to Simeon, and he developed a wonderful relationship with the old priest. Simeon's role at the Temple was to supervise the priests who circumcised male infants on the 8th day after birth. Normally this took place at the synagogue in the town of the parents, but with such a large throng in Jerusalem for Pesach, the number of firstborn males born in Jerusalem this week increased dramatically. Additionally, many families had come to Jerusalem several weeks ago to register for the census ordered by Caesar Augustus. The steady flow of families kept Simeon busy most of the morning. Families were told to bring their child by the 3rd hour just after the morning sacrifice. Simeon made a habit of waiting at the entrance after sacrifice to receive, bless and direct families to the rooms dedicated for circumcision. It was easy work and it allowed Simeon time for prayer and study in the afternoon hours.

Occasionally a family would arrive in the afternoon and he would be called from his day room to welcome them.

Each day, Nicodemus grew closer to the lamb. At night it would lie down next to him and keep him warm, and each morning it would beg for a few scraps of food as Tela ate his morning meal. Just before lunch Nicodemus would carry the lamb out the eastern gate. Together they would walk the path down to the Kidron Valley and ford the small stream. In the olive grove opposite the city they would laugh and chase each other around the trees before resting in the shade of one of the spreading olive trees. Nicodemus knew what was coming later in the week, but he couldn't help himself. He loved the little innocent lamb.

After lunch, Nicodemus would leave some food for the lamb in a bowl next to his straw bed and go to the Temple and meet the priests in his father's room. There were always some who were resting or eating, and they quickly welcomed him into their circle. Simeon was almost always there, and they would talk about the Messianic verses in the Torah.

Wednesday evening, Benjamin sat down with Nicodemus and began the hard discussion about the preparation of the lamb for sacrifice the next day. *"Tela, you know why the Lord required us to select the lamb so many days ahead of the sacrifice, don't you?"* Benjamin explained to his son.

"Yes, I know," Nicodemus answered as he looked down. *"The Lord wants us to know that the price of redemption is high, but it is still hard."*

"You can carry the lamb to the Temple tomorrow. We'll go together." His father embraced him as Tela wept on his Father's shoulder. That night Tela held his lamb a little closer and fell asleep in the warmth of its fleece.

Chapter Four:
Nunc Dimittis

The morning walk to the Temple was one of the hardest that 10-year-old Nicodemus had ever taken. He knew his duty. He knew the law about Pesach, but he desperately wanted to be merciful to this little lamb. It had done nothing wrong. Why must it die? Is the law so harsh that it makes no allowances for our human attachments? It helped a little that his father was by his side, but he was also the one who would not allow him to do anything but the will of God. Nicodemus was tempted to run, run with the lamb to the hills and enjoy one more day of play among the olive trees. But it was not possible. He needed to make this journey and subject himself to the will of his heavenly Father, no matter how painful.

"Is this how Pesach is supposed to feel?" he asked his father as he carried the lamb in his arms. As he spoke the lamb looked up into his eyes and licked his face. The affection from this little one only made him weep. *"Tela, obedience can sometimes be difficult,"* his father answered. *"The Lord knows how you feel. Remember the story of the first Pesach. Our ancestors used the blood of that first lamb to save their families from the angel of death. In some small way, this lamb's blood does the same for us."*

"But the lamb has not done anything wrong. Why does it have to suffer for me? That's not fair." Tela spoke through his tears.

"It may not seem like it to you now, Tela. One day you will see this day much differently." Benjamin responded.

As they entered the Temple, Nicodemus asked his father to take the lamb. He could not watch, and he bolted for the day room, running down the Colonnade. Hot tears streamed out of his grieving heart. He pushed through the door, bumping into Simeon who was seated just inside the room. He was dressed in his priestly robes and praying.

"Hold on, Nicodemus. What's going on? Why the tears?" the old priest consoled Nicodemus. *"Pe . . . Pe . . . Pesach!"* Nicodemus

stammered his voice cracking. *"My lamb is being sacrificed! And Father doesn't even seem to care."*

"Sit down here, Nicodemus; I know just how you feel." The old man took a deep breath as Nicodemus' tears slowed and he quieted to Simeon's kind words. *"May I tell you a story?"*

"Sure," Nicodemus eventually said as he sat and looked at the ground.

"When I was a small boy I was not as disciplined and obedient as you. In fact, I had a habit of talking back to my father. I bet you didn't think I was that kind of boy, did you?" Simeon asked. Nicodemus shook his head.

"Well, I was. I didn't understand how serious my sin was. I didn't know much about God's justice. Then one day my father taught me an important lesson that I have never forgotten. Maybe it will help you. One day I had spoken rudely to my mother, who wanted me to wash the cooking pot. I was headed out the door to play with my friends when my father caught me by the arm. He took me inside the house and picked up a long stick that was propped in the corner. He used this stick to discipline the oxen in the field when he wanted them to turn. I had seen him use it very often and I was sure he was about to use it on me. I knew I had done wrong and probably deserved it. Do you know what he did?"

"He whipped your bottom!" Nicodemus looked up at the old priest.

"No, Tela. He removed his robe to his waist, knelt on the floor and gave me the stick and said, 'Sin must be punished, Simeon. That is God's unchanging justice. You sinned, and you deserve to be punished; but because of my love for you, I will take your punishment. You will punish me for your sins. Now take the stick and punish me.' He bent over as I had done many times and said, 'punish me'."

"What did you do?" Nicodemus asked Simeon in amazement. *"Did you really beat your father?"*

30

"At first I just said 'No'. But he kept insisting. Finally, I gave him one stroke very lightly. He looked up at me sternly and said, 'No, not like that! Beat me Simeon! Do it!' He kept shouting at me until I started to cry and through my tears I beat my father... for my sin."

"I don't understand. Your father didn't do anything wrong. You deserved to be punished." Nicodemus responded.

"Exactly, Nicodemus. That incident changed me. I never wanted to go through that again."

"But what does that have to do with...this," Nicodemus pointed to the courtyard where countless Passover lambs were being slaughtered.

"Our Father in heaven has responded to our sin in the same way my father did." Simeon continued, *"He places our sin on the innocent lamb and has mercy on us! Do you see? The blood of the lamb washes away the sin of each and every family. That is why the lamb is spotless and perfect. It is a picture of the innocent dying for the guilty! Today, you have experienced the perfect love of your Father in heaven. Instead of running from it, embrace it; learn from it. Let it cleanse you. One day very soon, Messiah will come just like that lamb and carry our sin. I am sure you memorized the words of Isaiah the prophet, 'We all like sheep have gone astray, each of us turned to his own way; and the Lord has laid on him the iniquity of us all.'"* Isaiah 53:6

"You mean Messiah will die... like my lamb, Simeon?" Nicodemus asked, lifting his head for the first time.

"We will see what the Lord has in mind, Nicodemus, but I know redemption is coming soon and with it, forgiveness."

There was a knock on the door. Simeon's attendant opened it and looked at Simeon, *"A young couple is here for circumcision and presentation, sir,"* the young man announced.

"I'll be right there," Simeon responded.

"Does that story help, Tela?" Simeon met Nicodemus' eyes with a smile.

"A little, but it still hurts," Nicodemus answered. *"Yes, I know,"* Simeon nodded. *"Sin brings pain."*

With that Simeon left the room to meet those requiring his services. As he exited the door and glanced at the Temple, an overwhelming feeling of fulfillment touched him. He placed his hand over his heart and stood still.

"The Lamb has come," a voice whispered.

Simeon turned around to see who had spoken to him. At first, he thought it might be Nicodemus, but he was still inside the room.

It repeated, *"Come, the Lamb is here!"*

Simeon walked the Colonnade, his spirit light and filled with anticipation. *"The Lamb?"* he asked himself. *"Could it be? Could it really be?"* He picked up his pace as he entered the courtyard and there just inside the entrance were a number of families with infants who had come to have their firstborn male children circumcised. He was led to one of the young couples and the mother handed him the 8-day old infant. Simeon lifted the child heavenward as all around watched. His words flowed from somewhere deep inside. Without even a thought he spoke,

> **"Sovereign Lord, as you have promised, you now dismiss your servant in peace. For my eyes have seen your salvation which you have prepared in the sight of all people, a light for revelation to the Gentiles and for glory to your people Israel."**
> Luke 2:29-31

Nicodemus had followed Simeon out into the courtyard to look for his father. He watched as Simeon approached the young couple and from a distance heard the old priest praising God. The words seemed to fill the courtyard, and all around him had turned to listen. Just then an elderly woman whom Nicodemus did not know came up to the family and also began praising God. He heard her say to the priests next to him, *"Redemption has come."* Nicodemus turned again to where Simeon was standing. The priest lowered his arms and handed the child back to the mother, whispering something to her and directing them to the room for circumcision.

Nicodemus was no longer thinking about his lamb. He stood transfixed at the sight of this young couple and their baby. The words of Simeon in the room had been like salve on an open wound in his heart, and he longed to know more about what he had just overheard.

Nicodemus watched Simeon as he continued his work helping and directing couples to attendants who led them to private rooms where their baby boys would be circumcised. The joy radiating from Simeon's face was unlike any Nicodemus had ever known. Nicodemus knew this precious event, that he still didn't fully understand, was one that he could never forget.

The old man looked tired from the encounter and he walked slowly down the Colonnade. Nicodemus wanted to follow, but just then his father approached. Mercifully, Benjamin had attended to the sacrifice of the lamb and, as priests were allowed some flexibility in Pesach observance because of their duties, he left the lamb to be roasted and eaten by his attendants. One of the other priests staying in their house was in the same line for sacrifice and had offered to share his lamb with all in the house.

"How are you son?" Benjamin asked as he approached *"Are you angry with me?"*

"No, father," Tela responded with a smile. *"Simeon and I talked; he explained Passover in such a nice way. It still hurts. But wait until I tell what just happened right here!"* Nicodemus pointed to the ground where Simeon had raised the infant.

"What?" Benjamin asked.

"The best news possible!" The two began to leave the Temple and Nicodemus continued, *"I'll tell you as we prepare for Pesach."* The previous evening Benjamin had swept the house clean of any possible leaven. So, the only preparations Simeon needed to worry about were buying the bitter herbs and unleavened bread. This they did as they walked back to their house. As they walked they could

33

both smell roasting lamb down every street, and when they entered the courtyard of their home two of the priests had already set up a fire and spit for roasting the lamb whole. Tela was just glad it was not his lamb. The priests had already made arrangements with all in the house, including the landlord and his family, to join them for the meal. Pesach tradition required that the meal be shared by 10-20 people, so it just made sense to roast one lamb for all 12 in the house. All helped to prepare the meal and the landlord had purchased 10 jugs of wine for the evening, more than they would need.

Pesach was a celebration meal for God's people. It was a time for joy. No longer did they eat it standing as their forefathers did in Egypt on the first Pesach. It was the first of three festivals for which all males were bound to appear in Jerusalem. The other two were the Feast of Tabernacles and the Feast of Weeks. The Hebrew word "Pesach" literally meant "to step over" and referred to the ancient history of the celebration in Egypt when the angel of death, on seeing the blood of the lamb on the door-post and lintel, "stepped-over" that house and did not slay the first-born male. It was celebrated on the 15th day of the first month in the Jewish calendar, Nisan. It was not uncommon for more than 250,000 lambs to be sacrificed in the temple on Pesach. The city was bursting at the seams, and thousands upon thousands camped outside the city walls since accommodation inside was normally filled to capacity. Pesach actually began on the 13th evening when the head of every household would take a lighted candle and search the whole house for any yeast (leaven) where it was normally kept. The search was conducted in complete silence. Before beginning the search, the household head was to pray,

"Blessed art Thou, Jehovah our God, King of the Universe, who hast sanctified us by Thy Commandments, and commanded us to remove the leaven."

After the search was completed he was to pray again, *"All the leaven that is in my possession that which I have seen and that which I have not seen, be it null, be it accounted as the dust of the earth."* The unleavened bread could be baked with one of five grains: oats, wheat, barley, spelt or rye.

The official time for removing of leaven was actually at noon on Passover Day when the second of two cakes was removed from a bench in the temple, signaling the time for burning of all leaven in Jerusalem. However, households were allowed to sweep their homes on the night before also.

The divisions of priests formed two long lines from each side of the altar of burnt offering for the slaying of the lambs by the head of each family or company. As the neck of the lamb was cut, the blood was caught by a priest in a golden or silver bowl and passed to another priest, which he exchanged with an empty bowl. He then carried the bowl of blood to the priest at the top of the great altar. This priest received the bowl and in one motion poured the blood before the altar and returned the empty bowl to the priest. The blood flowed all afternoon along a channel coming from the altar and found its way into the Kidron River, which flowed red with blood for the remainder of the day on Passover. Anyone crossing the Kidron any time after 2:00 PM on Passover would certainly have his feet stained by this river of blood. During the slaying of the lambs, Levitical choirs would sing the Hallel which included Psalms 113-118. The Hallel would be repeated as long as each Division of priests was on duty.

Nicodemus had celebrated this feast every year, usually at the home of friends of his parents. But the atmosphere of this celebration was quite different. This was the first time he observed Pesach with his father. He didn't know how he would feel eating the lamb, but it was a little easier after he drank some wine. The meal consisted of four glasses of wine and because of his age, his glass had been watered down considerably. All the participants gathered in a semi-circle with the bread, herbs and lamb on plates in the middle. They ate while reclining on large cushions provided by the landlord. Each one rested his head on his left hand while eating with the right hand. Zechariah spoke about the unleavened bread, its history from the Exodus and its symbolic meaning as the absence of sin. Benjamin spoke about the lamb and the redemption of God's people by the blood of the lamb. He glanced at Nicodemus several times and Tela nodded. The unspoken communication acknowledged acceptance and trust. The landlord spoke about the bitter herbs and recalled the 430 years of slavery endured by God's people as well as the bitterness of anger and revenge toward the current occupier of Israel: Rome. In between the group sang psalms and discussed the day's events. They laughed and told stories. One of the priests even shared a story he had heard from a pilgrim who was camped outside the city on the slopes of the Kidron Valley. With great drama he shared how a Roman soldier had been on patrol there, slipped into the Kidron River and was drenched from head to toe in lamb's blood, flowing from the Temple. Repeatedly he tried to stand up but with the weight of his armor, he lost his balance several times and fell back into the river. Everyone laughed at the image of a Roman caught in a river of blood and unable to right himself. *"Can the blood of a lamb cleanse even the sin of a Roman soldier?"* Nicodemus asked. He had asked the question in all seriousness, but all the men laughed at the idea of a Jewish lamb bringing cleansing to a Roman.

As Pesach commenced the stories continued between songs and wise words from the priests. When Zechariah raised the third cup, the

Cup of Blessing, he recited the traditional verses from the Psalms calling for God's judgment on the nations,

"Pour out your wrath on the nations that do not acknowledge you
On the kingdoms that do not call on your name." Ps. 79:6
"May their place be deserted;
let there be no one to dwell in their tents" Ps. 69:25
"Pursue them in anger and destroy them
from under the heavens of the Lord." Lam. 3:66

Benjamin stood as Zechariah was reciting and opened the door. This was to admit Elijah the prophet, the forerunner of the Messiah. A space and even a serving dish had been reserved for Elijah. At this, Nicodemus perked up and caught Zechariah's eye.

The two exchanged a smile and a knowing nod as a man burst into the room breathing heavily. Bending over, he tried to catch his breath. Between gasps he managed to say, *"It's Simeon! Come quickly!"* It was Simeon's attendant. Zechariah and Benjamin excused themselves as they left quickly with Nicodemus trailing a few steps behind. *"We found him on the floor in his day room,"* Nicodemus heard them say as they walked quickly to the Temple.

Chapter Five:
Slaughter

Nicodemus rose early the day after Pesach for his first day of class in the Temple. He made the short walk from the house to the Temple. Joshua had made it clear that students would only be allowed to be out of school for the three major festivals. The Feast of Unleavened Bread which began on Pesach was not one of them. They would meet even on Sabbath, as education and learning were supreme. Besides, Rabban Joshua was from the School of Hillel, which did not take such a restrictive view of the Sabbath as other schools.

Class would focus mainly on the Torah with additional focus on the great prophets Isaiah and Jeremiah as well as the Psalms so that students would be able to worship in the Temple with understanding. Nicodemus, who had already learned a number of Psalms from Rabban Terah at Beth Sepher in Ein Karem, was ahead of most of his classmates. Nearly all of them were a year older than he. His humble and timid personality made him well liked.

There were 25 in his class, and they sat on the floor in a semi-circle with Rabban Joshua at the center. The class had been focusing for the last one month on those Scriptures that described the Passover observance. Rabban Joshua announced that they would be studying the Feast of Unleavened Bread for the next one week. *"We will have the opportunity to worship and observe the daily sacrifice in the Temple. Each day, 2 young bullocks, a ram and seven lambs will be sacrificed. The sacrifices started today and will continue until next Friday, so on the last day we will spend the day in the Temple in worship."* The class copied the relevant text from Leviticus on their personal scrolls as Joshua read from his copy.

Nicodemus was still coming to terms with the death of Simeon the priest. He had only had a few conversations with the man, but he had been very consoling over the sacrifice of his Passover lamb. He could not erase the image of the priest lifting that small baby in the

Temple. His first words still echoed in his heart and mind: ***"Lord, now let your servant depart in peace..."*** (Luke 2:29) He had followed his father and Zechariah to the Temple the day before as they rushed to keep up with Simeon's attendant. He had waited outside while they attended to the old man. His breathing was shallow yet there was such a look of peace on Simeon's face. He seemed to know exactly what was happening. At one point, Zechariah bent over to listen to Simeon whisper something in his ear. Zechariah sat up after listening and the two men shared a broad smile. Nicodemus eased his way slowly into the room to see Simeon raise his arm. He appeared to be reaching for something or ... someone. At that he closed his eyes and took one long final breath. As he exhaled a look of peace enveloped him and Zechariah took his arm and laid it across his chest. He rose and said to Father, *"He is at peace now and has his reward."*

As the three of them walked slowly back to their home, Nicodemus took his father's hand. He wanted to know what Simeon had said to Zechariah, but there would be time for that discussion later.

"He was so wise and gentle," Benjamin said as he turned to Zechariah. Zechariah seemed to be deep in thought and was still smiling.

"Yes," Zechariah responded, *"That gentleness came from what he saw yesterday."*

"The sacrifice of the Passover lambs?" Tela asked.

Zechariah stopped, turned to Nicodemus and said, *"THE lamb, Tela."*

Nicodemus was not quite sure what Zechariah meant but he would ask him about it later.

With that the three of them walked back to their home to finish Passover. Simeon's attendant would see to it that the family was contacted and burial arrangements made for Simeon. The body would be buried just outside the Shechem gate in one of the garden tombs owned by the family.

Later that evening on the rooftop, Zechariah shared some of his memories from serving in the Temple for many years with Simeon. During a lull in the conversation, Nicodemus asked, *"May I ask something, Zechariah?"*

"You can," Zechariah responded, *"what do you want to know?"*

"Will you share with us what Simeon whispered in your ear just before he died?"

A smile returned to the priest's face. He paused and glanced at the night sky. Just then the bright star overhead shone through a break in the clouds. He smiled again, turning his head toward Nicodemus. He replied, *"Simeon said, 'The Lamb is here...prepare your son.'"*

For a while Nicodemus had trouble focusing in class. Over the next week he spoke with his father about Simeon and even the identity of the baby whom Simeon lifted in the Temple. Benjamin told Nicodemus about the many conversations he and Simeon had over the years. Unlike most priests, Simeon stayed inside the Temple itself, day and night.

"His duties were very light because of his age," Benjamin told his son. *"He spent most of his time reading the Scriptures. In the past six months he talked more and more about his visions promising that he would see the Messiah before he died. They started just after the vision Zechariah had in the temple more than a year ago."*

"And the baby in the Temple?" Nicodemus asked, *"How could that be the Messiah? The parents were poor. I saw them present just two doves for the mother's purification. And when the man talked, I could tell they were from Galilee. How can the Messiah come from Galilee?"*

"Yes, the prophet Micah is clear. The Messiah is to be born in Bethlehem. It doesn't fit the prophecy does it?!" Benjamin added, *"But remember, all of King David's descendants were to be in Bethlehem for the census. It could be that the Galilean couple are descendants of David."*

40

"But he must be near because Gabriel told Zechariah his son would prepare us for him." Nicodemus noted

"The best you can do right now, Nicodemus, is to study the Scriptures faithfully, and the Lord will make all this clear in his own time."

At the end of the Feast of Unleavened Bread, Benjamin said goodbye to his son and headed for home with Zechariah. He left money with the shopkeeper and told Nicodemus he could get whatever he needed from him. There would be a new pair of priests from a new division staying in the house every week, and Benjamin had already informed them that his son would be staying there. Nicodemus' Aunt Leah lived in Jerusalem also and promised to look in on the boy and make sure his laundry was washed every week.

Education for secondary school training by a Rabbi at the Temple was expensive. Many rich aristocrats sponsored promising students. Religious education was viewed as of primary importance to wealthy residents of Jerusalem. Benjamin, however, had no need of outside support for Nicodemus. Benjamin's father had been a wealthy landowner, as well as a priest, and supplied Jerusalem with some of its finest wines. His connections at the Temple allowed him to sell his virgin olive oil for worship and sacrifices. Benjamin had inherited his father's vast vineyards and orchards. One day it would all belong to Nicodemus. However, money had never been the family's first love. Service to God and religious education by the best teachers came first, always. Nicodemus had no idea just how wealthy his father was, and Benjamin protected his son from that information. *"Love of money is the root of all evil,"* he often told the men and women in the synagogue gatherings in Ein Karem.

In the months that followed, Nicodemus proved to be not only a good student but was well respected for his thoughtful questions, his sincere devotion to his lessons, and his humility with his classmates. He already knew the Scriptures better than most of his 24 classmates when he started, and most of them were a year or two older. He loved the worship in the temple and singing in the boys' Levitical choir.

Rabban Joshua made good on his promise to take his class on "learning trips" as he called them. The first was to the ancient city of Jericho and to the place Joshua felt God's people had crossed the Jordan under his name's sake's leadership. They had camped on the west side of the Jordan precisely where the standing stones had been placed by the ancient elders of each tribe. Nicodemus loved learning at the historic sites he had only heard about.

Six months after Joshua began his studies in Jerusalem, an entourage of strangely dressed men on camels entered Jerusalem. The entire city was on edge. The 12 men were riding on camels with 80 well-armed soldiers escorting them. It was not an invasion, but some in the streets speculated that perhaps the Parthians were once again inciting a border conflict to test the Roman resolve. The long-time residents of Jerusalem had lived through several conflicts between the Parthians and Romans in their homeland. Herod himself had regained control of Jerusalem in a battle with the Parthians that went on for three years. The African adage proved to be true for the Jews in Judea: "When two elephants fight, it is the grass that suffers."

The Magi were known to be powerful priests for the Parthians. But their influence dated back to the days of Daniel the prophet. The Magi had been head of the hereditary priesthood of the Medes. They had unprecedented historic and religious knowledge, and when Darius took note of their ability to interpret dreams, he gave them control over the state religion of Persia. Daniel himself had been named "Rab-Mag" (Chief of the Magi). Daniel, according to tradition, had entrusted to a secret sect of the Magi (A Greek word transliterated from the Persian "magoi") a Messianic vision to be ushered in with the appearance of a "star." In their priestly and governmental roles, they became extremely powerful as The Council of Megistanes. They had complete control of the choice and election of king of the realm, and so came to be known down through history as "king makers."

The political unrest caused by their appearance was enormous. It was the topic of every conversation on every street corner, and the news spread like wild fire. It reached Ein Karem the next day and led Benjamin to pack a few things immediately and head for Jerusalem to make sure his son was safe. Fearing Herod's reaction, Rabban Joshua cancelled classes until further notice. Roman soldiers were everywhere. A centuriae (80 soldiers) had been summoned to Herod's palace, with regular patrols moving throughout the city ready to put down any revolt. Gatherings of more than 3 people on the street were immediately dealt with. Word had gone around that Herod feared that these Parthian priests might be in Jerusalem to collaborate with Jewish revolutionaries.

Nicodemus took advantage of the off day to trail along with several of the priests staying in the house. They had headed for Herod's palace. He too, wanted to get a glimpse of this strange site. He was not disappointed. Outside Herod's Palace was the contingent of Parthian soldiers who had accompanied the 12 men still inside the Palace. They knew this because a number of Arabian steeds and camels were just outside Herod's stables. Just as they reached the Palace, they saw several high-ranking priests from the Temple, along with several prominent Rabbis accompanied by Temple soldiers, approaching the Palace. Nicodemus heard the priests with him say that these men had been summoned by Herod. They had no idea what this might mean. It was still fairly early in the day, so Nicodemus and the priests decided to wait and see what might be going on inside the Palace. Normally an audience with Herod was short. He was quick tempered and did not like conversations where he did not know the outcome or purpose.

Within an hour 10 Parthian soldiers exited the Palace accompanied by the 12 men. They were talking excitedly with each other. They were out of earshot, so Nicodemus could not hear what they were saying. The 12 men in flowing robes mounted their camels. A Roman centurion who had been inside the Palace came out immediately after the Parthian guard and ordered his men to mount up and accompany the group to Zion gate. The Romans proceeded to clear the street that led to the gate on the southern side of the city. They galloped past the crowd where Nicodemus was standing, followed by 12 Parthians on Arabian stallions, then the 12 men on camels flanked by more Parthians, followed by the remaining 60 Parthian soldiers. It was a dazzling display and Nicodemus stood transfixed by the scene. What did all this mean? Why were they here? They couldn't be here to crown Herod King of the Jews. The Roman Senate had already done that. Where were they going now? Back to Parthia?

Benjamin had just arrived as the enormous contingent of soldiers was leaving. He had come via the "Jaffa Gate" which was near Herod's Palace. He had taken the quickest route into the city and saw the last of the soldiers leaving the court in front of the Palace when he spotted Nicodemus in the crowd on the opposite side of the court. As soon as all the Roman soldiers were clear, he walked across the courtyard to speak with his son.

Benjamin immediately went into the Temple to learn what he could about the visitors from Parthia. He took Nicodemus back to the house first and then went to speak with some of the chief priests. He had learned that these "king-makers" had come to inquire of Herod about the birth of the one called "King of the Jews." Experts in the Scriptures had been summoned by Herod to give their expertise on the subject. Many in the Temple guessed Herod had another motive. They believed he was looking for any sign that these priests were in the midst of fomenting revolt in collaboration with Messianic revolutionaries. The answer given to Herod was given without elaboration. The prophet Micah spoke of the Messiah being born in Bethlehem. This was a long-standing tradition that any ten-year-old knew, including Nicodemus and every boy in his class.

"Why did Herod allow these men to leave?" Nicodemus asked his father that evening as they sat around their evening meal.

"I don't know if he has," his father answered. *"Some of the priests observed some of his spies following the 12 Magi when they left the city."*

"Where are the Magi going?" Nicodemus asked. *"Back to Parthia? Or could it be true that Messiah has come and was born in Bethlehem?"*

"We'll know soon enough, son," his father replied, *"but right now I'm concerned how Herod will react to all of this. I just don't trust him. He's killed his own children fearing he might lose his throne. I'm afraid more bloodshed is coming."*

"If it really is Messiah, even Herod won't be able to stop him, will he, Father?" Nicodemus asked.

"You're right son, but others may get hurt in the process. That is why I'm here. I want to make sure you are safe." Benjamin added, *"Let's get some sleep now. In the morning I want to hear about your trip to Jericho."*

Five days later, the news reached the Temple. Herod had struck again. In a fit of rage, he had ordered soldiers to go to Bethlehem. Once there, they slaughtered--on Herod's command--every boy two years old and younger. It was done in secret and in the middle of the night. Soldiers with torches and swords flashing burst into homes, executing the infant boys of Bethlehem. It had been reported that 20 boys had died at the hands of this bloody tyrant. The Parthian priests had escaped, and no one knew if they had found the One they were searching for.

Chapter Six:
The Law

As Nicodemus began his training under Rabbi Joshua, he often heard the famous saying of the day by the most famous teacher Hillel: *"If I am not for myself, who will be for me? If I am not for others, what am I? And if not now, when?"* It was discussed in detail as the study of the "Oral Torah" began. It reflected the high moral standard of the Jewish people. It was contrasted with their conquerors, the Romans. Rome liked to elevate its own morality, but out here in Judea, far from the seven sacred hills of Rome, might made right! The only truth was power! It was reflected in Roman/Jewish relations as well. Many in the Sanhedrin had already been influenced by Rome's power and wealth. Even the Chief Priest and the Nasi (President) of the Sanhedrin were now appointed by Rome. But there were still some in academic circles who answered to a higher ethic than the denarius. The School of Hillel wielded great influence still. But as the Jewish teachers strove to hang on to their ethic, the pendulum began to swing ever so imperceptibly toward legalism. For most, Moses became the standard bearer, not Abraham. Sinai usurped Mt Moriah as the oracle of truth. God's sacred covenant with Abraham became seen for its physical and genealogical implications. The spiritual truths of the covenant were emphasized less and less. The result of this shift allowed mercy to be sacrificed. Even the Messiah was seen more as the restorer of the Law of Moses and less as the Suffering Servant of Isaiah's prophecy.

Nicodemus never even noticed how his tender heart was being affected. The more he sat at the feet of Rabbi Joshua and dreamed of one day being a great teacher himself, the less he thought about the spiritual impact of the Passover lamb. Gradually he began to compartmentalize that first image of the lamb dying at the hands of the priest for evening sacrifice. He did the same with his memories of Simeon and his final words: *"The Lamb has come."* Obedience became preeminent. But still, whenever he would travel back to Ein

Karem and speak with his father and Zechariah, he felt a spark of something deep inside, like an ember glowing under his mother's cooking pot. He could not explain it. It would grow dim every time he returned to school, but it never really was extinguished.

The strong legalistic tendency of the major schools was seen also by the aristocratic Jewish families as the only way to defend against the moral vacuum that was Hellenism, as well as the Roman abuses of the individual. In truth, it was the Jewish people and their strong ethical upbringing which stood as a beacon of morality in the cesspool that was the Roman Empire.

The Greek influence was still visible throughout Israel with its deification of individual pleasure. The pursuit of pleasure as an ideal was not limited to Asia Minor; the tentacles of Greek philosophy had reached the most remote regions of the empire. Greek style theaters — adopted by Rome — were built even in the heart of the Galilee. Sepphoris was in the process of being rebuilt by Herod Antipas during the early education of Nicodemus in Jerusalem. The Romans had even employed local Jewish teknon (stone masons or carpenters) in its construction. The son of the late Herod the Great, Herod Antipas — tetrarch of Galilee — was also building Tiberius as his new capital in Galilee.

Rome exerted its influence by power and might but also by the flow of wealth and the corruption of the Jewish Ruling Council. The Sanhedrin was allowed to govern over religious matters by the Romans. By controlling the appointment of the High Priest and the religious leaders, Rome had an uncomfortable yet pragmatic system in place. Revolt was limited to minor skirmishes as it was made clear by the Roman governor that any threat to their power would bring the swift and merciless end to the Sanhedrin. In this way, an unholy alliance was created that maintained the peace. Still, factions continued to exist in the Sanhedrin. Serious spiritual leadership was rare. Even priests in the temple often bilked the common people, overcharging them for sacrificial animals and gorging themselves on animals sacrificed in the temple, even Passover lambs.

Nicodemus was initially oblivious to all this. His father was one of the rare priests who took his service seriously and reared his son to be the same. Ein Karem was just far enough away from Jerusalem to be isolated from the spiritual hypocrisy of the city. Benjamin had been mentored by Simeon and truly missed his genuine and devout presence in the Temple. Benjamin visited his son regularly in Jerusalem even when he was not on duty. They would have long conversations about the topics introduced by Rabban Joshua.

One of Rabban Joshua's favorite techniques after thorough study of one of the books of the Torah was a concept called Remez (hint). It required a brilliant mind and total recall not only of a few verses of Scripture but entire chapters and the context. The technique involved the introduction of a topic or question. Then a phrase from the text would be quoted by a skilled Rabbi that only partially addressed the question at hand. The key lay in the context of the verses that surrounded the quoted text. Only the brightest students would be able to see the inference from the quoted text. In this way the most gift students in the class would teach the slower students. Sometimes the teacher would also introduce a topic for discussion about a finer point of the Law's application and not quote any text. He may only make a hand gesture that alluded to a text. Nicodemus loved this style of teaching as he had already memorized most of the Torah and the Psalms. He was not only gifted in recalling large sections of Scripture, but he perfectly applied the context to discussions.

Nicodemus would often test his father with this technique during their long discussions in the evenings when his father visited. On one occasion after Joshua had led the class on a long discussion of Ezekiel 34, Nicodemus decided to introduce a topic. As they sat under the full moon on the roof of their house in Jerusalem enjoying fresh grapes from Benjamin's vineyard, Nicodemus began: *Father, sometimes shepherds on the hills of Bethlehem care little for the sheep. I have even heard stories that some corrupt, hired shepherds slaughter a lamb, roast and eat it and then tell the chief shepherd that the lamb was attacked by a wild animal. How does the Lord respond to unfaithful, corrupt shepherds?"* Nicodemus had thought long and hard about the question to ask after crafting the story. He wanted to leave the question vague enough that it could lead his father to think he was discussing the requirements and responsibilities of a priest in the Temple or a Rabbi. He expected his father would be led to the book of Leviticus and to one of the finer points of the law. He assumed his father would get the analogy. Only the dullest in his class thought that Joshua was talking about literal sheep and shepherds when he had described the same scene in class. However, Nicodemus knew he was alluding to the prophet Ezekiel and the unfaithful shepherds of Ezekiel 34. But the real focus of the chapter was the Messianic element introduced with the words, *"I myself will shepherd my people."* (Ezekiel 34:15)

As Nicodemus asked the question, his father paused, looking off into the distance, and a puzzled look came across his face. Of course, this was pretense. Benjamin knew exactly where his son was leading, but he played along. Benjamin was very familiar with the teaching concept of Remez and decided to quote a text from Genesis 22, hoping it would confuse his son. *"God himself will provide the lamb,"* (Genesis 22:8) his father finally said with a straight face, trying not to laugh. He had intentionally quoted a Messianic verse from the sacrifice of Isaac, thereby hitting the issue even more pointedly than his son could imagine. After a long pause, his father began to chuckle as his son sat bewildered, not knowing how to respond to this perfect response. Nicodemus could hardly contain himself and began to laugh uncontrollably at how brilliant his father was in not falling for the elaborate trap. *"How did you know I was describing a Messianic image,"* Nicodemus asked between laughs.

"Ah," his father responded, *"you are in your last year with Joshua and he is known for using that story to confuse his class and keep them humble after they have finished studying Ezekiel. By the way, how many students did he trip up this year?"*

"Every single one!" Nicodemus responded with a chuckle, *"Even me!"*

Chapter 7:
The Baptist

In the second year of Nicodemus' schooling at the Temple, Rabban Joshua had organized a second educational trip to the Jericho site. They had planned to camp again beside the Jordan River at the traditional site of Israel's crossing a thousand years before. This time they spent two days recounting the destruction of Jericho and had even marched around the ancient ruins as God's people had done. They recited the verses that described how God had brought down this mighty city. In the glow of their evening fire by the Jordan, Rabban Joshua talked about how God had used even Rahab the prostitute in Jericho to accomplish his purposes. Many of the boys disagreed with Joshua's application of this text. They could not understand why God would save a sinner and they refused to agree that mercy was a quality God wanted them to show toward the "sinners" in Jerusalem. Nicodemus found himself coming to the defense of Joshua. *"Who of us is not in need of God's mercy,"* he challenged one of the oldest boys.

"I'm not and you shouldn't be either, Nicodemus," he replied, *"mercy comes after repentance not before!"*

Joshua quelled the argument between the two with a quick retort, *"That is up to God, not you, young man! Scripture is the expression of God's will, not yours!"* The disagreement between Rabban Joshua and his brightest pupil was not new. It was a constant battle. But this was the first time that Nicodemus dared to oppose the hard line older boy.

News spread from travelers the next day that King Herod had come to Jericho. His illness, which had been the talk of Jerusalem for months, had driven him to his Palace retreat under the swaying palms along the river. Some said he was being eaten alive and nothing brought him relief. Many were of the opinion that the curse of Jericho was the cause of his disease. He had built a palatial palace at the ancient site, something God had expressly forbidden.

51

Numerous times in the last millennium, others had done the same and felt the effects of the curse. Rabban Joshua decided that it would be safer to go back to Jerusalem and not be near this tyrant whose violence and hate could lead him to do anything. On the road back to Jerusalem, they met Roman soldiers who were transporting prisoners to Jericho. Two were priests and friends of Joshua's. He later learned that Judas and Matthias -- known as zealot priests -- had organized a band of 40 men to pull down the immense golden eagle that hung over the great gate of the Temple. It had been put there by Herod to the disgust of every Jew in Jerusalem. The two priests had willingly surrendered when they were surrounded by Roman troops from the Antonio Fortress, but not before they had removed all signs of Herod's rule. Many of the Roman soldiers hated Herod almost as much as the Jews did, but allowing for any signs of unrest simply was not tolerated in Jerusalem, no matter who was king. The 40 men and the priests were eventually burned alive in the theatre in Jericho after a mock public trial where Herod, carried in on his couch, served as accuser and judge. The next week Herod returned to Jerusalem and, upon receiving permission from Rome, promptly executed his son Antipater on charges of murdering his half-brothers Alexander and Aristobulus. Buoyed by this violence, Herod rallied for a few days and ordered his sister to round up respected aristocrats and imprison them in the Hippodrome with orders to execute them at his death, which followed just five days later. She was unable to follow through with the orders. One of the few remaining children of Herod, Archeleus was urged by the army to take the throne. Wisely he resisted until Rome agreed. But when it became known in Jerusalem how the zealots and the two priests had been burned alive, resistance followed with demonstrations in the Temple courts. Archeleus responded in typical Roman fashion; he slaughtered more than 3,000 Jews on the most sacred site of the Temple itself. The following weeks were filled with intrigue as a large Jewish Roman contingent that exceeded 8,000 went to Rome to express a desire that the entire Herodian family should be deposed. It didn't happen, and

Archeleus was declared "ethnarch" and imposed new taxes. While this was going on, fresh revolts broke out in Jerusalem and Philip, Archeleus' stepbrother, left orders that any revolt should be met with executions and crucifixions.

Before the violence broke out, Rabban Joshua sent all his students home until further notice. Benjamin had arrived in the city shortly after word reached him of Herod's trip to Jericho. He brought Nicodemus home to Ein Karem to continue his studies under Rabban Terah.

Nicodemus spent time at the home of Zechariah and even helped little John take his first steps. For Nicodemus it was like having a younger brother, and the two became inseparable as John grew. When John reached his third birthday, Nicodemus even taught John the Hebrew alphabet with a mnemonic song he had made up himself. By age five John helped Nicodemus in his father's vineyard when Nicodemus was not in school. They often could be seen walking hand in hand through the vineyard picking up branches heavy with grapes. Having fallen into the dirt, they tied them to the trellis so that the branches would be in the sunlight and produce more fruit. Rabban Terah had often used this analogy, describing God as the Good Keeper of the Vineyard who not only pruned his people but rescued those who had fallen into sin, empowering them with the radiance of his glory once again. As they worked, Nicodemus would share this parable with John who was always very eager to learn the Scriptures already as a toddler.

Nicodemus remained in Ein Karem and never returned to school in Jerusalem. He was only one of three students his age in secondary school under Rabban Terah. His knowledge expanded quickly throughout his teen years. At thirteen he began Bet Midrash, which included a study of all the prophets and the other sacred writings, including the Proverbs of Solomon and Ecclesiastes, as well as the historical books of Scripture: Joshua, Judges, Chronicles, Kings and Samuel. By the time he was fifteen, Nicodemus had committed most of these books to memory. He knew the context and circumstance of each book and became adept at Remez, often defeating Rabban Terah in this challenging technique of debate. By this time John had also joined Beth Sepher. John and Nicodemus would often walk through the vineyards after school singing psalms and discussing Scriptures. John could not have had a better mentor and friend. The boy's long hair set him apart and often other children would stigmatize him for his different ways. Nicodemus not only sympathized with John but encouraged him in his unique calling as a Nazarite.

Nicodemus continued his studies while helping his father with the vineyard. He spent a lot of time in the vineyard, especially during the summer months. School was limited to four hours a day during the summer because of the heat, so Nicodemus would spend time with the workers in the vineyard tying up branches to the trellis. By the time he was 20, Nicodemus was the most learned student of the Scriptures in Ein Karem, surpassing even the aged Zechariah. He could now interpret Scripture adeptly. Only one step in his academic life was yet to be attained: Talmidim (Disciple). Benjamin's influence and wealth in Jerusalem gained him access to the most venerated of Rabbis. The greatest by far was Gamaliel, who not only headed the School of Hillel, but every three years would ask 12 of the most promising students to become his disciples. Becoming a talmid, or student, meant more than just learning what the teacher knew. It meant becoming like the teacher in every way. That meant watching, listening and imitating how the Rabbi lived, how he interacted with others, how he applied the Law in his life. It was an intense emotional and educational commitment.

The day Benjamin heard from Gamaliel that he was interested in asking his son to become his Talmidim, he could barely contain himself. He wanted to immediately leave Jerusalem and return home with the good news, but Gamaliel restrained him.

"I must ask him myself, Benjamin," the Rabbi told him. *"This has been the custom of our school for generations. It must be done face to face and while he is engaged in his daily duties. This is to emphasize that he is walking away from his life to devote himself*

54

entirely to this endeavor. If he hesitates or asks for time to consider or wants to finish something he is working on, the offer is rescinded. He must respond by dropping any tools of his trade on the spot. I will describe to him in a few brief sentences the nature of the calling and then will speak just two words to him: 'Follow Me!' He knows this, as do you, Benjamin."

"You are correct, Rabbi. My excitement got the better of me. When will you do this?" Benjamin asked.

"Tomorrow at first light I will walk to your home alone. You are to remain here and may follow in a few hours. If Nicodemus is with me as we walk back to Jerusalem, you may greet him when we meet, but for the next three years he will be staying where I stay along with the 11 others I will ask to join me. You will be welcome to visit us, and we will travel and teach in the synagogues of Judea and Galilee. If all goes well, when we finish after three years, Nicodemus may choose to become a Rabbi himself in our school. I am hoping he will and I promise I will counsel him along the way. There is a growing influence of Rome among us, even in the Sanhedrin. We need devout scholars. And I am hoping that one day Nicodemus will join us in the Sanhedrin when an opening becomes available. We need sincere and devout learned men who have not been seduced by Roman money and power."

"I am most pleased Rabbi. This has been a mutual desire of Rachel and me for some time, Nicodemus also! I know for sure what he will say!" Benjamin responded.

Benjamin could hardly contain his joy. He so wanted to share the news with his wife, but there would be time for that tomorrow after he met Nicodemus and the most learned scholar in all of Israel on the path from his home. *"Talmidim! What a blessing!"* Benjamin whispered as he walked from the Temple courts where he had spoken with Gamaliel. A broad smile crossed his face as he descended the southern stairs and headed for his home in Jerusalem.

The next morning at dawn Gamaliel left his home and headed for Ein Karem, the home of his friend Benjamin. Benjamin followed one hour after sunrise. As Gamaliel rounded the bend in the Roman road just one mile from the Shechem gate, he noticed a crowd that had gathered on the roadside. Several men had helped an injured traveler onto his donkey, while his traveling companion was unmoving and lifeless beside the road. Robbers often ambushed travelers at this dangerous corner in the road. It was apparent that this couple had been beaten severely. Just then Benjamin arrived and recognized the priestly garments of the man. He quickened his pace, arriving just as Zechariah lifted his head from the neck of the donkey. Blood had stained the donkey's gray coat and was dripping onto the pavement stones of the Roman road. He looked into the eyes of Benjamin and tried to talk. Benjamin drew close as his old friend whispered in his ear, *"Take John!"* Then the old priest let out a groan and collapsed onto the donkey. He was barely breathing.

"I found them under an olive tree just down there," Gamaliel pointed to a dip in the road that curved around an olive grove, *"Must have happened shortly before I arrived. They killed Elizabeth with one blow to the head. Zechariah must have fought them off. His hands are bloodied and there is bruising on his forearms. I found him barely breathing."*

"Quick, take them to my home in Jerusalem," Benjamin shouted to the men who are leading the two donkeys, *"I'll run ahead and get the physician."*

But by the time the donkeys arrived with their burden, Zechariah had already died. Benjamin spent the rest of the day arranging for his dear friends to be transported back to Ein Karem. His mind was filled with how he would tell Nicodemus and little John. A 10-year-old boy should not have to deal with such sorrow. At 20, Nicodemus had already witnessed just how violent Judea was. He would be better suited to handle this shock, but Benjamin worried about John. He and Zechariah had talked many times about John's future. His father did not expect to live long enough to see his son fulfill his calling, so he had shared his intent for John's preparation. *"If I die before the boy is 12, I want him to continue in school here at Ein*

Karem. Then I want you to search for a certain Rabbi in the wilderness near En Gedi among the sect of the Essenes. He will know what to do." These were the words of Zechariah to his friend Benjamin, spoken just days earlier. Did he know the end was near for him? For now, John would come to live with him while he finished school. With a heavy heart, Benjamin turned these thoughts over in his head as he followed the oxen pulling the cart which carried these two dear friends back to Ein Karem for burial. He had forgotten entirely about the joyful anticipation that had filled his heart at sunrise. He couldn't imagine Nicodemus leaving John now to become a Talmidim under Gamaliel. He would speak with Gamaliel in a few days, after things had calmed down.

The oxen could not take the normal route to Ein Karem. They were too wide for the narrow path that led through the olive and grape farms. Benjamin took them on the long route that lead north of Ein Karem and approached the hilltop village from the other side of town. Nicodemus was working in the vineyards with John when he heard the oxen cart rumble through the village and come to rest at the home of Zechariah and Elizabeth. He and John came running from the vineyard when they saw Benjamin untying the cart.

"What have you brought, father?" Nicodemus asked as he walked around to the rear of the cart, followed by John. Benjamin held out his arm to restrain his son, but Nicodemus was taller and stronger than his father now. Immediately Nicodemus noticed the blood-stained linen sheets and the outline of the faces of his dear friends. He jumped onto the cart and pulled back the sheet. *"No!!!"* he shouted to the heavens. *"No!"*

John just stood still, his long hair blowing in the breeze as tears streamed down his face. John seldom wept. He always had demonstrated complete control of his emotions, unlike Tela. John had always been a rock, even when he endured teasing from other children for how different he was. He would even confront his tormentors, look them in the eye, and tell them to stop. But now events were beyond his control. The shock of loss left him frozen in place. There was no one to tell, *"Stop!"*

He fell to his knees, looked down and covered his face with both hands, *"Lord, God, give me strength!"* he whispered.

Chapter 8:
Essenes

John lived with Benjamin and Rachel for the next two years as he continued his studies under Rabban Terah along with Nicodemus who was 10 years his senior. It was traditional for students to learn in their home village from a community hired teacher or rabbi. Even though Nicodemus had spent some time in Jerusalem under Rabbi Joshua, this was quite unusual and only the wealthiest could afford this. Nicodemus was much happier staying at home these past years and he was now a special blessing to John. The tragic death of John's parents had a sobering impact on the boy. He seemed to withdraw into himself and when he did speak in class, he did so with intense focus on the subject. He and Nicodemus would still stroll through the vineyards and tie up vines in the summer time. Their conversations never returned to light subjects however. Nicodemus took even more care to protect John from the taunts of his classmates. He would watch carefully as he sat in the back, copying texts from the prophets, noting any tension between John and another student. Several times Nicodemus spoke privately with John's classmates and warned them about any teasing or bullying. But as John grew, he needed this less and less. He developed a "fire in his soul for righteousness," which was how Nicodemus described it to his father. When he looked at you, you could not help but feel the full measure of God's displeasure with your failings. The two would often accompany Benjamin to Jerusalem. Nicodemus particularly missed the wisdom of Zechariah's words during the 4-hour walk. Rabban Terah gave John much leeway in his school schedule as Benjamin had shared with him the plans Zechariah had for the boy in the desert of Judea.

As the day drew close for John's transition, Nicodemus would initiate conversations about the future. Nicodemus himself was still unsure whether he wanted to pursue a life in the spiritual cauldron of Jerusalem or a quiet life keeping a vineyard. John was less indecisive, even though he was only 12 now. He spoke openly with Nicodemus about visions from God and even dreams of a coming kingdom.

"A day of judgment is coming, Nicodemus," John told him one day as they walked among the olive grove below Ein Karem. *"I sense it in my spirit, and I know I am to play a role."*

"I know John; you have the temperament for it," Nicodemus responded. *"I'm sure your father shared what Gabriel told him about you!"*

"He did tell me, but not everything. He said the Lord would make it clear," John stated.

*"'**To make ready a people prepared for the Lord.'** (Luke 1:17) That is the phrase I have always remembered from your father's description,"* Nicodemus recalled. *"Somehow you will be involved in this time of preparation for the arrival of the Messiah."*

"Yes, Nicodemus. It is like my life is a painting, and in my visions and dreams, I can only see the broad strokes of a brush. My time with the Essenes will make that clear, I believe."

Just then Benjamin came walking through the olive grove and greeted his son and John. *"Good morning boys. How goes the work?"* he asked.

"Not much work today, Father. John and I were just talking about the future, his and mine." Nicodemus responded.

"Good topic," Benjamin stated looking at John. *"I remember well when I was the age of each of you. Everything in front of you, wanting time to hurry up, as if the future held some secret to certainty. Time, I have found, however, is a trickster. It tempts us into thinking our future is up to us and just the right decision will change everything. But you know what David wrote in Psalm 31! We sang it in the temple when my division was on duty!"*

"My times are in your hands; deliver me from the hands of my enemies!" (Psalm 31:15) Nicodemus sang the familiar Passover worship tune as John added his voice to the second line. The two would often sing the mnemonic tunes Nicodemus had composed for the Scriptures while they worked in the vineyard. John particularly liked this Psalm as he felt a kind of kinship with David. Both he and David waited on the Lord to see how He would shape their future in the kingdom. John was not running from an evil king, but he sensed that someone just like Saul was in his future.

"Let your face shine on your servant; save me in your unfailing love.
Let me not be put to shame, Lord, for I have cried out to you;
But let the wicked be put to shame and be silent in the realm of the dead.
Let their lying lips be silenced,
for with pride and contempt they speak arrogantly against the righteous." (Psalm 31:16-18)

John and Nicodemus continued singing the familiar Psalm, John's voice dropping off during the last line. Something about those last words brought a disturbance inside him. When they finished, Benjamin added, *"I knew you two would know that Scripture. I believe it is particularly relevant for both of you right now. It is especially true since we will be going to Passover next week. I've been asked to assist with the many pilgrims coming, and that Psalm will be sung in worship. Then I'll be traveling down the Jericho road with you, John, and leaving you with the Essenes. Nicodemus, you can stay at our home in Jerusalem. There are some friends in the Sanhedrin who would like to speak with you after the Sabbath following Passover."*

"What's this about, Father?" Nicodemus asked.

"You'll see soon enough." Benjamin answered, *"But it is something I've been working on for some time. We'll talk more about it after they've spoken to you. One of the men is Joseph from Arimathea, just so you know. He is a high ranking member and quite influential. Just listen to what they have to say."*

"My, I can only imagine what this is about. Is it about becoming a talmid again?" Nicodemus prodded his father.

61

"Just wait son... it is better than that." Benjamin hinted. Benjamin had been in discussion with Joseph and Gamaliel and several wealthy aristocrats in Jerusalem concerning the vacancy in the Sanhedrin. Sanhedrin members were nominated by the wealthy Jewish families in and around Jerusalem. These families took the responsibility seriously to nominate only the keenest minds. The nomination would be presented to the Nasi (Ruler) in the Sanhedrin. It was a formality, as the Nasi seldom would object. Most members of the Sanhedrin were there because of family connections to the wealthy Jewish families who had funded their education. Some had risen from poor families to the most prestigious positions and none of them were inclined to bite the hand that provided. Nicodemus was well known to most of the members, the Temple priests, and Rabbis. He had shown an adept knowledge of the Scriptures and had progressed through school well ahead of his peers. His integrity was beyond reproach and this is what particularly drew the attention of the Sanhedrin members like Joseph. There had been not only a cultural invasion of Hellenism in Israel, but it had infected even the Sanhedrin. Oddly enough it was particularly pervasive among the members from the School of Shammai — a school that taught a strict interpretive approach to the Torah. There had been many debates in its chambers about observance of the Sabbath particularly. These debates took place regularly in the Temple courts. Rabban Terah and Joshua, whom Nicodemus had sat before, were strong proponents of the School of Hillel. This school of thinking took a more reasoned and liberal approach to the Torah. In the heated debates between these two schools, the School of Shammai had been accused of teaching that "man was made for the Sabbath," not Sabbath made for man.

Benjamin and his influential friends wanted Nicodemus to fill the vacant position on the Sanhedrin. They planned to present him with Joseph as his mentor. He would school him as a Pharisee while he served as a junior member. It would be hard for the Nasi to object to this as it had been done many times before. But the real sticking point would be that Nicodemus was not married. It was not written anywhere that a Sanhedrin member had to be married, but every one of them was married and it was an assumed prerequisite. Nicodemus and Benjamin had talked of this, and he was currently enamored with a young girl named Rachel in Ein Karem. However, none of the details had been discussed between the families. Nicodemus also needed to build his home on the family complex. The requisite engagement period would be another obstacle to his nomination. Nicodemus did not know any of this maneuvering behind the scenes, but the motivation was particularly strong in the School of Hillel members to fill this position with this gifted young man. Joseph and Gamaliel were particularly motivated because a promising brilliant student in the School of Shammai was emerging as another candidate. However, this young man was also not married, and the rumor had gone around that few women had any interest in him. His name was Saul of Tarsus, and he was a brilliant debater. The popular opinion was that his skill would have been a match for Satan himself in Eden. But what Nicodemus lacked in intensity, he more than made up for in the knowledge of Scripture and his ability at interpretation. This ability and authority to interpret called "S'mikhah", was normally given to only the most brilliant Rabbis. Rabban Terah had gone through this formal process with Nicodemus when it became apparent that Nicodemus had already shown the ability to interpret Scripture. Most Rabbis were allowed to only repeat accepted interpretations, so it was particularly unique for Nicodemus to be granted this exceptional authority so young. To make a new interpretation was referred to by Rabbis as "having authority!" Rabban Terah had presented his prize student in Jerusalem for this honor when he was only 21. Gamaliel had been one of the Teachers of the Law who sat on the examination committee. The young man amazed the committee not only with his flawless recitation but also his ability to deftly divide the text and suggest the will of God behind the text. The two-day examination took place at the Temple. Candidate Nicodemus stood before a semicircle of 12 learned teachers—some were Sanhedrin members--

and answered every question without hesitation. It was this and his humility before the text that so impressed Gamaliel and made him regret how the circumstances of Zechariah and Elizabeth's untimely murder kept Nicodemus from becoming a *talmid* under him. But now his appointment to the Sanhedrin was even more critical.

Benjamin, Nicodemus and 12-year-old John left for Jerusalem on the Friday before Pesach. John's life would be a simple one among the Essenes. He would only need an extra linen tunic. All else would be provided on his arrival. So, it did not take long for John to pack. The walk through the vineyards and olive groves brought back memories of the journey Nicodemus had taken with his father 12 years earlier with Zechariah. Anticipation and the discussion of Gabriel's appearance to the old priest had filled Nicodemus' mind. Now his mind was preoccupied with the departure of John. This would most certainly be his last walk on this trail with John. Nicodemus tried to engage John with fond memories of their journeys and walks along these paths, but John seemed to be in another place. He seemed to know that the significance of his life was before him and the memories of his days in Ein Karem were just that; memories, nothing more.

Passover week went smoothly. Nicodemus choose the lamb on Sunday and put John in charge of the lamb for the week. The lamb seemed to follow John everywhere immediately. They were inseparable all week long. It reminded Nicodemus of the time twelve years earlier when he experienced his first Passover. John prepared the lamb's meal and his bedding. The lamb would even follow him through the market. Other lambs would wander from their owners in the confusion of the myriad of people in the streets of Jerusalem but not this lamb. John used the Hebrew word for calling attention: "Hinneh" (הִנֵּה) when he would turn a corner in the market or on the Mt. of Olives. Immediately the lamb would raise its head and follow John's lead. Even when John walked to the Temple for the sacrifice of the lamb, he used no rope to keep it from running away. It walked dutifully behind John. Even when the priest approached to slit the lamb's throat, John had trained the lamb to raise its head at his signal. When the priest raised his knife, there was not even a single bleat even as the lamb bled and died in John's arms. *"So he opened not his mouth!"* (Isaiah 53:7) These words from Isaiah leapt to Nicodemus' mind as he watched. John seemed to know that there was something prophetic in all of this. The painting was becoming clear.

The day after the Passover Sabbath, Benjamin left with John, walking out the Eastern Gate and down the 17 mile Jericho road. The return would be a bit tougher for the aging man. It was a steep and dangerous road, climbing almost 3300 feet in elevation between Jericho and Jerusalem. Robbers often hid in the bushes around interior bends of the road as it snaked along the Judean hills. Benjamin took along a shepherd's rod just for this kind of journey. He did not wear his priestly robes. It was better to wear something less conspicuous and less valuable. Nicodemus remained behind in Jerusalem. Later that morning he would meet a man named Joseph who would share the news that his father had kept secret.

Nicodemus said a quick prayer for his father's safety as he headed for his meeting in the Temple with Joseph. The city streets were still empty but would soon be filled with travelers headed home after Passover. The week would be much different as the city adjusted to its normal population after swelling to more than 2 million during Pesach. Nicodemus climbed the Southern Steps to the Temple. Joseph approached him along with Gamaliel.

"Shalom Master Gamaliel." Nicodemus went to one knee in respect for the learned teacher.

"Shalom, and greetings young man, I have been looking forward to this meeting. This is Joseph from Arimathea. He has only served in the Sanhedrin for a few years but has proven himself faithful." Gamaliel motioned to the tall, slender man in his early thirties next to him.

"Greetings and Shalom, Nicodemus. I have heard much about you from Master Gamaliel." Joseph extended his hand and greeted Nicodemus.

"Thank you, Joseph. May I ask the subject of this meeting?" Nicodemus responded.

"Right to the point, I like that," Gamaliel continued. *"Let's find a private room where we can talk."*

The three walked along the Colonnade and passed by a number of teachers, priests, and Rabbis who were engaged in a deep conversation with a young boy about John's age. In fact as Nicodemus passed by, he thought at first that it was John. The features of this boy were strikingly similar to John except John's hair was long. They entered an interior room where visiting priests prepared for service. It was empty now with the end of Passover and lent itself to privacy.

"This won't take long," Gamaliel began. *"You may not be aware that about two years ago I was on my way to your home when I came upon your dear friends, Zechariah and Elizabeth. How is John doing by the way? I hear he is a special boy and that your father and Rachel took him into your home."*

"Yes, John and I became quite close over the last two years. Father has taken him to an Essene community in Qumran just this morning," Nicodemus explained. *"But I did not know you were coming to Ein Karem. You were coming to visit Father?"*

"No, to see you, as a matter of fact," Gamaliel smiled at the prospect of leading into his announcement by building on just how much he regarded Nicodemus. *"I was coming to invite you to become a Talmidim."*

"I am humbled," Nicodemus sat down on one of the long benches used by the priests. *"Really?"* He looked up at Gamaliel, visibly stunned.

"That should not surprise you. You are highly regarded among the teachers of the Law. Many on the Sanhedrin feel the same. In fact, we have been discussing you as the one to fill the vacancy. I

have been asked by a group of influential leaders to ask you to join us."

"Doesn't one normally have to have already become a Pharisee or at least a priest? And I am not married." Nicodemus' honest humility was clearly apparent in his response.

"Exceptions have and can be made to procedure," Gamaliel interrupted. *"As for marriage, your father tells me you have an interest in that area?"*

Nicodemus blushed and chuckled, *"Well...yes. But there are some logistics and I...uh, we—father and I—have not yet negotiated the bride price with the family."*

"What are your plans in that area?" Gamaliel asked directly.

"I love her and actually had in mind to speak with Father once we are home again after Passover." Nicodemus composed himself but could feel the blush across his face.

"With that in place," Joseph interjected, *"we could present your name to the Council from the committee in charge of nominations as early as our meeting after the Feast Days."*

"I would be much honored." Nicodemus responded with a slight bow.

"You will discover this soon enough," Joseph added. *"There are movements in the Sanhedrin that are disturbing. You know well the make-up of the Council of 71. We do not lack for politics. The Roman influence is what we really fear. A few among us are in the procurator's pocket. That is why we see your appointment as important right now. Hellenism is also becoming more and more influential at the highest levels, especially among the sect of Sadducees in our midst."*

"That is dangerous and spiritually disturbing," Nicodemus added. *"So how can I be of help there? I am young, inexperienced in such matters, and certainly lack the authority and reputation to be influential."*

"Yes, you are young," Gamaliel responded. *"In fact you would be the youngest ever. You will have Joseph here as a mentor. I will*

train you on the finer points of the Pharisees and the Law. You are already adept at debate. I have heard you. You were most impressive in your interview for "S'mikhah. But it is your sincerity and heart for the Law that is lacking in the Sanhedrin. Age can bring wisdom if one is humble enough. But in many it has made them subject to the manipulations of the political operatives. Joseph will school you on the various agendas of each member. He knows them well. So, tell us when you and your Father have decided with Rachel's family on the length of the engagement and we will move forward. Agreed?"

"How did you know her name?" Nicodemus asked with a look of incredulity.

Gamaliel just smiled and motioned to the door as the three left the inner room.

The three passed the priests and rabbis in discussion with the same young boy. The group had grown to several dozen. He heard several of them on the periphery of the group say, *"Amazing! How does a Galilean boy get such learning?"* and *"He reminds me of a young Gamaliel!"* and *"He even interprets Scripture. Do you know who his Rabbi is in Nazareth?"* Nicodemus paused to listen to the discussion going on between the boy and Rabban Joshua. They were discussing one of the toughest subjects that stumped even the most learned of rabbis.

"Does one become a child of Abraham by faith or circumcision?" Nicodemus heard the boy ask Rabban Joshua. Nicodemus had heard this topic debated numerous times in the Temple courts by some of the keenest minds in Israel.

"Circumcision is an expression of a covenant relationship. Faith is our life and attitude in response to that covenant," Joshua responded.

The boy's response to Joshua's statement stunned Nicodemus and the gathering, *"So righteousness is attained by an act of man? Is an olive tree an olive tree BECAUSE it produces olives?"*

Every teacher went silent. Nicodemus looked around the circle. Stunned expressions. Puzzled looks. This young boy had answered his own question. They were stumped. Their theology—Nicodemus' learning included--emphasized that a fruit filled life of righteousness pleased God and was the foundation of the Law and relationship with God. With this one analogy, this boy had exposed the weakness of this perspective. *"An olive tree was one because it was created that way,"* Nicodemus thought to himself, *"the olives are a product of the tree God created. So, faith is the tree and olives...come... from the faith...God created?"* As Nicodemus ran this thought through his head, he walked slowly around the group trying to discern these words. The boy then quoted the verse to the song he had written long ago: **"Abraham believed God and he credited to him as righteousness."** (Genesis 15:6) Nicodemus stepped around the group and into the sunshine just outside the Colonnade. A ray of sunshine struck his face as he stepped out of the shade. He turned his head and looked at the boy as he passed. Their eyes met as the boy smiled and nodded.

Chapter 9:
Samaritan

Two days passed, and Benjamin still had not returned from Qumran. He had told Nicodemus he would only spend one night to make sure John was settled. He should have returned on Monday and now it was Tuesday evening and Nicodemus was becoming worried. He planned to leave for Qumran early the next morning to check on his father.

He had spent the last two days sitting in the Temple court listening to the conversations between the Galilean boy and the best minds in Jerusalem.

Such learning was not rare in Galilee; in fact it was more common than Judea. But there was a definite bias among the Judean teachers against them. Rabban Terah had often spoken to Nicodemus about this. Terah had visited the synagogue in Capernaum many times. The Rabbi there by the name of Jairus was an impressive scholar and so were the other Rabbis in the hill towns overlooking the Jezreel Valley. The Galileans were much more exposed to the outside world as the Via Maris bisected Galilee, while Jerusalem and its teachers were actually the ones isolated among the hills. The Galilean people were more educated in the Bible and its application than most Jews. More famous Jewish teachers came from Galilee than anywhere else in the world. They were known for their great reverence for Scripture and the passionate desire to be faithful to it. This translated into vibrant religious communities devoted to strong families and their country. Their synagogues echoed with debate and discussions about keeping the Torah. They resisted the pagan influences of Hellenism far more than did their Judean counterparts. So neither Terah nor Nicodemus were as shocked at the home area of this boy. But the boy was not just wise. He was humble and had a reverence for the Temple as if it was his home. Nicodemus sat with Terah listening to the debates about the Torah, Sabbath, and

Passover. The current topic being discussed was the meaning and intent in animal sacrifice.

Terah leaned over and whispered to Nicodemus, *"Were you this brilliant at 12?"*

Nicodemus shook his head and mouthed the word *"No!"*

The next morning Nicodemus headed out the eastern gate, into the Kidron Valley, ascended the hill to Bethany and down the long and winding road to Jericho. There were few travelers along the way as most had already departed days earlier when Passover was over. He carried along a few provisions and a skin of fresh water. The Judean wilderness could quickly heat up, and the walk would take him at least four hours before the first water source near Jericho.

He had not even walked for an hour when he met an exhausted and frantic couple. They must have left Jericho before daybreak to already be this close to Jerusalem. He heard them talking as they approached.

"Where should we go first to look for him...the Temple?" The young woman asked her husband.

They met each other at a place where the path was so narrow that only one could safely pass at a time. Anticipating this, Nicodemus walked back uphill to an interior bend in the path where travelers could easily pass each other or rest on the large stones. They had been placed there to keep flash floods from washing away the path.

"Shalom and thank you," the husband said, pausing to rest on one of the stones. He was much older than his young wife, who was clearly very disturbed.

"Can I be of assistance?" Nicodemus asked genuinely.

"We are looking for our missing son," the man said. *"We came for Passover with the boy along with many friends and relatives. On the way home we discovered him missing. We have been walking for two days and don't know where to begin looking in the city."*

The woman looked up into Nicodemus' eyes. She had been crying, and her face was stained with tears. She gave him a half smile and begged, *"Did you happen to see him? He is only 12 and a very polite boy.* " Something in the way the woman talked reminded Nicodemus of someone, and he couldn't quite place her.

"No, I am sorry," Nicodemus replied. *"I'm also looking for my missing father. He passed this way on Sunday and was to have returned to Jerusalem by this time. I'm headed for Jericho and Qumran to look for him".* *"Wait..."* Nicodemus thought. *"Could the boy in the Temple be their son? Too much of a coincidence."*

Suddenly he placed the woman's voice and mannerisms. Elizabeth, yes! She was younger but could easily have been her sister.

"In the place where we stayed last night," the man responded, *"there was a man recovering from an attack by robbers along this road. I believe he said it had happened only a few days ago. You might start there."*

"Thank you so much! Was he badly injured?" Nicodemus asked.
"When we saw him, he was clearly recovering," the man answered.

"Great. Thank you!" Nicodemus was overjoyed and quickly headed down the trail. After walking to the bend, he suddenly remembered. He shouted back to the couple, *"Try looking for your son in the Temple! I'm not sure but I may have seen him there."* The couple waved, thanked him, and quickly continued on their way as did Nicodemus, buoyed by the news that his father had been seen. There was only one public inn between Bethany and Jericho, a little more than half way down the road. Benjamin could be there in less than an hour. As he hurried down the trail, his mind returned to the couple. They had seemed familiar, like he had seen them someplace before. It had been a long time ago, but he couldn't quite place where or when. *"It will come to me,"* he thought as he walked.

Benjamin was overjoyed to see his son walk around the bend on the Jericho road and approach the inn. He had just walked outside for some sun. It had been two days since leaving John in Qumran. He remembered being hit from behind and nothing more until he awoke to a stranger's face leaning over him, wiping his forehead with a cold wet cloth.

"My boy!" Benjamin shouted and immediately regretted it, holding his head.

"How are you father?" Nicodemus smiled, clearly overjoyed at the site of his father. They embraced for a long time and whispered in each other's ear: *"God be praised!"*

Finally, they sat in the finely carved acacia wood chairs that sat outside the inn. Benjamin proceeded to recall for his son what he could remember. He focused mostly on his rescuer, a Samaritan who had helped him up the steep trail to this place, even paying for his care and staying with him and changing his bandages.

"While I was sleeping yesterday, he must have slipped away," Benjamin related, *"but the Lord provided a precious couple who stayed here late last night. They were from Galilee, and even though they were clearly worried about their missing son, they were very compassionate toward me and changed my bandages this morning before they left very early. They seemed as surprised and pleased by the compassion of the Samaritan man as I was."*

"Yes, I met them just up the road. I think I met their son in the Temple, father. In fact, he has been there since Passover and has impressed all the teachers of the Law. Rabban Terah, Gamaliel and Joseph were all there listening to him and asking him questions. I'm sure they will find him there today."

"Good, I'm glad," Benjamin sighed. *"Good people! That reminds me, how did your meeting go?"*

"I completely forgot about that. I am very pleased by the honor," Nicodemus replied.

"You will accept, right? And marriage?" Benjamin inquired. *"Are you and Rachel ready for that step?"*

"Yes father. As soon as you are well enough to travel," Nicodemus added. *"We can sit with her parents and discuss the bride price. They are not poor people so there won't be an issue there, I am sure."*

"Give me a few more days here." Benjamin said as he leaned back in his chair. *"In fact I would like to find the Samaritan man and repay him. The innkeeper here said he stayed up all night with me, stopped the bleeding, and dressed my wounds with expensive ointment. Look at my arms, they are healing very quickly. I must find him. He has changed my attitude toward Samaritans. When we go home, I'll leave word with the owner of this house. He said the man is a trader in healing ointments from the East and comes through here often. He deserves a reward for his selflessness. Maybe I can connect him to some of my business friends in Jerusalem. I'm sure he finds it challenging to sell in Jerusalem as a Samaritan."*

"Father, if you are strong enough, I would like to hear about the Essene community where you left John," Nicodemus inquired.

"I'm feeling a bit tired, but let me share a few things. It is an ascetic sect, very serious people. I arrived on Sunday morning prayers. They do not normally accept any outsider and it was rare for them to even allow me to stay the night. When John was just 7 or 8, Zechariah told me that the Lord had sent one of them to his house. That same man welcomed me and only after sunset did he speak. He shared something of their order and that he had a dream that he was to travel to Ein Karem and speak with a priest there. Of course, that was Zechariah. He said that John would be a powerful prophet and that it was his duty to prepare John for this. John's oath as a Nazarite would be intensified under this sect, he told me. His mind and body purified. He would devote himself to prayer and join the division among them called Vathikim or "strong ones" who are devoted to prayer every morning at dawn. In addition, John would not eat meat or oil and drink no wine. He would never marry and remain chaste and pure, living in poverty with only the most simple of provisions in his home. The priest who visited Zechariah said that John would leave their company when he reached the age of maturity. He would be sent into the desert to fulfill his calling from God. The one meal I shared with the group was very unique. The young men served those seated. They were seated according to age

and rank, with only the oldest speaking but very quietly. They dressed only in white linen."

"Do you trust that John will be safe among them?" Nicodemus asked.

"I have no doubt," Benjamin responded. *"In some ways I envy their life of simplicity and purity. There is no sign of the corruption that infests Jerusalem. They have chosen to remove themselves from the entire system and focus on purity of mind and body. They have channeled water from the Judean hills and they bathe only in living water in their mikvehs. They do this several times a day. John is in good hands there."*

Benjamin remained at the small inn for four more days with his son, and they journeyed home after Sabbath. The journey was tiring for Benjamin. They stayed in Jerusalem for several days, resting, before making the four-hour journey back to Ein Karem. Nicodemus would miss John, their long walks, and singing the Scriptures among the olive groves.

But his thoughts quickly turned to Rachel, the girl who had captured his heart. After a month's time Benjamin was back to his old self. He and Nicodemus made plans to visit the home of Rachel's parents: Daniel and Sarah. Rachel was the youngest of six children and the precious apple of her father's eye. At sixteen, she was a beauty like none other. But for the last two years she never thought about marriage with any of her many suitors except the handsome and brilliant son of Benjamin and Rachel. She would not be tempted to be anything but faithful during the engagement period designed in Jewish culture to test the bride. Six months was the normal minimum amount of time for engagement. During this time Nicodemus would be required to build his home adjacent to his father's. Most Jewish homes were simple structures. Even the meaning of the Hebrew word for house, "Beth", meant a shelter. Most Jewish families spent most of their time out of doors and the house was used only for retiring from a long day. It was a place of rest. It also reflected a perspective about the faith of Jewish families.

They regarded their current house as only temporary and as such it was not adorned. It was only the wealthy Jewish landowners that spent time and effort in decorative tiles and paintings. Nicodemus found himself in between culture and expectation. He took time consulting not only with builders but with the elders of the community before starting to build his home. He finally decided on a simple home with an exterior that reflected his humble faith. The interior adornments would impress his new bride and the community. It took him the entire six months to build his home, and it included a tiled patio garden between his home and his parents. He had arranged for a new channel of water to flow from the spring in town to a fountain in the center of the garden. It was here that he intended to speak his vows to Rachel with her favorite flowers in full bloom. He could not wait.

Only Benjamin could decide when the house was acceptably prepared for the wedding. This was a father's duty and no one else, not even the bridegroom. Word was sent to Rachel's home that all was prepared. Nicodemus, with his father's blessing, rose early on a Wednesday, dressed in a new linen garment with a purple sash. Wednesday was the traditional day for a Jewish wedding, perhaps because it allowed the families to celebrate for three days before Sabbath, but also so that if there were any objections from the husband, they could be heard by the local council of elders before Sabbath. Benjamin had planned for a week of celebrations honoring the young couple, to be interrupted only by Sabbath. It was said that men married for one of four reasons: Passion, wealth, honor or for the "glory of God." The latter, rabbinical writings stated, produced children who "preserved Israel."

Rabbis also taught at the time that it was for man to pursue a woman, not a woman after a man. The argument went this way: since man was formed from the ground and the woman from a rib, in trying to find a wife, man looks for that which he had lost, the missing part of him.

Shortly after the meeting of Rachel's family with Nicodemus, official writings of betrothal (*shitre etrusin*) were drawn up by local officials and signed by the head of each family. It noted the obligations of both families, the dowry or bride-price, and other lesser significant details regarding living arrangements, children and the wedding plans. This ceremony also included the bridegroom giving his bride a single coin which expressed the debt of love between the two. The actual date of the wedding, which was always held at the home of the bridegroom, was never mentioned. This was solely determined at the will and good pleasure of the father of the bridegroom. The Chethubah, or statement of dowry, was a separate document and provided the minimum dowry of 200 denars for a young girl, almost always 16 or 17 years of age. 100 denars was the price for a widow. The priests in Jerusalem had set 400 denars as the price for the daughter of a priest. This was the absolute minimum. In the case of wealthy landowners, the price could be much higher. As Rachel and Nicodemus were both from wealthy land-owning families, the price was negotiated at 1000 denars which expressed more of a show of respect than compensation for the loss of an offspring.

As was custom, Nicodemus had chosen two groomsmen who served as intermediary emissaries. One attended to the groom, the other to the bride. These two, John and James, both married, would serve also the bride and groom during the wedding and the feast that followed. The *"friend of the bridegroom"* also had the custom of accompanying the couple to the bridal room after the wedding so that the chastity of the bride could be guaranteed. In some ancient writings, God himself is described as *"the friend of the bridegroom"* at the marriage in Eden. Moses is also described in Exodus as the same who leads out the bride, while Jehovah the bridegroom meets his bride at Sinai. (Psalm 68:7) In another rabbinical writing, the Almighty himself spoke the benediction, while Michael and Gabriel served as *friends of the bridegroom* to our first parents in Paradise.

Early on Wednesday morning Benjamin inspected the completed house Nicodemus had built. All preparations were completed in the tiled garden for the brief ceremony, including the planting of many white and purple flowers. It was then that Benjamin dispatched James, the friend of the bridegroom, to Rachel's home. Rachel had 10 young unmarried girls between ages 10-12 ready to receive her husband's attendant. Rachel's dress was a simple white dress, modest yet flowing with white silk lace. Her hair was tied up and covered with a silk veil covering her face. Her attendants received James, notifying their mistress that the time had come. Having been prepared for weeks, Rachel was ready within an hour. Her father had arranged for four attendants to carry her on a covered platform that sat between two poles. The journey would only take a matter of minutes. The bridal party was led by the 10 maidens who sang and danced in the front of the procession. Rachel's parents walked alongside. They were received by John, the bridegroom's attendant referred to as *"the friend of the bridegroom."* The platform was lowered for Rachel to step on the ground. With her head completely veiled, Rachel took Nicodemus' arm. Nicodemus' only assurance that this was Rachel was the gentle squeeze she gave to his arm as he led her. Nicodemus was very familiar with this gesture of affection. Before their engagement, Rachel would gently squeeze Nicodemus' arm and say good night. He could hardly contain the fullness of heart and the joy of anticipation this day had brought.

The ceremony that followed was simple. Rabban Terah awaited them in the garden under the arch adorned with white roses and olive branches. Still veiled, Nicodemus and Rachel stood before the Rabbi while Psalms of Praise were sung by Rachel's 10 attendants. Rabban Terah prayed and invited Nicodemus to speak his vow. In it he promised: *"It is my solemn vow to please, honor, nourish and care for Rachel."* Rachel repeated the same vow. At this, Rabban Terah poured a cup of wine into a golden chalice held by Nicodemus' attendant. He passed it along to Nicodemus and he drank, thereby sealing his vow. He then passed the cup to Rachel. Honor and commitment now passed to the bride. She could refuse to drink and thereby refuse the marriage. By drinking she accepted this formal and last expression of commitment to her husband. Under her veil, Rachel smiled and paused, looking into Nicodemus' eyes. He could not see her through the veil, but she could see the anticipation in his eyes. She lifted the cup under her veil and drank and returned the cup to him. She could not contain her joy and chuckled softly, squeezing his hand as she passed the cup. Nicodemus smiled broadly and returned the cup to John. Rachel, Nicodemus mother, sang a song based on a children's song she had sung to Nicodemus when he was very young. The song brought a smile to the face of Nicodemus. Rabban Terah stepped aside as John led the couple to the bridal chamber. As they slowly walked, two maidens stepped forward and lifted Rachel's veil and untied her hair. Rachel's long black hair tumbled down from the back of her head around her shoulders as the two entered the bridal chamber. They would soon return, and the festivities, toasts, meals, songs, dances and speeches would last well into the night. Each day different groups of people arrived for more celebrations. On the day of the wedding, only family and close friends from Ein Karem were in attendance. The second day, priests and Rabbis from Jerusalem arrived. The celebration was the highlight of the year in Ein Karem.

Chapter 10:
Contrasts and Contradictions

Jerusalem during the years following the marriage of Nicodemus and Rachel was one glorious contradiction. It was expressed in language, culture, population and religion. In reality, two worlds lived side by side in the holy city. There was Hellenism with its theater and Hippodrome, foreigners filling the court and crowding the city, and foreign ways and habits from the Roman procurator, newly appointed by Rome. On the other hand, there was the old Jewish world solidified in the Schools of Hillel and Shammai and overshadowed by the Temple and Synagogue. Each was pursuing opposing objectives and priorities.

Greek was the language of business. It was understood and spoken by most in the land. The study of Greek, while practiced, was actually forbidden by the Rabbis. But the language of the people was a dialect of ancient Hebrew: Palestinian Aramaic.

And just as there was a Jewish world and a Greek world living side by side, so was there piety and frivolity. Fortunes were lavished on the support of Jewish learning and on the advance of a nationalistic agenda. Next to this was priestly self-indulgence and avarice. The price of sacrificial animals was artificially raised and, at the same time, the rich would bring into the Temple the necessary sacrifices for the poor.

Citizens of Jerusalem–townspeople, as they preferred to be called– were polished, witty, and pleasant. Even the language of the city was different. The Jerusalem dialect was quicker, shorter and lighter. Their hospitality knew no bounds. No one considered his own house to be his own, and a stranger or pilgrim was always welcomed, especially for festivals. In the women's apartments, friends from the country would see every novelty of dress, jewelry and adornment, and could even examine themselves in looking glasses. A lady, it was said, could get anything in Jerusalem from a false tooth to a Persian shawl. The lavish lifestyle, however, led to the moral corruption of its people.

Politically, times had changed. The weak and wicked rule of Archeleus had lasted only nine years. Charges against him stuck and he was banished to Gaul. Judea, Samaria and Idumea were now incorporated into the Roman province of Syria under a Governor. However, the special administration of Judea was entrusted to a Procurator who resided at Caesarea on the coast. The new governor of Syria, Quirinius, after confiscating the wealth of Archeleus, ordered a census in Palestine with the objective of fixing a new tax code. A contingent of wealthy Jewish aristocrats had made this very overture to Caesar Augustus 10 years earlier hoping to rid themselves of the Herodian rule. What they received was worse. The Sanhedrin was stripped of its real power, though the Romans allowed for the Sanhedrin to continue to rule on religious questions. But the crackdown by Rome did not sit well with the populace and instead gave rise to a party of Nationalists referred to as Zealots, or Qannaim in Hebrew. Interestingly, the real home of the Zealots was not Judea or Jerusalem but Galilee.

In the 18 years that followed, the office of High Priest changed several times. Finally, Quirinius settled on Annas, son of Seth. Annas remained in this position for nine years before being deposed and his son-in-law Caiaphas appointed. The character of the High-Priests was described in terrible language. Words like self-indulgence, violence, luxury and even public indecency are included in the woes pronounced on the corrupt leaders of the priesthood. The house of Annas was particularly charged with "whispering"— or hissing like vipers. This implied a private influence on judges and their administration of religious justice.

Quirinius appointed a number of Procurators over Palestine following the rule of the Herodians. The first was Coponius, then Marcus Ambivius, Annius Rufus and Valerius Gratus. The Procurators' oppression by taxation was severe. However, they appeased the people by removing the image of the Emperor from the Roman standards when the army marched through the city.

There was a reckless disregard of all Jewish feelings and interests under the succession of Procurators. It actually worsened under Pontius Pilate. His administration was charged with judicial murder without any due process of law; violence, intimidation, theft, and torture. Former procurators at least respected the religious scruples of the Jews, but Pilate seemed intent on setting them purposely in defiance; and this not only once, but again and again, even beyond his jurisdiction. Such was the political condition of Jerusalem.

The ancient kingdom of Herod the Great was now divided between Pilate as a Procurator of Judea; the two sons of Herod: Antipas and Philip as tetrarchs; and Lysanias who ruled the small principality of Abilene.

Herod Antipas, ruler of the Galilee and Perea, ruled forty-three years. The vices of the father were certainly passed down and exaggerated in his son Antipas. He was known for his weakness of character, destitute of any religious feelings and easily manipulated by his wife. He was known to be covetous, avaricious and suspicious. His most extensive undertaking was the building of Tiberius in Galilee. The site, a burying-place, was avoided by devout Jews and had almost no Jewish population as a result. Antipas built his palace there and it was unrivaled in splendor.

Religion in the Roman world had degenerated into nothing more than superstition. The only religion which the State insisted on was the deification and worship of the Emperor. The ancient Roman religion had all but passed away. Public morals were entirely corrupt. The idea of conscience was unknown. Might was right. The sanctity of marriage was gone. Abortion, exposure and murder of new-born children were common and tolerated. Even the vice of the greatest of philosophers defies description. Slaves had absolutely no protection under law. Sick and old slaves were simply cast out to die from starvation. Charity toward the poor was regarded as questionable. The only escape which remained for the philosopher seemed the power to self-destruction. Society could not reform itself! Philosophy and religion had nothing to offer! Tacitus declared human life to be one great farce. Everywhere there was despair, conscious need, and unconscious longing.

Into such a world came a voice…crying in the wilderness!

Chapter 11:
A Den of Thieves

After the wedding, Nicodemus and Rachel took time to enjoy their new home and each other. They talked often over the next few months about opportunity in Jerusalem to become a member of the Sanhedrin. Nicodemus met several times with Joseph and Gamaliel again. But now he was married and enjoying his time as a farmer in partnership with his father and, of course, as a husband. The thought of leaving behind this peaceful environment to enter the spiritual battle in Jerusalem was becoming less and less appealing. Finally, he and his wife decided that the Sanhedrin could wait. The opportunity would return. Many of the members were elderly. Eventually he may even decide to become a priest like his father. As a Levite that was always his right. But for now, he preferred to dedicate his time to farm and family.

It did not take long before Rachel was expecting their first child. Two more followed in successive years. The years passed and eventually Nicodemus took over for his father who no longer could work his large farm. The vines and olives produced well. He had also built several olive presses within the orchard. This increased his profits as he no longer had to sell his olives to those near Jerusalem who specialized in pressing olives or "gat shmanim" (גת שמנים, Gethsemane). In Nicodemus' 32nd year Joseph came to Ein Karem to speak to him again.

He found Nicodemus in his olive orchard making repairs to the flat baskets that held the olives for pressing. *"Greetings, my friend,"* Joseph exclaimed as he approached Nicodemus, *"How is my favorite farmer?"*

"I am quite well, thank you Joseph," Nicodemus responded, *"How good it is to see you! It has been some time. Come; share a glass of wine with me at the house. Ours is the best in the area."*

"No thank you. I've been walking in the heat of the day and it may make me light headed. Besides, I prefer the privacy of the orchard." Joseph sat down on the huge stone called the "Gat" that would soon be pressing olives at the harvest. *"Can I ask you something?"*

"Sure, Joseph. What is on your mind?" Nicodemus asked.

"It has been ten years since our conversation on Passover about the Sanhedrin," Joseph began. *"I would still like to see you make use of the tremendous gifts God has given you. You passed your examination for 's'mikhah' long ago."* Joseph paused.

"Is there a question in there somewhere?" Nicodemus asked. *"Right to the point; I should have remembered,"* Joseph continued. *"I would like you to join me in our Chabhurah (Association) as a Pharisee. Your expertise in the Torah and your godly life already qualify you."*

"Wait a minute, Joseph," Nicodemus replied. *"I have no issue with the objectives of the Pharisee fraternity. My problem is with their reputation and inconsistency in practice. You've heard the insults of the Sadducees that 'the Pharisees would one day subject the sun itself to their laws of purification.' Not to mention the expression that is going around that 'a silly pietist, a clever sinner, and a Pharisee are ranked among the troubles of life'?"*

"That is why I have come, my friend," Joseph stated matter-of-factly. *"We need sincere, obedient lovers of the law like you to be the salt in our society. You know well the vows of Levitical purity and religious tithes that are part of our order. What you may not know is that there are seven types of Pharisees. I have found value as a 'Pharisee from love.' There are still a few of us in the Sanhedrin who seek to be what the 70 great men were to Moses. And the opportunity is there now. More and more Pharisees are members of the Sanhedrin now than ever."*

"So," Nicodemus responded, *"are you asking me to be a Pharisee or a Sanhedrin member?"*

"Initially just a Pharisee," Joseph explained. *"The opportunity in the Sanhedrin is not there presently. You would be a natural selection with a few years as a genuine Pharisee."*

The two walked back to Nicodemus' home on a hilltop in Ein Karem. They stopped in the town square and drank deeply from the natural spring at the well. When they reached the house, Rachel welcomed Joseph warmly and invited him to stay for the evening meal.

"My father's famous meat and vegetable stew is on the menu; you have to stay, Joseph," Nicodemus said with just a hint of pride.

"Besides you can greet the children who will be home soon from Beth Sepher. I'll go invite Father and Mother to come too."

"That is an invitation too good to refuse," Joseph said graciously.

The early part of the evening was spent enjoying Benjamin's favorite recipe. Then they reviewed the children's lessons from school and sang some of Nicodemus' favorite Psalms. As the sun went down, the children were sent to their rooms. The three men and Rachel enjoyed some of the best wine in the region from Nicodemus' vineyard. They discussed the appointment of the new High Priest, Joseph Caiaphas. He had only just been appointed by the Roman Procurator a year ago and his lifestyle was the talk of the priesthood in Jerusalem. The combination of a corrupt High Priest and a ruthless Roman Procurator was severe! Caiaphas was the son-in-law of the manipulative Annas, who had stepped down from his High Priestly duties. Officially, Annas still presided at the major religious festivals.

"At least the Romans didn't appoint one of his sons," Benjamin commented, *"the sons of Annas and even some of his sons-in-law control the flow of money and the sale of sacrificial animals in the Temple."*

"That is why we need Nicodemus in the Sanhedrin, Benjamin. We need a godly influence to at least temper the selfishness of the leadership," Joseph added.

"You remember the atmosphere in the Temple courts last Passover," Benjamin continued. *"It was atrocious. Weeks before Passover, on the 25th of Adar, money changers already had set up booths. I was there early and witnessed the cruel confiscation of property from poor pilgrims who could not pay the Temple tax. They could not afford the outrageous prices for a lamb that had been 'duly' inspected, which only increased the price. I've seen the price of a pigeon go as high as a Roman gold denar. Can you believe that? And you know who benefits from these abuses!"*

"Of course, it is Annas and his sons," Joseph answered immediately. *"They control everything: money changing, the temple tax, the inspection of sacrificial animals and the sale of the same. Roman avarice has nothing on the hypocrisy and greed of our own High Priest."*

Nicodemus knew all of this but his day to day life was filled with the peace of the countryside. His worst problem in Ein Karem was the heat of summer which caused his grapes to grow too quickly and reduce their quality. He sat quietly listening to the genuine concerns of these two well respected and honest men of God. He knew, in his heart, where his duty lay.

Nicodemus became a Pharisee that same year and fulfilled his obligations honorably. Three years later his name was presented by Joseph, Gamaliel, and his father Benjamin. For the next five years he was mentored by Joseph, who had been a member now for almost 20 years.

The Sanhedrin meeting place was in the Hall of Hewn Stones (Lishkat La-Gazit) on the south side of the Court of the Priests. They heard only religious disputes, having been stripped of any judicial authority by the Procurator years ago. They met every Thursday, except during Festival weeks. Rules of order for meeting were followed to the letter. The Council, as it was also referred to, numbered 71, including the Nasi or President who presided over the proceedings. In his absence the Vice-President (av bet din) would preside. Caiaphas the High Priest had been appointed by Pontius

Pilate himself as the Nasi. The court would normally only hear cases brought by a member or referred by one of the lesser Sanhedrin gatherings in Judea or Galilee. Most of the Members were priests, scribes or elders. Most were also Pharisees or Sadducees. The majority were Pharisees at the time. This created opposition that was palpable on both sides. Caiaphas, while serving as High Priest and Nasi, had tremendous influence. As a Sadducee himself, he faced opposition from Pharisees for his theological position as well as his enormous ego. He was known to be a puppet of Rome and maintained his position by keeping the peace for Pilate. But it was an uneasy peace both with Rome and the public.

Nicodemus made few comments during his first few years on the Sanhedrin. He served on a standing committee with Joseph, who investigated cases brought before the Council. He had felt the cold hard stare of Caiaphas one time when presenting the facts on one case. In his report he had referenced his friend from his youth in Ein Karem: Zechariah. Caiaphas the Sadducee disputed the existence of angels and, of course, the angelic vision of Gabriel in the Temple by Zechariah. The mere mention of the name Zechariah brought immediate murmurs from the Sadducee sect who sat on the opposite side of the gathering from the Pharisees.

All members of the Sanhedrin normally were required to be in Jerusalem beginning with the 15th of Adar and remain through the Feast of Unleavened Bread after Passover. Beginning with the 25th of Adar, the money changers had begun to set up their booths. People began arriving for Passover on the 25th day of Adar. The money changing booths in the countryside closed on that day and money could only be changed at official booths at the Temple. The Temple was filled with Jews from all over the Roman world. Most Galileans arrived with the beginning of Nisan. Judeans were the latest to arrive, just before Lamb selection day: The Sunday before Passover.

The abuses in the Temple had outraged Nicodemus. He dared not speak out in the Sanhedrin concerning these abuses, as the sons of

Annas who controlled the syndicate were also Sanhedrin members. They were known to be violent and it was not beyond them to both intimidate and threaten. The profit also lined the purse of Caiaphas, and was the mortar that bound Annas and Caiaphas.

The city was abuzz with word of a prophet from the wilderness of Judea who had begun preaching near the Jordan. Priests and Rabbis had been talking for several months about this man who preached repentance and baptism. There was talk of investigating this preacher who openly castigated the elite in Jerusalem including Caiaphas, Pilate and even Herod Antipas. It was reported by those who had arrived from Jericho that the man spoke against the abuses no one had the courage to address. Huge crowds, hungering for spiritual certainty in a sea of compromise, had gathered around him. As the week began, more and more pilgrims openly talked about "The Baptist." Some told their personal stories of being dipped in the waters of the Jordan. Even Roman soldiers, it was reported, came to hear him; some were even baptized. He filled a vacuum of spiritual authenticity that was lacking.

Nicodemus sat on the roof of his house discussing the talk of "The Baptist" with Joseph and his father.

"There is a hunger in Judea especially for the substance of his message!" Benjamin began. *"There is excess everywhere. We are no longer a people who pursue God and love him with all of our heart, soul and mind. I have watched it over the decades. We are a ship without a sail!"*

"My question is," Joseph added, *"is his message an end in itself or is there something on the horizon? Repentance without a trust in the mercy and forgiveness of God only leaves us without hope."*

"To make ready a people prepared for the Lord!" (Luke 1:17) Nicodemus spoke under his breath as he turned to his father. *"Thirty years ago, Zechariah described what is happening right now:* **In the Spirit and power of Elijah.** (Luke 1:17) *Remember, Father?"* Nicodemus paused and turned to the other men, *"Men, remember how Elijah appeared? He came from the wilds of Gilead. No one*

89

*knew where he came from. **'To turn the hearts of the disobedient to the wisdom of the righteous!'** (Luke 1:17) Those were the words of Gabriel to Zechariah."*

"We certainly are living in disobedient times, aren't we?" Joseph added.

"We need to go and see for ourselves." Nicodemus stood and looked to the east over the Mt. of Olives. *"Father..."* Nicodemus paused. *"Could this be John?"*

"It could very well be him. Sounds like an Essene gone public!" Benjamin responded. *"It would be best if you went after Passover. But do it quietly. Go in simple attire; leave your official robes here! His kind of message will incite the Sanhedrin, if it hasn't already! If he is not John, he may be a radical Essene; it is best you are discreet."*

On the day before Passover, in the morning, a priest would present two cakes on a bench in the court of the Temple. It was Benjamin's duty as the senior priest to present and remove the cakes on Passover morning. As long as they remained, pilgrims could eat food with leaven. Sometime between the fourth and fifth hours (10 AM —11 AM), one cake would be removed. This was the signal that all leaven should be removed in every household in the city. Precisely at noon, the second cake was removed from the bench, taken inside and burned. This was the signal for all of Israel to burn any leaven found in their homes. Priests carried out this sweeping in the Temple also. In the midst of the chaos of money changers and herds of animals — many having defecated on the floor of the Court of the Gentiles — hundreds of priests could be seen sweeping. This scene was witnessed by thousands of proselytes from around the world, all trying to pray as animals scurried about while the priests swept. Nicodemus and Gamaliel had joined Benjamin for this rite and were watching and discussing the hypocrisy of the scene.

"This is keeping the law?" Nicodemus whispered to Gamaliel as his father had removed the first cake. Gamaliel just shook his head at

the proceedings. An hour later Benjamin came to remove the second cake. The command went out from the Temple to burn the leaven.

Just then the two men heard a commotion on the far side of the court. A tall man in a brilliant white linen garment had begun shouting and leading the animals out of the court and toward the gate. As he drew closer, Nicodemus could hear him more clearly.

"Get these out of here," he said to those selling doves, *"How dare you turn my Father's house into a market!"* (John 2:16) Few dared to oppose him. All knew it was a desecration of the Temple, but none dared to oppose Annas and his sons. This man spoke not only for the masses who were cheated but also for those in the Gentile court who had come to pray. Priests who had just finished sweeping stood in awe of the scene. Many just dropped their brooms and smiled at the "cleansing", as many would call it later.

Gamaliel turned to Nicodemus and asked, *"Who is he? Look over there; the sons of Annas are sending their bodyguards to intercept him."*

None in the court dared stop the man! In fact, a cheer went up from the masses. *"Hallelujah!"* Some shouted.

The animals seemed to obey the man's commands to flee. They fled for the gates and into the city streets. Doves flew from their cages as their doors unlatched and flew open. Nicodemus noticed that the man had made a whip out of several ropes. He never struck an animal, but he was not so kind to the money changers. Turning over their tables, their coins flying into the air, he lifted his arm into the air and began to swing the whip. With each crack of the whip, another table would upend, seemingly, on its own now. Those tending the tables retreated and ran, as if caught in the midst of sin by the Almighty himself. Turning to the priests, he commanded them: *"Take these coins and put them into the Temple treasury!"*

Just then, the hired protectors of Annas and his sons approached him. The man's language had identified him as a Galilean. Knowing this, they asked him about his credentials: *"What sign can you show us to prove your authority to do this?"* (John 2:18) Any Rabbi with even the most minimal learning found this prejudicial and simplistic. The confrontation was only 10 feet in front of Nicodemus and Gamaliel.

Amused by this ridiculous question, Nicodemus whispered to Gamaliel, *"How about the Lord God Almighty and his servant Moses!"*

But his response left everyone stunned. He dropped his whip, pointed to himself and shouted so that all could hear plainly, ***"Destroy this temple, and I will raise it again in three days!"*** (John 2:19) With that he walked out of the Temple, 12 men following closely behind. The minions of Annas were left mumbling about how long it had taken Herod to build the Temple, but no one was paying any attention to them. All knew he was not talking about The Temple.

Nicodemus and Gamaliel were joined by Benjamin who had watched the events from the other side of the Temple court. They marveled at what they had seen and retired to their home to prepare for Passover the next day. They spent the evening on the rooftop once more discussing what they had all witnessed. Word had already been sent to them that the Sanhedrin would have a special meeting as soon as Passover was over.

"I'm sure that order came from Annas," Gamaliel remarked as they sat enjoying the cool spring air.

"To be sure," Benjamin added, *"his pocket is a little lighter tonight!"*

"Who cares about Annas," Nicodemus responded. He continued with a measured intensity, *"I want to know who that man was! Such courage and conviction! It should not be too difficult to find out. He is clearly a Rabbi from Galilee. His Talmidim were with him. Let's look into it before we go to Jericho on Sunday. I'm reflecting on some of his words."* Nicodemus paused for some time, and then remarked, *"He said, 'My Father's house,' not this house, not our house! My Father's House! Even prophets of old did not talk like*

that! They would never speak using a personal reference to the Lord Almighty!"

"You are right, Nicodemus," Gamaliel added. "I noticed that too. And his reference to resurrection was not just to irritate the Sadducees who were there, which it clearly did! I saw some of them scowl. They knew he was not talking about the physical structure. But why the almost fatalistic reference to his own death?"

"We need to know more about this man, and I believe we will soon enough!" Benjamin added, "This Rabbi is not going to go quietly into the night. Today was just an introduction. I also believe he is connected to the Baptist somehow!" Benjamin rose and headed for the stairs. He pointed at his son and repeated, **"To make ready a people prepared for the Lord!"** (Luke 1:17)

Chapter 12:
A Voice

Benjamin and Joseph had decided that it would be best for Nicodemus to visit "The Baptist" alone on Sunday morning without notifying anyone in the Sanhedrin or even anyone beyond their own circle. This seemed particularly appropriate since they suspected that "The Baptist" might in fact be John, the son of Zechariah and Elizabeth. Joseph would invent an excuse for his absence from the Sanhedrin meeting on Sunday. The expectation of all was that the most significant events had taken place in the Temple courts already on Preparation Day. Little did any of the men on the rooftop of Benjamin's house expect more news about the Rabbi from Galilee. But already at dawn, a friend of Benjamin arrived at the door with news. Evidently the Galilean Rabbi had been staying in the city at the home of one of his disciples named John. After the events at the Temple, the Rabbi had gone to the home and on the way had encountered a blind beggar and healed him. For the remainder of the day, the sick, lame and blind came to John's home and each one was healed. The priest had verified the healings before coming to Benjamin's home.

"These were people known to have serious physical ailments for some time, most of them since birth!" the priest reported to Benjamin as he entered the second story of the home. By this time Nicodemus and Joseph came from their rooms and were asking questions.

"Were these things done publicly in the street?" Nicodemus asked.

"Yes, some of them", he replied. *"After a large crowd had gathered, he went to the home of the disciple called John and people in great physical need were brought inside. A friend of mine reported seeing a lame man carried into the home and he came out dancing. A deaf child came out hearing. Most of them were from the lower classes. I even heard that some lepers were cleansed."*

"I don't mean to sound an alarm, Father," Nicodemus interrupted. *"But you know what this sounds like, these miracles? Isaiah's prophecy!* **"Then will the eyes of the blind be opened and the ears of the deaf unstopped. Then will the lame leap like a deer and the mute tongue shout for joy."** Isaiah 35:5,6

"It does," Joseph continued. *"But let's not get too excited too quickly. We need to hear this Rabbi. And you know the Sanhedrin will take this as a threat to their power. I don't expect anything to happen today, but I expect the meeting of the Sanhedrin to be raucous. Let us take measured steps and continue with our plan to send Nicodemus to 'The Baptist'. His testimony is even more vital now."*

"Isn't it more of a priority that we see and hear from this Rabbi first before we look for "The Baptist"? Nicodemus asked of Joseph and his father.

"Consider this, Nicodemus," Joseph answered. *"If this Rabbi is the Messiah, and I certainly am not suggesting that, but if he is, he won't be hard to find. Right now, I think 'The Baptist' is more of a target by Caiaphas and Annas. Let's start there and try to get ahead of this!"*

The men needed to be at the Temple for service. Benjamin's duty was light. His main responsibility at Passover was tending to the Preparation Day cakes, and that was finished. But he still needed to cleanse himself before entering the Temple. Joseph and Nicodemus were not priests and decided to go to the Temple early anyway and listen for news of the miracles. They found it significant that these events were taking place at Passover. Many Messianic scholars had predicted the revelation of the Messiah on Passover Day. The theme of deliverance fit the role. Needless to say, talk abounded among those arriving early at the Temple. There were a fair number of scoffers who dismissed the events as spiritual hysteria or demon possession. Miracle workers were fairly common. Few, however, had made such a demonstrative and public entrance as "The Galilean"—as he was now being called. The name was given not only because it noted where he came from, but it also betrayed the bigoted perspective of Judean Rabbis toward anyone from Galilee.

After the morning rumors began to repeat themselves, the three men retired again to their home for the Passover feast. The next day would be long and eventful. Eighteen miles was a long journey, even if it was downhill.

He set out at dawn the next day in an attempt to travel in the cool of the morning as he descended into the Jordan Valley. He reached the river before noon and began to inquire about the whereabouts of "The Baptist." Nicodemus was directed north to the springs of Aenon near Bethshean (Scythopolis), just on the border between Samaria and Galilee. He spent the night at a guest house along the way and reached Aenon the next morning. As he walked, Nicodemus was thinking to himself how dangerously brave "The Baptist" was. He could have camped much nearer to Jericho, which would have kept him some distance from Antipas, whom he had publicly rebuked for the taking of his brother's wife.

"The Baptist" could be heard preaching at the Jordon's edge near the Springs of Aenon, and Nicodemus saw him long before John saw him. His voice was deeper now, and his hair was much longer. His beard obscured his face. But the voice was most certainly that of John, Nicodemus' schoolmate and friend from youth. His heart warmed as he drew closer, remembering their long talks and songs in the vineyard. John did not notice Nicodemus approaching. The crowd was large, and it was obvious he was focused on his message of repentance and the kingdom of God. John had grown tall and strong. His skin looked weathered from extended time in the Judean sun. Nicodemus decided to sit and listen, waiting for the cool of the evening when the crowds would disperse, before approaching John. He wondered how long John had stayed in the Essene community. Nicodemus was only 22 when his father had taken John to Qumran. John had been 12. He was now 30, and Nicodemus 40 years of age. John spoke for two hours to the group of more than 1000 gathered on the sloping hill leading down to the Jordan. Nicodemus had never before heard such a wonderful treatment of God's giving of the law on Mt. Sinai, which was the topic of John's message. He spoke in detail of the images in the sacrifices, the impossibility of cleansing coming for the crown of his creation through the blood of animals.

"How can the finite redeem the eternal soul?" he asked again and again. *"Only the blood of one to come, the one whose sandals I am not worthy to untie, can wash away sin."* He then went on to speak of preparing our hearts like a road is prepared for the arrival of a King today. *"Only by repentance do we show ourselves ready to receive him."* Finally, as the sun was getting low on the horizon he invited those gathered to come down to the water for the Baptism of Repentance, as he called it.

"Like the living water of the Lord Almighty himself, this living water of the Jordan points us to the coming of Messiah, the King of Kings. May the Spirit of the Living Lord change your minds about the sin in your lives. The Kingdom of Heaven is near. Come and prepare for it!" John's words were powerful and only a few failed to go down to the River. When he finished he blessed them with Aaron's blessing. As he came up out of the water, he noticed Nicodemus standing on the shore. A broad smile filled his face and he ran to embrace his old friend.

After they finished embracing, they both stood back and looked at each other. Finally, Nicodemus spoke: *"If I may say, John, you have changed since Passover 18 years ago!"*

"Ha, ha, ha!" John laughed deeply, *"To be sure, but God has been good to me and preserved my life despite many challenges. Are you well Nicodemus? Are you married?"*

"Yes, John," Nicodemus answered, *"Rachel and I married shortly after you left for Qumran, and the Lord has blessed us with three sons. Can we find a place to sit and talk awhile?"*

"This IS my home, Nicodemus," John smiled and pointed to a cave on the other side of the Jordan. *"Most Jews won't cross over there so when I need time to pray and be alone, I stay there. It is just*

a little too close to the Decapolis for most. But the news we proclaim is for all, Jew and Gentile."

"Let's go. Where can we ford the river?" Nicodemus asked as they moved toward the river.

"I keep a small raft hidden just downstream. The Jordan is still too high to wade, but with my raft, I manage." John began to stride ahead of Nicodemus and the guard.

They managed to cross without too much difficulty. They walked up to the cave where John took refuge and started a fire to keep warm. As the sun set, John began to explain to his friend how he had spent eight years among the Essenes. The Rabbi had given John a lot of leeway even though he did not accept some of their teaching. John filled his day with prayer, reading Scripture, bathing and copying texts of Scripture.

"When I was about 20, I just knew my time there had finished," John explained. *"The Lord led me into the Judean wilderness. You remember how much I felt a kinship with King David? For the next ten years, that is how I lived, surviving on honey and locusts, moving from place to place in the wilderness."*

"And this is the calling the Lord has revealed to you now?" Nicodemus asked, *"Baptizing in the desert? Can I ask, what is God's objective for you?"*

"I am a voice of preparation," John replied with conviction. *"I am preparing God's people for one greater than I. It is not for me to speak of this. It is for you to search your heart and be open to God's leading. You will know him when you hear and see him! Don't be afraid, Nicodemus, just believe!"*

"I saw some men remaining after the baptisms today; are they your disciples?" Nicodemus asked.

"Yes, a few have remained," John answered, *"I have sent those who are from Galilee away and told them to wait for the Lord there. Two are with him now, John and Andrew."*

"I would like to speak with him when I return to Jerusalem; would it be possible to have an audience?" Nicodemus asked.

"Sure, I will send one of my disciples with you in the morning. He will introduce you to John. He will arrange a meeting." John answered, *"May I ask you something?"*

"To be sure," Nicodemus responded.

"Are you still working the farm in Ein Karem?" John asked. Nicodemus knew there was more to his question than just his question about the vineyard. *"I am in the Sanhedrin now, John. I am also a Pharisee and have been in the Sanhedrin now for five years. There are a few of us who are trying to lead God's people in a godly way."*

"You may one day find it incompatible," John stated abruptly, *"It is like this fire. When the fire is low, you can easily put it out with your foot without getting burned. But eventually it reaches a point where quenching the fire must come from something very different. Do you understand?"*

Nicodemus found John's words much different from the description given by those who had encountered him. He was reasoned and kind, with depth to his words. John snared a hare and cooked it for Nicodemus. John ate only from a clay jar filled with wild honey. They slept soundly protected by the cave from the cool night air. John had built a fire on top of several large stones. He buried them under a sandy area where Nicodemus slept. It was very comfortable. John spent several hours above the cave in prayer before coming into the cave later in the evening.

In the morning, John introduced Nicodemus to James, who would show him where the young man named John was staying in Jerusalem. As Nicodemus and "The Baptist" walked along the Jordan to where they would cross the River, it struck Nicodemus how humble and unselfish John was. It was not just his message of repentance that had drawn people to him; it was the sense that God himself was reaching out to his people through this wonderful man. Nicodemus reflected back on the work the two had shared in the vineyard twenty years earlier picking up vines that had fallen into the dirt after a heavy rain. Left in the dirt, the fruit would rot, and the vine would stagnate. Watching him preach and teach the previous day, it was like John was still working in a vineyard, picking up vines and washing off the dirt. What could possibly be better?

Chapter 13:
Born Again?

Nicodemus arrived back in Jerusalem late Thursday morning, accompanied by James. The Feast of Unleavened Bread was almost over. Nicodemus agreed to meet James and the Talmid of the Galilean called John. John had formerly been a disciple of "The Baptist." They would meet at the Temple so as to minimize detection. The busyness of the final feast day in the temple courts would provide an opportunity to hide in plain sight from the suspicious eyes of Annas and his sons.

John was much younger than Nicodemus expected. A Galilean also, John was one of the brightest of the Talmidim of the Galilean.

"Greetings, Master Nicodemus," James embraced him and introduced John. *"John is a trusted talmid of Yeshua of Nazareth."*

"Shalom, John," Nicodemus greeted John. *"I am Nicodemus."*

"Shalom, Master Nicodemus, I have heard of you. My father Zebedee often spoke of your father Benjamin. How is Benjamin, and how may I assist you?" John replied.

"Thank you, John," Nicodemus continued, *"Father is well. He is in the city for the Feast Days and still serves in the Temple at Passover. In fact, we all were there last week and witnessed the response of your Rabbi to the corruption in the Temple. I must say I was most impressed with his courage and zeal for the house of the Lord. Few have been willing to take such a strong stand against the abuses of Annas and his sons."*

Nicodemus found himself saying more than he wanted to on the subject, but he felt he needed to assure John that he was sympathetic with the stand of the Galilean and not a threat to him or an ally of the leadership in the Ruling Council. Nicodemus was also in his Pharisaical robes and knew this may have created some suspicion. He felt it best to be upfront and honest about his leanings politically and spiritually. *"I have just come from the Jordan where I met and spent an evening with a friend from long ago: John, called the*

Baptist. He used words to describe your master that have left me curious.

To be honest, I am extremely interested in speaking to him. He assured me that James here could arrange a time when he and I could meet and talk. Is that possible?"

"My goodness, you know the Baptist?" John answered. *"That is probably the one stamp of approval that is beyond question. I must admit, I had my doubts on coming here to meet you. There is already great opposition to our Master in your Council, particularly from the friends and family of Annas and Caiaphas. We are not here too many more days. Jesus has spoken of wanting to leave in the next few days, just after the Feast."*

"I have been away and missed the meeting of the Sanhedrin this past Sunday," Nicodemus replied. *"I know they intended to discuss the Baptist and, most certainly, the events involving your Master the day before Passover. But I did not know they had drawn any conclusions."* Nicodemus suddenly realized the dangerous step he was about to make. He so wanted to see and speak with Yeshua, but he would need to do it in a way that did not bring the wrath of Caiaphas on him and his family. Guilt was often by association as far as the Chief Priests and their followers were concerned.

"I don't want to draw attention to my visit and bring risk to you, your Master, or the other Talmidim by my presence," Nicodemus continued. *"Could I see him after the feast concludes today, after sunset? If you would prefer to keep your home private, we could meet here, and you could escort me to the place you are staying. I would completely understand your need for a bit of secrecy."*

"That would be most agreeable. Let us meet at sunset at the base of the southern steps?" John asked.

"Agreed," Nicodemus replied.

"May I ask you a question, Master Nicodemus?" John inquired. *"Absolutely!"*

"When you spoke with John, did he share anything about the encounter between him and Yeshua?" John asked.

"He did not," Nicodemus answered, "in fact, he never mentioned Yeshua by name, he only spoke of his work as one preparing for another, and that the one to come would increase and he would decrease. I found his humility quite stunning. You see, I knew John when he was only a boy in Ein Karem. After the death of his parents, he came to live in our home, and for two years we worked and studied together at the synagogue there. I knew the Lord had reserved him for a great work. His teaching is quite mesmerizing, the little bit of it I heard on the day we met. That was just a few days ago. Was the encounter with Yeshua the same?"

John smiled and even laughed a bit under his breath. "The same? No, it was quite unique. We are still discussing it among ourselves. Let us meet tonight at sunset. Come alone!"

With that John and James left, and Nicodemus walked to his home. He had already explained his visit with The Baptist to Joseph and his father. They were anxious to hear how this meeting with the disciple, called John, had gone.

Nicodemus climbed the stairs of his father's home. The sun made it too hot to have lunch on the roof, so they were inside in the common room.

"It's all set," Nicodemus began, "I'll be seeing the Rabbi from Galilee tonight. He is called Yeshua and is from Nazareth."

"Great news," Joseph responded. "How did John seem, suspicious at all?"

"No, not at all. I explained our association with the Baptist and that seemed to make all the difference. I think there is definitely a connection between the two. Do you remember I mentioned that the John I was meeting had once been a talmid of The Baptist? He asked me just now if The Baptist told me anything about the meeting between Yeshua and The Baptist. He seemed to be inferring that something significant happened between the two of them."

"That's very interesting," Benjamin responded. "Then the suspicions of the Sanhedrin – at least their hostile attitude toward both of them – have a real connection."

"True, and there is a spirit about the two of them. They do not fear either the Sanhedrin or the political power of Rome. Yeshua's actions last week demonstrate he cares nothing for the power and monetary might of Annas. The Baptist almost defies Antipas, setting up his preaching right on the border with Galilee. Antipas could roll out of the palace in Tiberius and be in Aenon in half a day, or less if he used Roman chariots!" Nicodemus was truly excited about what he was uncovering about these two men.

"Where will you meet Yeshua?" Benjamin asked.

"I'll meet John at the Temple and he'll take me to him. There are some concerns among his Talmidim that Yeshua's physical safety is an issue. Evidently, they have their own sources here in Jerusalem. He said they plan to leave in the next day or two!" Nicodemus answered.

"There is a large contingent still here from Galilee," Benjamin said. *"It would stand to reason some of them have connections."* He paused, *"How will you approach the Galilean tonight, son?"*

"I have been thinking about that on the way back from Aenon," Nicodemus responded. *"It is critical that I be respectful given the prejudicial and condescending attitude of most Teachers of the Law here in Judea toward anyone from Galilee. It is unfounded, prideful and based on the difference between us culturally. In fact, most Rabbis from the synagogues there I have found to be very scholarly. Actually, they are more seasoned in the law than Judean teachers. I believe if I just begin the conversation acknowledging him as a prophet, his answer will tell me much about whom he really is."*

"I agree," Joseph added. *"Given your role as a member of the Sanhedrin, you must not press him. We want a good relationship based on God's leading. Gamaliel would say that if he is a prophet, we need to let God lead and if not, he will come to nothing anyway. We have seen pretenders come and go. His words will tell us what we need to know."*

That evening Nicodemus was at the Temple well before sunset. He stayed in the Colonnade watching the closing of the Feast of

Unleavened Bread. Sabbath would soon be upon the city, and this too would provide him cover as people would be scurrying about in this hour before sunset.

John arrived a few minutes early. He too had wanted to walk in the busyness of the remaining pilgrims preparing for Sabbath as the Feast days concluded. He greeted Nicodemus in the hall and, without talking, the two departed. Nicodemus followed John as he kept pace with others rushing to their homes. In the midst of the crowds, Nicodemus felt he was being watched. Several times as they walked through the city streets, he noticed humbly dressed men stepping out of the shadows to follow them for a while and then turn a corner. This happened several times, and he finally said something to John.

"Don't worry," John responded. *"They are friends checking for anyone following you. Here, we have arrived. Take the outside stairs to the roof of this house. Andrew will meet you there. I'll wait down here with my friends and come up momentarily."*

Nicodemus climbed the stairs on the outside of the house. This was very typical of Judean homes. Families would spend time in the evening on the roof just as he and his friends did in his father's home. Andrew was sitting on the edge of the roof at the top of the stairs to welcome him.

"Nicodemus?" Andrew asked as he extended his hand to welcome him.

"Yes, shalom!" Nicodemus answered. A large group of men and women had gathered on the roof, reclining and enjoying the evening meal that had been spread on large platters in the center. He noticed a number of bottles of wine opened also. Andrew led him to the group and knelt behind the man Nicodemus immediately recognized as the Galilean from the Temple. He rose and approached Nicodemus. His penetrating eyes and flowing hair reminded him of The Baptist when he was very young. He smiled broadly and motioned for him to join the group.

"Welcome, Nicodemus, and Shalom!" the Galilean put a hand on his shoulder and invited him to sit next to him.

"Greetings and Shalom," Nicodemus responded as he walked toward the group. A few turned to see who was joining the group, others continued in conversation, some laughing, others eating from the food before them.

"We have a guest this evening," Yeshua raised his voice to get the attention of the group. *"Some of you know him."*

Just then John appeared from the same stairs along with several others. John passed by the Galilean, whispered in his ear and then went to sit in his open place. Nicodemus assumed he was reporting that no one had followed. *"Please welcome him and pour him a glass of wine. I believe he knows good wine!"* he smiled and looked Nicodemus in the eye, *"Join us!"*

Nicodemus only recognized one man beside John in the group, but could not place where he had seen him before. But he was here to speak with the Galilean.

"I bring greetings from John in Aenon," Nicodemus began as they sat on the floor where large pillows had been scattered, *"He spent two years in our home in Ein Karem when he was young."* Nicodemus had not planned to speak of John, but it just seemed natural to address their common connection initially.

"You and your family helped him at a very vulnerable time in his life," the Galilean replied. *"John is a great man! I am very grateful for what you did for him!"*

Nicodemus was not quite sure how to respond to these comments. He assumed that somehow the Galilean and John had a connection he did not know about, so he decided to move on.

"Rabbi, you are aware, I am sure, that I am a Pharisee and a member of the Sanhedrin. But I am here as Nicodemus the man. When John and I talked, he told me that he was born as one to prepare God's people for the kingdom of God!" As Nicodemus spoke, he chose his words carefully.

"To make ready a people prepared for the Lord!" (Luke 1:17) Yeshua corrected Nicodemus. As soon as the words touched his mind, Nicodemus felt a burning within him. He remembered vividly hearing those words from Zechariah's lips when he was 10 years old, and how completely convinced he was then that his son John would prepare Israel for the Messiah. Now he was hearing the words spoken to him by this Galilean Rabbi.

Suddenly it struck him that this Rabbi was employing Remez to their conversation. However, he was not quoting the Torah. He was quoting an angel. It left him completely stumped. He sensed that the Galilean was leading him in a Messianic direction. Should he follow? He was not sure. Over the years, Nicodemus' youthful certainty had been muddied by life's uncertainties. He desperately wanted things to be as simple as they seemed when he was 10 years old. And then there were the uncertainties about this Yeshua. Who was he really? Why was he quoting Gabriel's words? How did he even know what Gabriel had said to Zechariah? Was this all a trick of Satan? And what about his origin: Galilee? He had heard the mocking of people and even Rabbis while in the Temple as they discussed the Galilean's actions: *"What good thing could come from Galilee?"*

Nicodemus breathed deeply as Yeshua continued, *"My son, ask me what you came here to ask."*

There was just a hint of disappointment in his voice as Nicodemus felt the shadow of fear and uncertainty cross his heart.

"Rabbi, we know you are a teacher who has come from God. For no one could perform the miraculous signs you are doing if God were not with him." (John 3:2) Nicodemus finally said. It was not a question but a statement inferring a question. He had backed away from the personal and made the statement that, as he said it, seemed a little too official. He had retreated to a place of mere curiosity and debate. Deep inside, he regretted not responding to his heart's desire. Instead he posed a neutral statement, the answer to which would neither clarify nor offend.

"You are so close to the kingdom, Nicodemus," Yeshua responded, *"May I ask, don't you long for how simple God's truth seemed to you when you were a child?"*

This Rabbi had touched the very heart of what was bothering Nicodemus. He was on a search for truth but was afraid of where it would lead. His childhood faith was filled with certainty and truth that seemed to have been sacrificed long ago by the priesthood, the teachers of the law, and most certainly by those who claimed to be Shepherds of Israel. Oh, to be a child again!

"Can anyone go back to the certainty of childhood?" Nicodemus asked. He said the words before he had thought where they might lead or what this man would say. He had not planned for the conversation to go this way.

"I tell you the truth; no one can see the kingdom of God unless he enters as a child and is born again!" (John 3:3) Yeshua challenged Nicodemus. **"I tell you the truth!"** was the Aramaic expression prophets used to call attention to the absolute and important statement that would follow. There was so much uncertainty in Nicodemus' heart. Yeshua had just corrected him, as if he were a student in class who had said something foolish. Yeshua had challenged him to set aside all of his adult doubt, fears, and apprehensions. He knew Yeshua was inviting him to be a child again, to just believe. Nicodemus knew that something in him had been lost in all of the methodical learning, the debating, and the treating of the Holy Scripture as if it was just another endeavor like law or medicine. It was really the reason he had retreated into farming after his marriage. He told himself it was for family and the peace of farming. Really he had been running back to where things were simple and true. And now, talking to this Galilean Rabbi, he seemed to sense that a spark was being fanned into flame again, something he had not felt for a very long time. But…fear got the best of him and he retreated...again.

"How can a man be born when he is old?" Nicodemus asked, **"Surely, he cannot enter a second time into his mother's womb to be born!"** (John 3:4) As soon as the words were out of his mouth, Nicodemus regretted saying them. It was as if he had just betrayed himself and his vast learning. He knew Yeshua was not talking about physical birth. He was talking about the fresh and new feeling one gets when all is certain, true and beautiful; when God is love. It is like a child learning his first truths of Scripture. That certainty of faith flows from another place. Nicodemus knew it. He had felt the convincing power of God himself at work in the words of his promises. It had touched him once: body, soul and mind.

Yeshua answered, *"I tell you the truth, no one can enter the kingdom of God unless he is born of water and the Spirit. Flesh gives birth to flesh but the Spirit gives birth to spirit. You should not be surprised at my saying, 'You must be born again. The wind blows wherever it pleases. You hear its sound, but you cannot tell where it comes from or where it is going. So it is with everyone born of the Spirit."* (John 3:5-8)

This evening had started with Nicodemus wanting to know more about Yeshua of Nazareth; instead he was learning more about himself. And it was making him uncomfortable. He had never encountered anyone like this. Was Yeshua a prophet? For sure, in fact, at times Nicodemus had felt like he had come face to face with Isaiah the prophet of old who, despite serving a disobedient Judah, held out hope for a better day and for change within the people themselves. But the hope Isaiah hoped for would not originate in man. The temporary nature and powerless spiritual force of man was expressed so well by that prophet. *"All people are like grass and all their faithfulness is like the flowers of the field."* (Isaiah 40:7) Nicodemus knew the Scripture so well. And he knew how those verses ended: *"The grass withers and the flowers fall but the word of our God endures forever."* (Isaiah 40:8) But now almost 600 years after Isaiah, a religious system was in place, the effects of which stated with every increasing pride: "We are not grass! Our glory endures!" Nicodemus was living proof of how, even in the best of men, this spiritual shift had taken place and dominated their thinking. And here was this prophet calling him to account for the sin of a nation, his sin. They had replaced the glory of the Lord for their own: The creator with the created, the infallible with the mortal, mercy and forgiveness with laws and rules. It was a lie, but Nicodemus had been caught in it for so long he could hardly remember the simple truths from his childhood. Yeshua had opened the door a crack.

Oh, the joy of resting in the truths Simeon and Zechariah held dear! *"The Lamb has come!"* He recalled his father telling him those powerful words of Simeon as he entered God's glory. He was only 10 at the time. It had stirred his heart. Had he really drifted so far away from that day? It was like a memory so far in the distance, only a faint hurt remained. He knew the essence of it. But now, how could he get back there, and at what cost? He so dearly wanted it but didn't know how. So, he answered honestly to the confusion this Rabbi had unearthed within him:

"How can this be?" (John 3:9) Nicodemus asked. He braced himself for the reply. He had never asked, "How?" before. He always had all the answers. He was the best debater. He could master even the best teachers with Remez, when others were left stupefied. But on this, he did not know what to say. How does one get back to a place one longs for but doesn't know how to start?

"You are Israel's teacher," Yeshua said. *"And do you not understand these things? I tell you the truth, we speak of what we know and we testify to what we have seen, but still you people do not accept our testimony. I have spoken to you of earthly things and you do not believe; how then will you believe if I speak of heavenly things? No one has ever gone into heaven except the one who came from heaven — the Son of Man. Just as Moses lifted up the snake in the desert, so the Son of Man must be lifted up, that everyone who believes in him may have eternal life.*

For God so loved the world that he gave his one and only Son, that whoever believes in him shall not perish but have eternal life. For God did not send his Son into the world to condemn the world, but to save the world through him. Whoever believes in him is not condemned, but whoever does not believe stands condemned already because he has not believed in the name of God's one and only Son. This is the verdict: Light has come into the world, but men loved darkness instead of light because their deeds were evil. Everyone who does evil hates the light, and will not come into the light for fear that his deeds will be exposed. But whoever lives by the truth comes into the light, so that it may be seen plainly that what he has done has been done through God." (John 3:10-21)

Nicodemus sat back, his mind absorbing and rehashing what he had just heard. He felt humbled, repentant, and cleansed all at the same time. Yeshua turned and filled a glass with wine and passed it to Nicodemus. Yeshua's smile touched him. To Nicodemus, all this seemed so simple. After some time, Yeshua sat back and just enjoyed his wine. He tore off a piece of bread and opened a conversation with John and Andrew who were seated on the other side of Nicodemus. They talked about the Baptist. But Nicodemus' thoughts were far away, on a terraced hillside in Ein Karem, talking with his father and picking up vine branches and tying them to the trellis. He felt like he was that mature vine branch floundering in the dirt, unable to cleanse itself. He had been there for so long, it had become normal. Compromise, watching his words, being careful who was watching, and ...dirty! And with the words of this Rabbi, *"For God so loved the world!"* (John 3:16) he felt clean for the first time in a long time.

Chapter 14:
Living Water

"Whoever lives by the truth comes into the light so that it may be seen plainly that what he has done has been done through God." (John 3:21) These were the last words from Rabbi Yeshua to Nicodemus. And as Nicodemus walked back to his home, he felt their sting. *"Come into the light? Here I am sneaking around in the dark!"* he whispered to himself as he walked. For all his learning, he was living in darkness and fear. From the time he joined the Sanhedrin, his life was filled with hypocrisy and hiding. He told himself that it was his humility before the wise and experienced on the Sanhedrin. But it was not. He was afraid. Suddenly he felt ashamed. Only by going back to the simple and honest truths he loved as a boy would he ever be able to step out of the shadows and into the light. He knew one thing for certain! He needed to hear the Galilean again. But how?

The moon was almost full as he walked to his father's home. He didn't realize he had been with the Rabbi so long. As he climbed the stairs to the house he was welcomed by Joseph, his father and Gamaliel. All looked at him with anticipation.

"Well? Come inside and tell us," his father began. *"How did you find the Galilean? Is he for real or just another pretender?"*

"I don't quite know how to describe him. His words laid bare my soul," Nicodemus confessed. *"He is no pretender, father."*

"How did he respond when you said he is a teacher come from God?" Joseph asked.

Nicodemus motioned for them to sit. As he sat, he looked off into the distance and said, *"Strangest thing, he was more interested in talking about me. He said, 'No one can see the kingdom of God unless he is born again.'"* (John3:5)

"What did he mean? 'Born Again'?" Benjamin asked.

"He explained it in such a simple way. He said, 'Flesh gives birth to flesh but the Spirit gives birth to spirit.' (John 3:6) *He used the wind as an illustration. It blows wherever it pleases. 'So it is with everyone born of the Spirit.'* (John 3:8) *I believe he was addressing our preoccupation with the law as if we determine our spiritual fate by the law. He was saying: it isn't us! It isn't Moses! It isn't the Law! It is the Spirit of God! The Spirit gives us spiritual life. He opens the door to the kingdom; we don't."*

They all leaned back in their chairs and contemplated.

"I must say, it is in keeping with what I learned when I became a priest," Benjamin began. *"I remember my father telling me at my first sacrifice as a young priest: 'The truth here is that God is setting aside his wrath over sin by the blood of this animal. God is choosing mercy over punishment. As a priest you are merely facilitating God's activity. But animal blood is only the representation of what God is doing. The reality of forgiveness is in a sacrifice yet to be.'"*

"You said the same thing to me at my first evening sacrifice, Father!" Nicodemus responded. *"Remember how I wept over that lamb?"*

The three went on to discuss the words of Rabbi Yeshua into the night. But Nicodemus could not bring himself to address those final words of Yeshua: **"Whoever lives by the truth comes into the light."** (John 3:21)

Word circulated the next day that the Galilean had left Jerusalem. Pharisees in the Sanhedrin had discovered that he had gone with his disciples into the Judean countryside north of Jerusalem. Like "The Baptist" he was said to have begun baptizing also. It was said that a rivalry was developing between the two. Nicodemus had a hard time believing this. The man he met was not given to such egotistical and base temptations.

The Sanhedrin had discussed "The Baptist" on the Sunday Nicodemus was visiting him, and they had begun informal inquiries about him. They chose not to send an investigative team and did nothing officially. Gamaliel's cautionary words held sway. He advised letting the fervor die down on its own. Some mentioned that Antipas would not allow himself to be poked by this hermit. He would drown the man in his own baptismal waters if he continued to agitate the vindictive and vengeful ruler of the Galilee. The Rabbi Yeshua they had dismissed as a zealot who would meet his end without their intervention. Privately though, they were watching.

Nicodemus continued to wrestle with his conscience over *"stepping into the light."* Benjamin cautioned him not to do anything rash and risk his position. It was not only the challenge from the Rabbi that had moved Nicodemus; it was his genuine and humble words that spoke to his soul. He felt a burden lifted from his heart when the Rabbi told him, ***"For God so loved the world that he gave his one and only Son and that whoever believes in him shall not perish but have eternal life."*** (John 3:16) Could this be the answer to the meaning of the Lord's covenant with Abram in Genesis 15? The best teachers of the day taught that it was a reciprocal covenant, but it always bothered Nicodemus that there was no mention of Abram walking through the bisected pieces of the heifer, goat, ram, dove and pigeon. The teachers, including Joshua and Terah, were of the opinion that it was not a covenant unless both parties walked the blood trail. Still, it was never mentioned in the text that Abram was asked by the Lord to walk through the blood. Only the smoking firepot, representing the Lord himself, passed through the blood. Was Jesus saying that God loved man so much that if man broke the covenant, God would pay with his own blood? Such an explanation would be too good to be true. It could not be that easy. God does everything, and man does nothing?

Nicodemus kept spinning these truths in his mind and was getting nowhere. He needed to hear more from the Rabbi Yeshua. But he would need to be careful. The Pharisees had sent spies to follow the Rabbi. Nicodemus knew most of the Pharisees in Jerusalem and they knew him. After speaking with Joseph, the two of them decided to disguise themselves and pose as Judean trade merchants. In this way they could avoid detection and still follow the Rabbi. They left for

Jericho the next day and planned to follow the Jordan until they found him. Along the way they would question travelers about his whereabouts.

Within two days they had traveled the entire length of the Jordan and were almost within sight of the Sea of Galilee when they spoke to a Galilean who said he had been baptized by one of Yeshua's disciples. He said Yeshua and the disciples were headed southwest into Samaria.

The next morning, Joseph and Nicodemus rose early and headed in the same direction. Following a pass through the mountains, they arrived at the site of first capital of Israel: Shechem. Rabban Joshua had brought Nicodemus and his classmates here years ago. They had camped in the shadow of Mt. Gerizim. Joshua had wanted to expose his students to the history of this fertile plain. They had drunk from Jacob's well and read the Genesis account of Jacob purchasing the land and digging the ancient well.

It was late in the day, so they decided to find a place to stay, have a meal, and ask in the town square if anyone had seen the Galilean. Certainly, if he had been seen, people would remember. The two were careful to lengthen their speech so as not to give away their Jerusalem accent. That evening a man told them he had seen the Rabbi and his disciples earlier in the day. He said he believed they were staying nearby and were headed west. He told them to try near Sychar.

Just a half mile or so to the south of Sychar, Joseph and Nicodemus came to the Jacob's well. They arrived late in the day and had intended to stay in Sychar as they inquired about the Rabbi from Nazareth. A number of roads meet at the well. One goes south to Shiloh and Jerusalem. The same road goes north to Sychar. The roads were empty as Nicodemus and Joseph approached the well. From a distance they saw two men resting beside the well. As they drew closer, Nicodemus recognized the younger of the two. It was John, the disciple of Yeshua who had led him to his Rabbi. He said something to the seated man, and both rose and turned. Nicodemus was overjoyed to see Rabbi Yeshua smiling and waving.

"Good evening and Shalom, Rabbi," Nicodemus said as they approached. He had not given any thought to where he wanted to begin the conversation. Yeshua motioned to several stone benches under an acacia tree nearby.

"Welcome, Nicodemus! Good to see you again so soon. Traveling through Samaria, are you?" Yeshua smiled out of one side of his mouth. Nicodemus was not sure if the question was real or sarcasm. Judeans seldom were seen in Samaria, while Galileans often traveled through Samaria on the way to Jerusalem.

"This is Joseph from Arimathea, Master. And yes, in truth we have been looking for you." Nicodemus responded. *"Are you alone here?"*

"The others have gone into Sychar to buy food," John offered. *"In fact, we just arrived. We have been traveling for several days through Samaria. The Master is tired and decided to remain here while the others went for food."*

"How fortunate for us," Joseph interjected. *"May I draw some water for you? The well is deep and, since you are tired, I would be happy to draw you some water."*

"No thank you," Yeshua answered. *"Someone is coming to draw water for me."*

With that Joseph sat back down thinking that Yeshua meant the disciples would soon be back and draw water.

Just then a woman approached the well with a donkey and several large skins slung across its back. It was unusual for a woman to come to the well in the evening. Normally servant girls did this kind of work early in the morning. Women from a very poor background were the only ones who would draw water. This woman was well into her thirties and dressed quite well. She was no one's handmaid and was not poor. Upon seeing the four men, she quickly tied up her black hair and covered her head. She was clearly embarrassed.

Yeshua stood and approached the well. He asked her to draw him some water while Nicodemus and Joseph looked at each other, then at John. John just smiled and nodded. *"Watch and listen,"* John said quietly to the two men. They were close enough to hear the conversation but distant enough to give the Master privacy in conversation.

The woman was noticeably disturbed by the request. She had tied one of her skins to the rope, put in a large stone and lowered it. She was in the middle of pulling it up again. As she strained at the heavy load, she said under her breath. ***"You're a Jew. I'm Samaritan! You're asking me for a drink?"*** (John 4:9) There was more than a hint of sarcasm in her voice. The men already had an idea as to the occupation of the woman. She probably assumed Yeshua's request was more than a request for water. She looked experienced in dealing with men who had only one thing on their minds.

"If you knew the gift of God and who it is that asks you for a drink, you would have asked him and he would have given you living water." (John 4:10) Yeshua responded to the woman.

The men were shocked at Yeshua's response. First by the word he used in Aramaic for "gift of God." It was a word that described the joy and bliss of God's presence in heaven. He had taken the conversation from the gutter and elevated it beyond this world. And he was offering this "gift" to a woman of questionable reputation. Nicodemus and Joseph just looked at each other and then at Yeshua, whose back was to the men. They saw the look of amazement on the woman's face as she suddenly stopped pulling on the rope and held it with one hand. The skin had reached the surface. She removed it and began filling her other skins. The woman was strong and clearly was able to handle herself, even among Jewish men. After filling her containers, she lowered the weighted skin to the water again, turned to Yeshua and said, ***"Sir, you have nothing to draw with and the well is deep."*** *She motioned to her skin that was now filling at the bottom of the 100 foot deep well.* ***"Where can you get this living water? Are you greater than our father Jacob who gave us the well*** *and drank from it himself, as did also his sons and his flocks and herds?"* (John 4:11, 12)

Nicodemus recognized the conversation. It was so similar to the one he had with Yeshua. While Yeshua spoke on a spiritual level, she remained on a physical plane, almost refusing to see the obvious. He had done the same just a few days earlier when Yeshua had talked about being born again. Why was it so much easier to see resistance in others to the things of God?

The woman had pulled the skin from the well and was filling her second container. Yeshua bent over to hold it steady for her while she poured.

He replied, *"Everyone who drinks this water will be thirsty again, but whoever drinks the water I give him will never thirst. Indeed, the water I give him will become in him a spring of water welling up to eternal life."* (John 4:13, 14)

She stopped pouring and dropped the skin. The similarity of this conversation to the one Nicodemus had with Yeshua was uncanny.

"Whoever believes in him will not perish but have eternal life!" (John 3:16)

"The water I give him will become in him a spring of water welling up to eternal life!" (John 4:14)

At first Nicodemus thought that Yeshua was using the image of water to represent his teaching. Many Rabbis had used the same illustration in their writings. But never had any spoken of their doctrine as a "spring welling up!" Yeshua was speaking of something deeper, something more essential to salvation.

In the midst of sin and corruption, personally and professionally, Yeshua kept pointing heavenward. With Nicodemus, Yeshua had used the picture of the new life that comes from God. With this woman, he used the picture of the refreshment of cool water. The truth remained the same. God provides exactly what we need for time and eternity. Nicodemus and Joseph kept looking at each other as this drama unfolded in front of them. They could not imagine any Rabbi, priest, and certainly no member of the learned Sanhedrin, doing what this Galilean was doing. It was powerful and moved them deeply as they watched.

"He talked like this with you?" Joseph leaned and whispered to Nicodemus.

"Exactly like this," Nicodemus answered immediately, *"Exactly!"*

The woman finally stopped her work. She seemed tired.

"Sir, give me this water." (John 4:15) She paused as she turned to tie her burden to the donkey. Then she continued, **"So that I won't get thirsty...and...have to keep coming here to draw water."** (John 4:15)

She seemed to know what Yeshua was offering but could not bring herself to accept it. At that Nicodemus dropped his head. It was like looking in a mirror!

"She's afraid," he said to himself, *"Afraid she is not worthy! She feels dirty, like... a vine in the dirt!"*

"Go, call your husband and come back," (John 4:16) Yeshua told her.

"I have no husband," (John 4:17) she replied.

Yeshua said to her, **"You are right when you say you have no husband. The fact is, you have had five husbands, and the man you now have is not your husband. What you have said is quite true."** (John 4:17,18)

Nicodemus began to wonder if she would back away now. She had every reason to resist this direct confrontation about her lifestyle. Yet she seemed drawn to Yeshua, who had been willing to speak with her and talk about meaningful things. Most men only wanted to take from her. Yeshua was offering to give.

"Sir," the woman said, **"I can see that you are a prophet. Our fathers worshiped on this mountain but you Jews claim that the place where we must worship is in Jerusalem."** (John 4:19, 20)

The woman had responded in a way that neither Nicodemus nor Joseph expected. Samaritans recognized no prophet after Moses. The next prophet to appear, they believed, would in fact be the Messiah himself. Yeshua had revealed to her that he knew her past but did it in such a delicate way. He had no intention of stepping on this bruised reed. She felt dirty already. He simply acknowledged what she knew to be true. She was thirsty, and her life shouted it to the top of Mt Gerizim. But now Gerizim lay in ruins. There was no place for her to go. She only wanted him to clarify where she should go for the water she craved.

Jesus declared, *"Believe me, woman, the time is coming when you will worship the Father neither on this mountain nor in Jerusalem. You Samaritans worship what you do not know; we worship what we do know, for salvation is from the Jews. Yet a time is coming and has now come when the true worshipers will worship the Father in spirit and truth, for they are the kind of worshipers the Father seeks. God is spirit, and his worshipers must worship in spirit and in truth*." (John 4:21-24)

Joseph and Nicodemus listened and kept quiet. The words of Yeshua had fallen on the fertile soil of this woman's heart. This they could not dispute. It was obvious. She hung on his words like a baby to his mother. Could this Rabbi be the long awaited one? The genuine worship which focused on the Lord Almighty was exactly why Joseph had wanted Nicodemus on the Sanhedrin. Joseph smiled broadly as the woman responded to Yeshua's words, *"I know that Messiah is coming. When he comes, he will explain everything to us."* (John 4:25)

It was a leading statement. She was asking exactly what was on Nicodemus' heart. John had been distracted from the conversation at the approach of the 11 Talmidim. He missed Yeshua's response. But Nicodemus and Joseph did not. *"I who speak to you am he!"* (John 4:26)

Chapter 15:
Doubt

There was no doubt. They had heard it clearly: ***"I who speak to you am he!"*** (John 4:26) The woman too was shocked at Yeshua's words. John had walked down the road to welcome the other disciples and had missed Yeshua's words. For a few brief seconds, the woman stood still before Yeshua as he smiled at her. Finally, she fell to her knees, folded her arms across her chest, bent over and placed her forehead on the ground. Through her tears, Nicodemus and Joseph head her say several times, *"My Lord and my God!"* Gone was the sarcasm. Gone was the confusion. Her deep need for God's acceptance and love had been met in the most unusual place. She had come to this well as an outcast. She was not welcome at the more convenient well on the north side of Sychar. The "reputable" women of Sychar had made that very obvious. People whispered in the streets when she passed by. But here, in the midst of her attempt to hide from her sin and shame, she found cleansing, acceptance, and truth!

As the disciples approached, Yeshua reached down and took the hand of the Samaritan and lifted her to her feet. The 12 were only ten feet away when they stopped in their tracks and said nothing. Yeshua placed his hand on the woman's head and whispered something to her. Nicodemus could not hear what he said. As he spoke, the woman smiled and turned to see the disciples standing there. Nicodemus and Joseph could see the shock on her face, but it did not remain long as Jesus spoke again, *"Do not be afraid, only believe!"* She smiled and backed away, turned and ran down the road for Sychar, leaving behind her donkey and her water jars. All could hear her laughing as she ran down the road. Several times she stopped turned toward Mt. Gerizim, lifted her hands in the air and shouted, *"Ha! It's not you!"*

The Talmidim approached Jesus cautiously and began to converse. They spoke of bread and eating, and Jesus replied just as Nicodemus now expected. He took the physical and elevated it to a spiritual level. *"I have food to eat that you know nothing about."* (John 4:32)

After 15 minutes or so, a crowd of people could be seen coming from Sychar with the woman leading them. Nicodemus saw Jesus turn to the approaching crowd, point, and say, *"I tell you, open your eyes and look at the fields. They are ripe for harvest."* (John 4:35)

The rest of the day, Nicodemus and Joseph spent in Sychar. Countless Samaritans came to the house where Yeshua and the 12 were staying. Jesus taught them well into the night, opening their hearts and minds. Nicodemus and Joseph had never witnessed anything like this before, ever! A Jewish rabbi reaching out to Samaritans! And Samaritans showed not only hospitality but respect for a Jew. The cultural gap between the two was wide and animosity was mutual. But in this place, there was peace, brotherhood and forgiveness. And it came only because Rabbi Yeshua was present.

For the next two days, Nicodemus and Joseph watched and listened. Yeshua taught and healed the sick in Sychar. Many in the small village believed and worshiped him. On the third day, Yeshua and his Talmidim decided to leave for Galilee. They begged him to stay longer, but he insisted, *"I must be about my Father's business!"* The Samaritans gathered together in the town square and each of them came forward and placed a coin in a small leather bag. They offered it to the talmid called Judas as they left. Joseph and Nicodemus followed the 12 with Jesus until they reached the well and the road that went north to Galilee. As they turned to head north, Yeshua stopped and turned to Nicodemus and Joseph. *"Come, follow me!"* Yeshua motioned. Nicodemus knew what this meant. It was not a mere invitation to join them for a few more days. It was a call to discipleship. Learn from me, watch me and become like me! This was an invitation to become a Talmid under Yeshua. Nicodemus was conflicted. He had a family back in Ein Karem, a position in the Sanhedrin, a business to run. How could he leave that behind to join Yeshua? Noticing his hesitancy, Yeshua turned and began walking down the path, leaving Nicodemus and Joseph standing at the well. *"Shalom, God bless you!"* he shouted as he led his disciples down the road. They had hesitated and the call to be a talmid did not allow hesitancy.

"We should have gone!" Nicodemus turned to Joseph as they headed in the opposite direction.

"We hesitated," Joseph replied, *"But what we heard here at this well has changed me forever."*

"We cannot share this with anyone except Father and Gamaliel," Nicodemus continued. *"If what Rabbi Jeshua said to the woman is true, it will be explosive."*

For the next two days, Joseph and Nicodemus walked and talked. The farther they walked away from Yeshua, the more powerful doubt became. They battled between what they had seen and their background and training in the Law. As Nicodemus would address the law and its value to the society, Joseph would counter with the simplicity of Rabbi Yeshua's words and the power in his approach to people. On one thing they could agree, Yeshua was a prophet and a great teacher. But was he also Messiah? It was so outside the scope of their expectation. Could a simple Rabbi from Nazareth be the one? Nicodemus could not wrap his mind around the idea that the one who would sit on King David's throne could be born in poverty.

Upon reaching Jerusalem after being gone for a week, they quickly made their way through the Shechem gate, past the Antonio Fortress and into the home of Benjamin. Benjamin was overjoyed to see his son and anxiously awaited word from Nicodemus about the Galilean Rabbi. They greeted each other warmly and Benjamin asked, *"Tell me Nicodemus, did you find him? Talk is increasing among the chief priest Annas and his sons about Yeshua. They have not taken kindly to the fall off in revenue from the Galilean's actions in the temple court. Word is going around that they have sent their spies to search him out and challenge him."*

"Yes, Father," Nicodemus responded, *"After we had almost reached Galilee, we met a man who had been baptized by one of the Rabbi's disciples and he directed us into Samaria. Gamaliel should be present for this; is he in the city?"*

"He is at the temple I believe," Benjamin added. *"I can send someone to get him, or we can go there."*

"Probably best that I am seen at the Temple since I have not been at a meeting of the Sanhedrin for a long time. We can find a private room where I can share what we experienced in Samaria."

The three walked the few steps from the house into the Temple courts where they found the great teacher of the School of Hillel. Gamaliel had been leading a discussion in the Temple. Some listening to him were challenging Gamaliel on his teaching about ceremonial washing and the baptism of John. The debate became heated just as the three of them arrived at the Temple court. Gamaliel had maintained that the ceremonial washing was a simple act of purifying the body in preparation for service in the temple, but several men were very vocal in their opposition. They maintained that repentance was a key element of the Baptist's teaching. The washing, they maintained, reflected their changed mind to live differently. Gamaliel dismissed the crowd but spoke privately with those who had been with the Baptist. He wanted to hear more about this man who was turning Judea upside down with his teaching.

Gamaliel saw Nicodemus, Joseph, and Benjamin approaching, excused himself and anxiously approached Nicodemus. *"Let's go inside here,"* Gamaliel motioned to a nearby open room, *"I want to hear every word you have to say."* As they walked, Gamaliel confirmed what Benjamin had said. *"Things are really heating up among the family of Annas and the Sanhedrin members. What did you find out?"*

The four never bothered to sit down as Nicodemus and Joseph related their journey, the conversation with the woman at the well, and the subsequent teaching and healing by Rabbi Yeshua in Sychar.

Several times Joseph interrupted Nicodemus' story and mentioned Yeshua's statement claiming to be the Messiah.

Finally, Gamaliel asked Joseph when he mentioned it a third time, *"Do you believe he is the Messiah, Joseph?"* Joseph looked at Nicodemus and then at Gamaliel,

"Yes, I do!" he replied, *"His teaching has authority and power. He was never trained, yet has learning far beyond any of us. His miracles are a direct fulfillment of Isaiah's prophecy. We witnessed the blind, deaf, lame and mute healed by his hand. We saw an entire village flock to hear him, and these were Samaritans."*

"What about the Law, Joseph? Nicodemus interrupted, *"He told the woman, 'Just believe.' Did you hear him when he helped the woman to her feet? Believe? Is that all? Are we to leave behind everything we have learned about Moses and the prophets? No need for Sabbath laws!? No Passover? Just believe? I agree that Rabbi Yeshua is a prophet sent by God. Of that I am sure. Perhaps this is God's way of reforming our corrupt leadership. But Messiah, I'm not so sure."*

"I have thought about this for two days, Gamaliel!" Joseph continued, *"Nicodemus and I have debated every word of the Rabbi on our journey, his actions and teaching. I agree that he will be a powerful instrument of reform. But he will do much more than that."*

"Joseph, you know he will be rejected by all those in powerful positions!" Benjamin added. *"They will not so easily give up the prestige in which they pride themselves."*

"All the prophets were rejected," Gamaliel responded. *"But their word was proven true down through the generations. When something is of God, no one can effectively drown it out!"*

"I have to admit," Nicodemus paused before continuing, *"I feel torn inside. When I spoke with Yeshua almost a week ago, my heart burned inside me as he exposed my wrong thinking, my rationalizations. He spoke on a level I have never before experienced, yet he seems at home not just with the learned but with*

children. He is kind and humble. Not like any Rabbi or learned member of the Sanhedrin."

"So, what is holding you back, son?" Benjamin asked.

Nicodemus thought hard and said, *"It means I have been wrong for so long. It means I will have enemies in the Temple and the Empire. My comfortable life in the vineyards of Ein Karem will be no more. My future professional life will be gone. Do I wager everything on this man from Galilee?"*

"Unless he is whom he says he is!" Gamaliel responded. *"If he is the Messiah, isn't it better to stand with him than corrupt leadership?"*

"I need to pray and hear him again," Nicodemus finally said.

Over the next few months Nicodemus and Joseph talked often. They spoke not just about The Law but the personal sacrifice it would mean to be a follower of Yeshua. Joseph was ready to turn his back on his position in the Sanhedrin and his riches. He planned, however, to be a voice of reason there. If Yeshua was to take the seat of King David, he reasoned, nothing else would matter anyway. Nicodemus' heart was still torn. He feared more for his young family than position and influence. He had come into the Sanhedrin and become a Pharisee with a degree of reluctance anyway. It would not take much for him to walk away from it. However, he would be seen as an enemy of some of the most powerful men in the city. If Yeshua could not stand against the forces within the Sanhedrin that were becoming increasingly hostile toward the Baptist and Yeshua, then he and his family would be in serious danger. He had seen justice perverted time and time again. The added complication of the Roman/Caiaphas collaboration for peace made him fear even more. People disappeared without a trace under the new procurator. The Herodian family was gone from Judea, but the procurators had proven even worse. Anyone that threatened their power was eliminated.

Then word came that the Baptist had been arrested and put in prison in Galilee by Antipas. John had spoken openly about Antipas' sexual appetite, and his constant rebukes had not been received well by Herodias, his wife. Antipas had reluctantly arrested John but refused to have him executed. All this made Nicodemus even more hesitant about Yeshua. Nicodemus knew that Antipas could have his friend killed at any moment. He desperately wanted to see John, but it would be risky without authorization from the Procurator or Caiaphas.

The circle of Gamaliel, Joseph of Arimathea, and Nicodemus decided that the best course of action would be for Gamaliel to speak to Caiaphas and Annas. The two priests agreed that formal investigation by the Sanhedrin of the Baptist was now appropriate and might even garner good will with Antipas should he take the next step and have John executed. Normally there would be great opposition when a Roman tetrarch would imprison an innocent Jew, but the case of the Baptist was different. He, the Baptist, had offended Roman and Jew alike. Caiaphas also wanted the envoy to visit the synagogue in Capernaum as well and get input from Rabbi Jairus on Rabbi Yeshua. To this Gamaliel agreed quite willingly and suggested that Joseph and Nicodemus be appointed as the official envoy to the Capernaum synagogue. The papers were drawn along with a letter of greeting from the Council to Antipas.

The next day Nicodemus and Joseph were on their way to Tiberius.

Chapter 16:
Believe!

"The Baptist" had been arrested by Herod Antipas and taken to the prison in Julius in Perea before being transferred to the highly fortified prison in Machaerus. This word came to Nicodemus and Joseph of Arimathea just as they reached Jericho. While there, they were hosted by a Jewish man by the name of Zacchaeus, a wealthy tax collector in Jericho. Zacchaeus was privy to all the latest rumors regarding "The Baptist" as travelers would stay in his many lodgings in the Jordan River Valley outside Jericho. He was an honest man who had made a comfortable living collecting taxes on the Arabian traders who came through Jericho from Machaerus. Zacchaeus was experienced in discerning the intention of people and, through leading questions, discovered that these two men were not Pharisee spies or typical Sanhedrin members. Over a bottle of fine wine, he shared with Nicodemus and Joseph how John came to be imprisoned. It seemed "The Baptist's" message and condemnation of Antipas' adultery with his brother Philip's wife was only the tip of the offense that enraged Antipas. The two realized quickly that Caiaphas had not been entirely open about his involvement and plot to rid the world of "The Baptist." Fearing an uprising of the people and the consequential threat to his power and influence, Caiaphas had made peace with a contingent of Pharisees in the Sanhedrin, and dispatched them to Antipas with the intention of inciting him against "The Baptist." An uprising would not be in Antipas' best interest either, and he easily took the bait, already angered at "The Baptist" for calling him an adulterer.

After imprisoning him in Julius, Antipas quickly had John taken out of the immediate area and kept in the infamous Machaerus prison where many an outlaw wasted away. Fearing the people's love for John, Antipas did not have him immediately executed, which was the wish of Caiaphas. Prison was the next best option according to the High Priest. Nicodemus and Joseph found this information most believable, especially when Zacchaeus shared with them the story of his own baptism. From the beginning of John's arrival in the area, Zacchaeus had been attracted to John's teaching. There was depth, meaning and conviction in his words. Zacchaeus even referred to John as the modern-day Elijah, a comparison that did not escape the two. But then Zacchaeus shared a story that shocked the men.

"I was there when a certain Rabbi appeared and requested John to baptize him. You may have heard of him. I hear he recently created quite a disturbance in the Temple courts. His name is Yeshua from Nazareth. As he waded down into the River, I heard John shout to those on the bank, **'Behold, the Lamb of God who takes away the sin of the world.'"** (John 1:29)

"What did you say?" Nicodemus asked. *"The Lamb of God? Are you sure that is what he said?"*

"Yes," Zacchaeus answered, *"I am quite sure. I remember because as John baptized the Rabbi, there was a loud sound like thunder. And it is this same man who has been teaching and healing people in Galilee."*

"The Lamb of God," Nicodemus repeated several times to himself. With furrowed brow, he looked off into the distance and remembered his first evening sacrifice and his first Passover.

They talked well into the evening about the spiritual state of Israel, John's teaching, and the connection between John and Yeshua. Zacchaeus told story after story of changed lives: the baptism of Roman soldiers who laid down their weapons and waded into the Jordan, the throngs of people that followed John's every word and even how distraught his disciples were at his arrest.

In the morning Nicodemus and Joseph headed southeast toward Machaerus and crossed the Jordan. They followed the shoreline of the Salt Sea and finally headed east arriving in Machaerus late in the afternoon. The road up the hill from the valley floor was long and arduous. In many places it was more like a ledge with a steep incline on one side and a gorge hundreds of feet straight down on the other.

They discovered that Antipas was in fact in the palace but decided to find lodging and approach the palace in the morning. Few people in Machaerus were as engaging and open as Zacchaeus was the previous evening. They seemed to be in a spiritual prison that totally engulfed them. Living on the edge between the Roman Empire and the Parthians, there was an uneasy suspicion and closed mind about them.

Machaerus was an impressive city, built high into the side of a hill. Antipas' father, Herod the Great, had enlarged and fortified the city with walls and towers. Three hundred meters high above the city and separated from the city by a deep chasm, the castle was surrounded by walls and very high towers, some reaching 160 cubits. Inside the castle was a magnificent palace where Antipas resided when he was in Machaerus. He had at his disposal every offensive and defensive weapon known to man, along with storehouses and cisterns enabling the garrison on duty to withstand a long siege. Herod the Great had built this fortress for his comfort and as an escape route in case of insurrection.

The prison where John was kept was not in the castle but high on another mountain pinnacle across a deep valley from the fortress. It was built in such a way that the walls that surrounded it fell into deep ravines on all sides. It was approachable only in single file up a winding pathway of switchbacks. Antipas had allowed John's disciples to visit him frequently since his arrest, but they had now returned to Galilee and John was alone in his dungeon.

Nicodemus and Joseph dressed in their official robes the next morning for their audience with Antipas. They arrived and were told that the King was not yet awake, and they must wait. Whispers among the palace servants indicated that a night of revelry and drunkenness the previous night had left Antipas in a stupor. His attendants had, in fact, carried him unconscious to his bed long past midnight. His wife Herodias, however, came to welcome them. She was not given to such drunken pleasures. Her vice was ambition, and she had married Antipas for this very reason, assuming he was next in line for the throne of his father, Herod the Great. Caught in the web of her own making, her bitterness toward John was extreme. His words only reminded her of her failed attempts to achieve her ambition. She gave Nicodemus and Joseph a cold greeting. These two were just a reminder of the weak religious inclinations of her husband. She wanted "The Baptist" dead and his mouth silenced. But Antipas frequently brought John to the palace to hear him, something she detested. She would remain in her rooms until he had been returned to his dungeon. Each time he came, it meant she would have to deal with a remorseful husband who regretted John's arrest. At least today her husband would still be dealing with the after effects of his drunkenness the night before. She hoped these two "religious idiots"— as she called them — would grow impatient and leave before noon. But they did not, and after several hours of waiting, Antipas awoke and was informed that Sanhedrin members had requested an audience. He bathed, was dressed in his official robes by attendants, and was led to the welcoming hall to his gilded throne where he would receive his guests. He was not in a mood to listen. His head was pounding and he sent an attendant for wine to clear his head.

"Now what does Caiaphas want from me," he said aloud as he took a long gulp of wine. *"I've put the man in prison, why can't he just leave me alone?"* He contemplated that perhaps Pilate might be behind this visitation. *"Perhaps, they have been rebuffed by the procurator,"* he thought, *"and are playing on my long-standing feud with Pilate."* He could not hold the thought for long in his current mental state and motioned for the two men to be brought.

Joseph and Nicodemus entered, went through the requisite machinations before the tetrarch, and presented their official papers from Caiaphas. Antipas was relieved that they had no other request other than a visit with "The Baptist" to confirm he was still in the dungeon. They preferred to visit John themselves rather than having him brought to them, which normally would have made Antipas suspicious. But as he was more concerned about relieving himself

131

and retiring to his bed, he motioned to his attendants to call the guards to accompany them to the prison.

Nicodemus and Joseph had only heard rumors about the prison in Machaerus. No one had ever come out who had entered, and those who managed to visit prisoners told stories that seemed too horrific to be true. They found the stories to be accurate. They followed the guard down long winding stone stairs. Lit only by the torch the guard carried, the dungeon was putrid, damp and much cooler than the palace. As they reached the bottom of the stairs they could hear singing coming from inside one of the rooms. The guard opened the heavy iron door, placed his torch on the wall and lit another. The two men entered the small room just as "The Baptist" had finished singing one of the Psalms of Ascent. Nicodemus recognized it immediately as one of the Psalms he and John had sung together in the vineyards of Ein Karem. John had just finished singing the chorus to which Nicodemus had written the tune.

"If you, O Lord, kept a record of sins,
O Lord, who could stand?
But with you there is forgiveness; Therefore you are feared"
Psalm 130:3,4

John smiled and embraced Nicodemus before he could say a word. Nicodemus could tell that John was much thinner. He had been here less than a month. He introduced Joseph, and John began to apologize, *"I'm sorry I am not able to offer you a seat or a glass of wine my friend."*

Nicodemus smiled. His heart broke to see this strong man, his friend from home, in such a state. They talked of his arrest by Antipas. Several months prior, two Roman soldiers had visited Aenon. They had been sent to hear him preach. They had even been baptized, waiting for all others to leave before taking him captive. Within a few days he was transferred here to Machaerus in the middle of the night.

132

Then John began to talk about Antipas. *"He lives in the shadows,"* John began. *"He longs to hear the truth; in fact, we have had many conversations about sin and righteousness. Several times he has been close to the kingdom. But he retreats into the shadows. He fears the light. He knows the truth, but the disobedience of his past keeps him in the dark. I have encouraged him often that there is nothing to fear in the light of truth. But fear has a grip on his heart. Plus, his wife controls him spiritually. It is often when she is traveling in Arabia that he calls for me."*

Nicodemus and Joseph kept quiet as John talked and John could tell his heart was heavy. *"What is troubling you, my friend?"* John asked Nicodemus.

"Your words about Antipas," Nicodemus responded, *"they remind me of something Rabbi Yeshua said to me!"*

"You've spoken to him?" John asked. *"My disciple James introduced you to John then? And he took you to him?"*

"Yes, I spent an evening with Yeshua and we talked at length." Nicodemus responded. *"Is he the one, John? Or do we wait for another?"*

John just smiled at Nicodemus. *"Your life is complicated by many things, my friend. One day, all those things that bind you will be gone and only one thing will remain. Remember the story you told me about your first Passover in Jerusalem? You were only 10. You spoke with my father along the road. He told you about Gabriel and his vision. You were so certain then! Remember? And your Passover lamb, you did not even bring it to the Temple! Your father took it to be slaughtered for you. Remember what the priest Simeon told you when you ran away from the Temple courts and met him inside his room?"*

"Yes, I do John," Nicodemus responded hesitantly, *"but I was a child. We are not children anymore."*

"But sin and evil remain," John continued, *"Truth and believing is child-like! It does not change when we grow up; it becomes even more vital!"*

They both sat quietly for a long time. Tears began streaming down Nicodemus' face as Joseph watched and listened to John minister to Nicodemus' heart. Joseph was even more convinced by John's words, how he said them and more pointedly, WHERE he said them. A prisoner was encouraging a free man. Or was it the other way around? Despite the depths of this place, the damp desolation of the Machaerus dungeon, John was free, and he lived and spoke as a free man. It was as if God himself was here! And John needed no one else and nothing else.

Finally, John took Nicodemus' hand and said, *"Don't be afraid Nicodemus, just believe!"* Again, the words of Yeshua leapt to the mind of Nicodemus. He had said the same to the woman at the well, *"Don't be afraid, just believe!"*

Nicodemus smiled and looked up into John's weathered and worn face. *"Thank you, John! God has used you powerfully today. I came here to encourage you and you have encouraged me! I will seek out Yeshua with an honest and open heart."*

With that the guard returned to the doorway. *"Time's up!"* he shouted.

They embraced for a long time and smiled. *"Shalom, John,"* Nicodemus finally said to his friend as he turned to leave. Joseph embraced John and left. Nicodemus turned at the doorway to look once more at his friend.

They both smiled as John said, *"Step into the light, Nicodemus. Don't be afraid!"*

Nicodemus didn't say much as he and Joseph were escorted back to the castle. Several times Nicodemus looked back over his shoulder at the prison. Each time he silently prayed that the Lord would deliver him. He repeated the opening words of the Psalm John had been singing when they arrived,

"Out of the depths I cry to you Lord; O Lord, hear my voice. Let your ears be attentive to my cry for mercy." Psalm 130:1, 2

"Mercy!" Nicodemus whispered several times as they climbed the steep hill back to the castle, *"Lord, have mercy!"*

The two spent another night in Machaerus before departing the next morning for Capernaum. It would be a four-day journey and there would be much time for discussion along the way. They talked often as they walked. John's testimony was powerful, and they often returned to his encouraging witness to the truth despite living in the deplorable circumstance that was the Machaerus dungeon. As they walked along the Jordan River Valley north toward Galilee, they discussed the objective of their mission and the hypocritical motivation of Caiaphas. It was obvious to them that Caiaphas was trying to use them. He had intentionally withheld his involvement in the arrest of John. They must be careful. If Caiaphas had already dispatched his spies to get rid of John, it was obvious he could be doing the same to Yeshua in Galilee. John was right, Nicodemus thought; his life was increasingly complicated. How would he unravel it all, save his family from danger, maintain his position and still hold on to truth without fear. When he was with John and Yeshua, it all seemed so easy. Then he would enter his world again where things were complex and involved.

Capernaum was a very small town, just a fishing community really. Such a small town would seldom have a synagogue. However, there was a Roman centurion who lived in the area and had found the Jewish way of life and the honest integrity of the local fishermen most appealing. He had used his wealth and position to build a synagogue for the people, and he often attended synagogue gatherings on Sabbath when he was at home. The head of the synagogue was a well-respected Rabbi called Jairus. Nicodemus and Joseph were warmly welcomed at his home. Jairus was married and had two children. The youngest was only twelve and had just been taken ill. Nicodemus and Joseph offered to stay elsewhere during this challenging time, but Jairus refused.

"We have plenty of room," he said. *"You have traveled many days and I am anxious to hear about your visit to The Baptist."*

135

The next morning however, the girl took a turn for the worse and while Jairus was out, she died. One of Jairus' servants was dispatched to find him and give him the sad news. Jairus' wife, who had welcomed them so warmly, was now distraught. Nicodemus and Joseph tried to console her, but she was beside herself with grief.

"If only the master was here," she kept saying. Nicodemus assumed she was wishing her husband had not gone out that morning, until he returned and noticed immediately that Jairus had gone to seek the help of Yeshua. Later he discovered that not only did Jairus know Yeshua but he had witnessed many of his miracles of healing, even the servant of the Roman Centurion who had built the synagogue. Throngs of people crowded around the Galilean Rabbi as he approached Jairus' home. Already many neighbors and friends from the synagogue had arrived and had begun wailing at the news of the death of the girl.

As Yeshua approached the door of the house, he was met by Nicodemus and Joseph, who had been trying to control the crowd in Jairus' absence. He entered along with three of his Talmidim and greeted the two men. He refused to allow the crowd to enter and admonished them, ***"Stop wailing, she is not dead but asleep!"*** (Luke 8:52) As he closed the door, they could hear laughter and scoffing coming from outside. He took Jairus and his wife by the hand and led them to the upstairs bedroom where the girl had been laid out. As Yeshua climbed the stairs to the upper level, Nicodemus heard him say to the parents, *"Don't be afraid, just believe!"* The six of them entered the girl's room and closed the door. Nicodemus and Joseph were left on the lower level. They could hear the crowd outside murmuring about Yeshua's words.

One said, *"Asleep! Asleep? How cruel to say that to Jairus!"* Others responded with hissing disappointment.

Despite the high drama, the symbolism was not lost on Nicodemus. He had been feeling caught between faith and doubt for some time. Now, here he stood, listening to ridicule and disbelief as Yeshua was only steps away.

Within a matter of moments, Nicodemus and Joseph were puzzled by the sounds coming from the upstairs room. Laughter! Praise! *"Hallelujah! Hallelujah!"* they heard Jairus' familiar voice. The door opened and the three Talmidim, Peter, James, and John, came out with astonished expressions, shaking their heads, mouths agape, and coming down the stairs ahead of Jairus and Yeshua. Jairus was weeping and laughing at the same time. He embraced Yeshua for a long time, stood back and fell to his knees, lifted his hands to heaven and cried out in a loud voice, *"My Lord and my God!"*

John approached Nicodemus with a big smile on his face and shook his hand vigorously. *"Come,"* he said to the two, *"see for yourself."*

Nicodemus and Joseph climbed the stairs to hear Yeshua raise his voice for all to hear, **"Tell no one what you have seen here,"** (Luke 8:56). He looked at each of those gathered. This did little to temper the enthusiasm of the three Talmidim. They led Nicodemus and Joseph to the upper level. Inside they could hear voices, a mother and child talking. They entered the room to see the girl sitting upright eating a piece of fish. The color was back in her cheeks. She was smiling at the men as they stood in disbelief at the foot of her bed.

"This is my youngest daughter!" her mother said to the men as if introducing them, *"She's alive! The master has come. He brings life and light wherever he goes! Rejoice with me! This daughter of mine was dead and is alive again!"* She rose to her feet and embraced the two men, laughing and crying at the same time!

Chapter 17:
Sukkot

Nicodemus and Joseph of Arimathea were deeply impacted by the powerful miracle of Yeshua. They spent the next few days with Jairus as he shared some of the teachings of Yeshua on the Law of Moses. He also related some of the miracles he himself had witnessed. This is what motivated him to search out the Master when his daughter became so sick. He told them stories of a paralytic, a leper and even the servant of the Centurion who had built the synagogue in Capernaum. All were healed by Yeshua.

"He is no respecter of persons," Jairus told them one evening. *"Jew and Roman, rich and poor come to him! He even healed the wife of Cuza, who manages the household of Antipas in Tiberius!"*

The miracle and the conversation with Jairus only confirmed Joseph's faith in Rabbi Yeshua. Nicodemus was deeply moved by the sincere belief of Jairus and the testimony of his little girl. The girl described the moment of "awakening" — as she called it — as being surrounded by love and song. And when she saw the face of Yeshua, she said it was like HE became the song.

The next day in the synagogue, Joseph recognized a group of five Pharisees from the Sanhedrin. They were known as "The Fierce Five" and were the same men he suspected had visited Antipas and incited him to arrest "The Baptist." Their presence shocked him and could only mean one thing: Caiaphas had sent them to directly confront Rabbi Yeshua. Joseph noticed that the men had been scanning the gathering as if looking for someone during the reading of Scripture. Many in the assembly were still talking openly about the teaching of Yeshua and his many miracles. Joseph whispered to Jairus to be careful of these men.

"They are dangerous," Nicodemus added.

The two men decided to leave the same day but, being the Sabbath, could not journey far; so they stayed in a small guest house just outside Capernaum along the lake. The owner welcomed them warmly, and when they shared that they had come from the home of Jairus and witnessed the raising of his daughter by Yeshua, he suddenly became more open.

"Be careful as you continue on your way south," he warned, *"I have heard that Antipas has dispatched an envoy to search for Rabbi Yeshua! Some say he only wants to speak with Him. But he arrested John, and no one has seen him since. Just stay clear of Tiberius!"*

The two men did not need any more encouragement to leave quickly. They took the long road around Tiberius, preferring not to come into contact with any Roman or to desecrate themselves by walking through a city which had once been a burial site.

They spent the next three days on the journey discussing the report they would give to Caiaphas. Reporting and confirming John's imprisonment and the cold welcome of Herodias would be the easy part of the report. They knew "The Fierce Five" would mention having seen them in Capernaum, so they would have to choose their words carefully about the raising of the daughter of Jairus. They finally decided to report the incident without any conclusion. Their recommendation would simply mention that there was need to hear from Rabbi Yeshua directly and not rely on hearsay testimony of those with a bias one way or the other. They hoped that Yeshua would be present for the fall festival of Tabernacles, one of the three which required the presence of every male in Israel.

As they approached Jerusalem, Joseph mentioned that he had friends in Bethany and wanted to visit them for an evening!

"They have been friends of our family for a long time. The parents have passed away and the two sisters live with their younger brother!" Joseph explained as they reached the rise of the long winding road from Jericho, *"They are called Mary, Martha and Lazarus, and they are sincere children of Abraham. I have not seen them in several years. I am anxious to hear what they think of Rabbi Yeshua!"*

"I believe I know the place," Nicodemus responded, *"Are they part of the Essene hospice that cares for the unclean and sick in Bethany?"* (Bethany — Beth Anya — means House of Misery and may have been named for the hospice.)

"Yes, they are," Joseph answered.

"Father has supported the hospice for some time, but I have never met the caretakers. They must be very gracious people," Nicodemus added.

"They are," Joseph responded, *"The two women are widows of men who were quite wealthy, and they have dedicated their wealth to helping the poor. Their home is large and comfortable and will be a good place to rest from the journey and finalize our report."*

Joseph and Nicodemus spent several days in Bethany resting and visiting the hospice to which Mary and Martha had dedicated their lives and their wealth. Lazarus, who was much younger than the sisters, also spent time at the hospice. Nicodemus was genuinely touched by the heart of the three for the poor and unclean. They discussed the Rabbi Yeshua as well and marveled at his teaching. They had been at the temple for the cleansing on Pesach.

After presenting their report to Caiaphas, Nicodemus decided to take some time at home in Ein Karem. He planned to return to the Temple for Pentecost in a few weeks and then manage his farm until Sukkot. There would be a lot of work to do as Sukkot (Feast of Tabernacles) coincided with the harvest of grapes and olives. It was always his busiest time of year at home. His farm had provided the wine for the Sukkot offering, and the first pressing of the olives would light the large menorah in the Temple along with the other lights in the Temple. But Nicodemus was more concerned about taking some time to prayerfully consider everything he had witnessed and heard in the past weeks. He had kept a mental list that was growing:

1. His deep conversation with Yeshua at night.
2. The woman at Jacob's well and the two days in Sychar listening to Yeshua teach and heal

3. Visiting John in Machaerus.

4. The raising of the daughter of Jairus.

The evidence was mounting and yet he could not bring himself to acknowledge what Joseph expressed without hesitation. *"Yeshua is the Christ?"* he said to himself as he worked the fields. Deep inside he felt the tug of war between his training and what he had experienced during the past few weeks. He shared what he had seen and heard with Rachel, and they would talk long into the night over a bottle of wine. She did not have the background in the Torah that Nicodemus did. She was quick to accept that Yeshua was the long-awaited Messiah. Her most powerful argument Nicodemus could not refute: *"If he is the Christ, is he not able to protect us from whatever forces of evil may oppose him in the Sanhedrin? And if he is, do you want to be left sitting on the fence when he arrives in Jerusalem to take his throne?"*

Sukkot was fast approaching, and Nicodemus stayed busy in the fields managing his staff for the olive and grape harvest. He wanted it completed before going to Jerusalem with his family for The Feast.

The week-long Sukkot Festival followed the harvest of figs, pomegranates, dates, and grapes. Following God's command, the people built booths of olive, palm, and myrtle branches. The booths provided shade, but there needed to be enough space in the branches, so the people could see the sky, reminding them of their years in the wilderness. These booths, or sukkot, gave the feast its name.

For seven days, the people ate, lived, and slept in these booths. This was one of the three feasts for which everyone was commanded to come to Jerusalem. Thousands of people crowded the streets of the city, and there were sukkot everywhere. The children especially loved it.

The Pharisees had adopted another custom. They took the branches of the three trees, olive, palm, and myrtle, and tied them together. Holding this cluster of branches — called "lulavim" — in one hand and a citron in the other, they carried them to the temple for each of the seven days of the festival. Here the people, and even the youngest children, would wave their "lulavim" joyously, as they danced, sang, and chanted the Hallel. A procession of priests, who made the festive sacrifices and carried water and wine to be poured into the silver channels on the altar as drink offerings, would lead the men and boys around the altar in the priests' court in front of the temple. Whenever they came to the Hosanna, they waved their lulavim toward the altar as they sang, *"O Lord, save us! O Lord, grant us success!"* After several hours of intense rejoicing before the Lord, the people returned to their booths to rest, eat, and prepare for the next day's celebration.

The significance of Tabernacles was only magnified by several historical celebrations. One thousand years earlier Solomon's Temple was dedicated during Sukkot and the Ark of the Covenant was brought into the Temple and placed in the Holy of Holies.

Two hundred years ago the Greeks had dominated Israel. Their king, Antiochus, had outlawed the study of the Torah and all Jewish worship. He had even placed his own image in the Holy of Holies and extinguished the Great Menorah. He sacrificed pigs on the altar. Judah Maccabee, however, led a group of freedom fighters against the far stronger Greek army. These rebels miraculously defeated the army of Antiochus and reclaimed the city of Jerusalem. Though only a small supply of sacred oil remained, Judah ordered The Great Menorah relit. Miraculously, it burned for eight days.

Four great Menorahs were constructed and placed in the Court of the Women. They stood 75 feet tall as a remembrance of the Great Menorah that burned miraculously for eight days. Sukkot also included an emphasis on water as it was held at the end of the dry season and included a prayer for the rains to return for the next planting season. This part of the ceremony involved a procession of priests, accompanied by flutes. Priests marched from the temple to the Pool of Siloam. The High Priest filled a golden pitcher with water, and the procession returned to the temple. The priest carried the pitcher, entered the priests' court through the Water Gate and at the blast of the shofar, approached the altar. He made one circle around the altar as the crowd sang the Hallel. Then the priest climbed the ramp and stood near the top of the altar. As the crowd grew silent, the priest solemnly poured the water. In this way, they asked God for life-giving rain for the next planting season.

The celebration grew in intensity each day, climaxing on the seventh day. When the seventh day of the feast arrived, the courts of the temple were packed with worshipers from all over the world. Chants of praise were heard throughout the city, and hundreds of thousands of "lulavim" waved in the air. The priestly procession once more went to the living water of the Pool of Siloam. Thousands of people jammed into the temple courts as the procession circled the altar seven times. Then there were three blasts on the trumpets, and the crowd grew still as the priest poured the living water into the funnel. Now the chanting became even more intense. The waving of the "lulavim" reached a frenzy as branches were beaten against the ground until the leaves fell off.

Nicodemus had plans to build his booth for the Feast of Tabernacles or Sukkot in the courtyard of his father's house in Jerusalem. His three boys were now old enough to enjoy the festivities, the enthusiastic worship that would fill the city, and particularly sleeping outside under the stars. His elderly father would have his own booth next to his. His age and many years of service as a priest allowed him to stay in the house, but Nicodemus knew he would refuse this comfort. *"No elderly person had a permanent house in the wilderness!"* he would always tell his son, *"so, neither will I!"*

On the last day of the Feast, Rachel took the boys to the Court of the Women so they could see the Four Great Menorah being lit. Just before they were lit, all other lights in the courts were extinguished. In complete darkness the blazing torches illuminated the court one by one, and when they were all lit, the crowd repeatedly shouted in unison, *"Hosanna! Lord, save us!"* The boys thoroughly enjoyed shouting at the top of their lungs and beating the lulavim which

143

Nicodemus had made for each of them. Rachel smiled at just how much each of them was like their father.

Nicodemus had heard the whispered questions among the members of the Sanhedrin. All wanted to know if Rabbi Yeshua had been seen. Joseph had heard he was staying with his disciples in Bethany, but this news was kept within their small circle of friends.

At the same time the Menorahs were lit, the High Priest Annas poured the water and wine at the altar into the silver channels while the people chanted. Just as the crowd began to quiet down, a disturbance could be heard on the far side of the temple courts and a crescendo of *"Hosannas"* began to rise. Yeshua had come! His disciples were clearing a path through the great throng of people. Hundreds of his followers surrounded the twelve Talmidim. They had raised their "lulavim" in the air and had resumed their shouts of *"Hosanna, Lord save us!"* Some held them out toward Yeshua; others threw them on the ground in his path. Still more threw their outer garments on the ground in front of him as he approached. They passed directly by Nicodemus as they approached the great altar!

The Galilean raised his hands trying to quiet the crowd. People jostled to get a glimpse of him and to hear what he was about to say. The great throng of priests who had come with the water from Siloam stood still. Annas, who had carried the golden pitcher of water, stood on the platform above the altar and looked down with a scowl on his face.

Yeshua lowered his hands, raised his voice and shouted, ***"If anyone is thirsty, let him come to ME and drink. Whoever believes in me, as the Scripture has said, streams of living water will flow from within him."*** (John 7:37) Immediately the crowd erupted, some with shouts of *"Hallelujah"* and *"Hosanna."* Nicodemus noticed a group step forward. They were the Samaritans from Sychar. They fell on their knees before Yeshua and worshiped him. The woman from the well stood in front of them, raised her hands to heaven and shouted, *"Yeshua is the Christ!"* Others began to say the same as a group of Pharisees tried to silence them. Temple guards attempted to work their way through the multitude, but the density of the crowd and the wall of Yeshua's followers did not allow them to pass!

"Let him come to me and drink!" The invitation could not have been more clear and obvious. Just then Joseph came up behind Nicodemus. He put a hand on his shoulder and said, *"Yeshua IS the Christ!"*

Chapter 18:
Dust

Nicodemus and his family spent the evening in Jerusalem along with his father and mother, Benjamin and Rachel. Nicodemus had invited Joseph and his wife, along with Gamaliel, to stay with them as well. The men spent the greater part of the evening on the rooftop talking about Yeshua. His statement alluding to himself as the "living water" was the topic.

"That is a clear reference to the Messiah!" Joseph stated emphatically.

"When he spoke of himself as the source of the springs of the water of life," Gamaliel added, *"I was reminded of Jeremiah's words when he says, 'My people have forsaken me, the spring of living water.'"* Jer. 2:13

"You are very quiet tonight son," Benjamin stated, looking at Nicodemus. *"Deep in thought over all this?"*

"I'm reflecting on all those Samaritans from Sychar who boldly bowed down before Yeshua in the Temple courts! Such simple humble faith!" Nicodemus spoke slowly and deliberately as he looked at the ground. *"'The humble will rejoice in the Lord!' Isaiah says."* (Isaiah 29:19) He stopped and looked up at each of the men. *"Could we have had a clearer fulfillment of those words than what we saw today?"*

"What are you saying, Nicodemus?" Joseph interrupted.

"In that same portion of Isaiah, he says, 'The wisdom of the wise will perish; the intelligence of the intelligent will vanish.' (Isaiah 29:14) *We are...I am proud of my education."* Tears began to flow down Nicodemus cheeks as he swallowed hard. *"Has my wisdom blinded me?"*

Benjamin smiled. He recognized the wounded lamb in Nicodemus coming out for the first time in a long time. *"Son, you are quite correct. Wisdom for its own sake is wrong and leads us away from true worship."*

"That is my very point, father. I'm saying I have been obeying the Law and missing the ONE behind the Law," Nicodemus confessed. *"The blind, deaf, lame and mute heard the voice of Yeshua today. They rejoiced and worshiped. And I stood there ashamed. I felt my wisdom vanish just as Isaiah said!"*

For a long time, the men sat quietly and contemplated Nicodemus' honest confession. Even Gamaliel, the wisest teacher in all of Judea, sat and nodded at Nicodemus' honest humility.

Early the next morning, a special meeting of the Sanhedrin was called. The Feast of Tabernacles had concluded, and the many booths constructed throughout the city and on the hills surrounding it were being dismantled.

Caiaphas convened the Council in the Hall of Hewn Stones. *"We are here to discuss the problem of Yeshua!"* Caiaphas announced as he called the meeting to order. *"We have a false prophet in our midst."*

One of the "Fierce Five" stood and dominated the floor, *"We all saw the Samaritans worshiping him and hailing him as Messiah yesterday. This is blasphemy. Samaritans in our Temple courts worshipping a Rabbi from Galilee? Are we to allow this? I suggest we issue a statement from this body declaring that man from Galilee to be a false prophet, demon possessed and a deceiver from Samaria!"*

"Wait a minute," Gamaliel interrupted, *"this motion is out of order! We cannot simply condemn a man out of hand! It is beneath the distinguished nature of this body to take such action. I suggest…"*

Nicodemus, who was seated next to Gamaliel stood, put his hand on the great teacher's shoulder and interrupted, *"If I may, most distinguished Nasi Caiaphas, High Priest Annas and honored members, last year I spent time in Galilee and spoke to Rabbi Jairus at the synagogue in Capernaum. Yeshua frequents that synagogue. Jairus spoke most favorably of his teaching and service toward the poor in Galilee. I believe it is most appropriate for us to hear from*

147

him. The Law of Moses does not allow us to just condemn a man without the benefit of two witnesses. This is our sacred duty. **Or does our law condemn anyone without first hearing him to find out what he is doing?"** (John 7:51)

At this, Sadducees aligned with Caiaphas shouted Nicodemus down.

"Samaritan lover!" some shouted. *"Go back to Galilee!"* others shouted.

"Look into it, and you will find that a prophet does not come out of Galilee!" (John 7:52) still others responded.

Hisses and boos erupted from the strict Sadducee sect despite objections from the other side of the assembly. They stamped their feet in disapproval until finally Caiaphas called for order.

Just then Caiaphas pointed to the Temple guards at the door and motioned for them to come forward, *"You were given an assignment, if I am correct? Where is he?"* he asked them. **"Why didn't you bring him in?"** (John 7:45)

At this Nicodemus and Joseph looked at each other shocked at this revelation. Had Caiaphas ordered the arrest of Yeshua? It seemed unthinkable even for him.

"The crowd did not allow us near him, sir," one of them answered.

So it was true!

"Certainly, you had other opportunities before the final Feast Day yesterday?" Caiaphas was now angry and began to pound his staff on the stones!

"No one ever spoke the way this man does!" (John 7:46) the other guard offered sheepishly.

"What? What did you say?" Caiaphas fumed. **"You mean he has deceived you also? Have any of the rulers or the Pharisees believed in him?"** (John 7:48) Caiaphas gestured around the assembly, stopping and pointing with his staff at Joseph, Gamaliel and Nicodemus. **"This mob,"** he continued, **"knows nothing of the law — there is a curse on them.** (John 7:49) *Are you siding with those*

Samaritans?" Caiaphas was ranting now. His temper was infamous, and the guards retreated as he continued on about the offense of the Samaritan presence in the temple courts the previous day.

The Hall erupted. Normal procedures of discussion were now no longer possible. The members from both sides of the Hall shouted at one another as they exited the hall without any conclusion about Yeshua, at least officially. Rumors ran rampant that a plot to execute Yeshua had been given.

Nicodemus refused to engage anyone who hurled insults his way. Instead, as the three men walked into the temple court on their way to their house, Nicodemus again quoted aloud from Isaiah, ***"The ruthless will vanish, the mockers will disappear, and all who have an eye for evil will be cut down."*** (Isaiah 29:20) But the confrontation between the hostile Caiaphas and Yeshua was only beginning.

Very early that morning, temple guards had dragged a woman out of her home. She was known to be the mistress of one of the sons of Annas. Caiaphas was planning to arrest Yeshua that very morning while the Council met. He had not expected, however, the meeting to end so quickly.

As Nicodemus, Gamaliel and Joseph reached the far side of the temple courts, they discovered that Yeshua had come and a large crowd had gathered around him. He had taken the position of a traditional Rabbi and was seated with many sitting around him listening.

Just then two of the "Fierce Five" and a group of teachers of the law approached the gathering of people around Yeshua. One of them had the arrested woman by the hair and was dragging her across the court to her screams of protestation. He had a cord in his other hand and was beating her into submission. With a single motion, he threw the woman on the ground in front of Yeshua. Several in the group tried to help her but were met with the crack of the whip. Two other Pharisees grabbed the woman by each arm and made her stand before Yeshua. She looked down, sobbing and humiliated!

Objections were immediately raised from those who were sitting around Yeshua, including his Talmidim. Yeshua raised his hand and all fell silent immediately. A Pharisee stepped forward to address Yeshua, *"Rabbi,"* he said with a hint of sarcasm, *"this woman was caught in the act of adultery. In the law, Moses commanded us to stone such women. Now, what do you say?"* John 8:4, 5

The question was calculated. Several Pharisees had concocted this idea in direct response to Yeshua keeping company with and eating with tax collectors and prostitutes. They needed a way of arresting him for violations of the Law. But they needed at least a semi-legitimate reason because of his popularity among the people. They had planned on waiting until the next Festival of Pesach in the spring to set their trap. Then they could be assured Yeshua would be in Jerusalem. But when Caiaphas saw Yeshua in the Temple courts just after dawn, he quickly put the plan into motion with the intent that he be brought before them that very morning and condemned as a heretic. But the Council did not meet long enough for the Pharisees and Teachers of the Law to put the plan into motion. The woman had actually not been caught in the act of adultery that morning. One of the sons of Annas had been having an affair with her for a long time and the woman had threatened to expose him if he did not pay her for her silence. She was dragged from her home early that morning on orders directly from Annas, who was privy to the entire plot and was using this situation to free his son from his indiscretion.

John, the talmid of Yeshua, mumbled under his breath as the woman stood before Yeshua and the assembly of about 100 people, *"Where are the witnesses and where is the man?"* Yet he dared not interrupt Yeshua, who had taken charge of this confrontation by raising his hand and asking for silence. But Yeshua had not spoken a word. He had been seated while teaching the gathering. He had been elaborating on the words of Jeremiah who described the Father as a bridegroom who had been abandoned by his unfaithful bride. The irony of the circumstance before them was not lost on the Talmidim as this unfaithful woman stood before Yeshua. But who was the real unfaithful one?

For a long time, Yeshua said nothing. He just sat and looked at the ground. Nicodemus, Joseph and Gamaliel whispered to each other. *"It's a trap,"* Joseph said to Nicodemus, *"if he says she should be stoned, they will report him to the Procurator. We are not allowed to execute anyone by Roman decree."*

"And if he says she should not be killed," Gamaliel continued the thought, *"they will accuse him of opposing the Law of Moses."*

"But this is highly irregular," Nicodemus responded. *"Such cases are not heard by a Rabbi. The Council is in charge of spiritual discipline."*

"Let's just see how it plays out first before we object," Gamaliel answered. *"Yeshua has handled this kind of situation before. Let's just see who gets humiliated!"*

The Pharisees continued to taunt Yeshua, mocking his authority. *"Where did you pass your "S'mikah"?"* one said as he laughed.

Another was even bolder, *"You spend time with these types of women; maybe you know her too well!"* They all laughed, pushed the woman closer to Yeshua and began to spit at the feet of the woman.

Yeshua still said nothing. Instead he went to one knee and began to write in the dust on the temple pavement stones. Several Pharisees boldly stepped forward to see what he was writing but it was not legible to them. Several of the older Rabbis stepped back immediately, with shock on their faces.

At first this surprised the three, but Nicodemus just smiled and turned to Gamaliel, *"You see what he is doing"* Nicodemus whispered, *"He is using the highest form of Remez! He is responding! But it is the most clever and controlled response! It is a reference to the prophet Jeremiah. He is writing in the dust. Jeremiah said,* **'Those who turn away from you will be written in the dust because they have forsaken the Lord, the spring of living water.'** *(Jer. 17:13) You see what he is doing? He is connecting what*

151

he said yesterday about living water to what these men are doing today! Clever! Very clever! He is calling out their hypocrisy! And see the men in back? They understand exactly what he is doing. But these younger guys in front don't have a clue."

Just then Yeshua stood and looked the nearest Pharisee in the eye. *"Here it comes!"* Gamaliel whispered to Nicodemus.

"If any of you is without sin, let him be the first to throw a stone at her." (John 8:7) Yeshua's eyes burned with intensity. He stared straight at the man who had mocked his authority. He paused and looked at each man. He then calmly went to one knee and began writing in the dust again. The Pharisees in front watched Yeshua kneel and looked at the others. They were clearly confused! The oldest man in the back turned and walked away.

"Thomas! Jacob!" he called over his shoulder. The men in front just watched as the older men in back whispered to each other and motioned with their head toward the exit. The younger Pharisees looked shocked, but they dared not defy their older mentors. They looked down. The older men left one by one. Finally, the younger Pharisees sneered at Yeshua who was still looking down and writing in the dust, turned and left.

The crowd began to chuckle under their breath. The Talmidim just smiled at each other.

John caught Nicodemus eye and mouthed the word, *"Jeremiah."* Nicodemus nodded slowly and responded, *"Yes, written in the dust!"*

After all the men had left and were out of the Temple, Yeshua stood and looked at the woman. He reached out and lifted her chin, looking her in the eye. He smiled and said, ***"Woman, where are they?"*** (John 8:10) He motioned behind her and she turned to see that those who had dragged her from her bed that morning were not there. She turned back to Yeshua to hear him say, ***"Has no one condemned you?"*** Jn 8:10

***"No one sir,"* she said.** (Jn. 8:11)

"Then neither do I condemn you," he said, **"Go now and leave your life of sin."** (Jn. 8:12)

She smiled, looking at the Talmidim, turned, and began to walk away. After a few steps she began to run, laugh and shout, *"Hallelujah! Yeshua is the Christ!"*

Chapter 19:
Lazarus!

The Feast of Tabernacles and the events that surrounded it finally convinced Nicodemus that Yeshua was indeed Messiah. The wicked and corrupt spiritual leadership of Caiaphas along with the convincing testimony of Joseph of Arimathea had convinced him on a moral level. But for Nicodemus, it went much deeper. If Yeshua can raise someone from the dead, then he is the source of life, he reasoned. No devil or charlatan can restore life, only the one who gave life. Origin was important to Nicodemus, but it was not everything. The way that Yeshua dealt with the Pharisees' attempt to trap him in the temple courts showed him a loving and caring Rabbi in Yeshua. He protected and restored the dignity of the woman caught in sin. And he had used the most amazing technique to do so! Remez was not just a debate technique to Yeshua, a way to best someone in an argument over a spiritual point. It brought meaning and purpose to the woman. This is what touched Nicodemus so deeply. He felt like a child again in his faith as he watched the woman dance and shout in the temple courts. It was Yeshua who had freed her from guilt and shame and given her peace and joy. And Nicodemus remembered the same joy he felt in his father's vineyard as a boy, singing Psalms and reciting Scripture. He had found joy and meaning again after getting lost in the Law.

But more than anything else, what touched Nicodemus and changed his heart was watching Yeshua defend the spiritual value of others. He had seen Yeshua demonstrate the value of the individual. So often the Pharisees had placed obedience over the value of the individual. Nicodemus had come to believe that the Law was made for man; man was not made for the Law. This was a restoration of the Law to its proper place in society, according to Nicodemus. Watching Yeshua defend the helpless woman who was being manipulated by the teachers of the Law showed Nicodemus a Messiah who truly cared about all people.

Joseph and Nicodemus followed Yeshua everywhere for the next year and a half. They brought their wives and children as well.

While in Galilee, Yeshua had taken Nicodemus' youngest son Benjamin and placed him in the midst of his Talmidim. ***"Unless you change and become like little children, you will never enter the kingdom of heaven. Therefore, whoever humbles himself like this child is the greatest in the kingdom of heaven,"*** (Matt. 18:2-4) he had told them. Nicodemus would tell Ben later, *"That was the greatest experience of my life, watching Yeshua use you as a lesson for his Talmidim!"*

Even though Yeshua never invited Nicodemus to become a talmid again, he considered himself a follower. Each day his faith grew deeper and richer as he listened to parable after parable. Some of them were familiar and had been used by many Rabbis before him. Yeshua however, adapted them, deepened, and elevated the spiritual content. Nicodemus favorites were the three "lost" parables. He loved the intellectual wisdom, the natural crescendo of value in each, the rhythm and easily applicable circumstance, and the correction of Pharisaical pretense. But Nicodemus particularly loved the life giving, restorative power of God illustrated in each, especially the lost son parable! Nicodemus saw himself in the rebellious eldest son. He had never taken his father's inheritance or plunged into the depths of depravity as the younger son had. But his heart had wandered away from the perfect father, just like the oldest son. He had deceived himself into believing he deserved God's love because of his loyalty to the Law. He had become a champion for justice. He pursued righteousness and obedience. Yet he was not at peace. In Yeshua's teaching, he learned to long for mercy, and it was there that he found forgiveness and peace.

Nicodemus and Joseph had debated long into the night after those parables. How beautifully Yeshua had crafted a story that included both the sinner and the quasi "saint" as lost. Yet the Father was gracious and compassionate with both. It was beautiful!

155

Nicodemus made regular journeys to Galilee and became well known in the synagogue in Capernaum. He would return to manage his vineyard for a few weeks but would quickly feel a longing to sit at Yeshua's feet again. He would often contribute to the support of Yeshua and the Talmidim, as did Joseph as well. His sons didn't spend much time in Beth Sepher that year, but Nicodemus knew they were benefitting much more from their time listening to Yeshua teach. Crowds in Galilee flocked to hear him. Entire families came. Children particularly loved his stories and the warmth of his presence.

A few months before Pesach, Nicodemus had returned to Jerusalem with his family and Joseph's family. They stopped in Bethany to visit Mary, Martha and Lazarus as they often did. But on this occasion Lazarus was sick with an unknown illness. No treatment had been working, and he had been confined to his bed for several weeks. It was Sabbath and Lazarus' condition worsened throughout the day. Joseph arranged for one of the workers in the Hospice to search for Yeshua, who had withdrawn into Perea because of an attempt on his life the previous winter during the Feast of Dedication. Yeshua had left word with Mary and Martha as he traveled through Bethany, where he would be for the next few weeks, so it was not difficult for the servant to find Yeshua and give him the news about Lazarus. It was a full day's journey into Perea from Bethany. Nicodemus had given the servant his own donkey so that he could reach Yeshua faster. He left the next morning. At best Yeshua could be expected to arrive Monday evening, Tuesday at the latest. But Sunday evening Lazarus weakened considerably and died late that night.

His sisters were beside themselves with sadness and regretted not sending for Yeshua sooner. Early the next morning, word was sent to Jerusalem of Lazarus' death. Mary and Martha were well known among the followers of Yeshua. He had been a frequent guest and had taught in their home many times. He had healed many in the hospice, even lepers. It did not take long for friends to arrive to comfort the sisters. Lazarus was laid out in the home and would be buried later in the day on Monday, as was tradition. Normally, the body would have been buried the same day, but Lazarus had died late in the evening and everyone was exhausted. But first there would be a time of prayer in the home. Mary had asked Joseph if he would address the gathering, which he did. This traditional address was extremely important, and Joseph was honored to be asked. He spoke on the words of Psalm 34. Aware that the faith of Mary and Martha was being tested by temptations of doubt, he spoke on the words, *"The righteous cry out and the Lord hears them; he delivers them from all their troubles. The Lord is close to the brokenhearted and saves those who are crushed in spirit."* Ps. 34:18, 19 His message was encouraging and direct. He reminded all present that life is inconsistent because of sin, but the Lord remains holy and trustworthy. *"The Lord is with us,"* he repeated throughout his message, *"take refuge in him."*

As the body of Lazarus was carried to the tomb in the very garden Lazarus had planted, several mourners began to wail. Mary, who was leading the procession arm in arm with her sister Martha, raised her hand and asked for silence. *"Yeshua taught us not to mourn as those who have no hope,"* she stated. *"We will meet Lazarus again on the last day. May this day be a day of faith and hope. Be not faithless but believe!"* Her words were powerful and effective. It was unusual for women to be in a funeral procession. Normally the men in the family would bury the body and the women would come in a separate procession to anoint the body. But since Lazarus was the last remaining male in the family, Mary and Martha led the procession. Nicodemus and Joseph began to sing The Psalm of David, as it was called. Psalm 23 was normally sung in the Temple by the Levitical boys' choir for a Festival of Praise, and the words and melody touched all in the procession as they joined in the chorus: "The Lord is my Shepherd!"

They laid Lazarus in the family burial cave, carved out by Lazarus' own hands. It was six feet wide and nine feet deep with three niches — called Kukhin — on each side. His body had been prepared with various spices, myrtle, and aloes. He had been wrapped in strips of linen with a burial cloth 12 feet long and 3 feet wide covering and supporting him. Six men, three on each side carried him, gripping the cloth that held him. The six men bent at the waist to enter the cave and placed Lazarus' body in a kukhin on the left side. After one year, these same men would enter the cave again and place Lazarus's bones in an ossuary box. His bones would be tied with cloths after being anointed with oil and wine — symbols of joy and gladness — then placed in his own ossuary.

After the men left the tomb, Mary and Martha entered. Mary had carried the cloth in which their Isaiah scroll was kept. As a wealthy family, they had copies of the Torah, Psalms and Isaiah. Lazarus loved the book of Isaiah and had memorized most of it. It was traditional for this cloth to be placed on the body of the deceased. Mary laid it across Lazarus chest. She quoted his favorite words as she did so, *"You have been a refuge for the poor, a refuge for the needy in his distress, a shelter from the storm and a shade from the heat."* Is. 25:4 As she stepped back from the niche, she began to weep and rested against her sister Martha. Regaining her composure, she turned again to Lazarus and said, *"Rest in the Lord, brother. We shall meet again."*

When Mary and Martha exited the tomb, all those who had come to comfort the sisters proceeded to enter the tomb, passed by the body of Lazarus and said, *"Depart in Peace."* After the procession, the six men rolled the large stone across the front of the cave and sealed it. A potted rose was brought forward and placed in front of the stone, marking it as a new grave.

The next three days were filled with visitors from Jerusalem coming to express their sorrow at the death of Lazarus. It was one of the most binding rabbinic traditions for friends of the family to mourn with the family. Typically, the mourning would last for 30 days with the first three the most intense. Mary and Martha however insisted that there was to be no wailing. Joseph and Nicodemus had to intervene several times with groups of women who had come for that specific purpose. Early on the fourth day, the messenger Joseph had sent to Yeshua returned. He told Joseph that he had found Yeshua and given him the message. Yeshua's response, according to the servant, was, *"This sickness will not end in death. No, it is for God's glory so that God's Son may be glorified through it."* (Jn. 11:4) Joseph chose not to relay this information to Mary and Martha. The servant did say that Yeshua was on the way and could be expected later the same day. He had rushed ahead once Yeshua had decided to come.

Nicodemus and Joseph were outside enjoying the cool of the evening air and the breezes that were common on the hills of Bethany. When the hospice servant told Nicodemus that Yeshua was on the way, he sent several lookouts to watch the road and notify them when he was near. Martha had just come outside to thank Joseph again for his wonderful words on Monday. As she spoke, a man came running and announced to them that Yeshua was spotted coming up the Jericho road and would be there shortly. Martha immediately began running down the road toward the junction with the Jericho Road. Nicodemus and Joseph followed with several others who happened to be outside at the time. Before they reached the junction, Nicodemus could see Martha on her knees before Yeshua. By the time the men reached her, Yeshua had raised her to her feet. She kept repeating, *"I'm so sorry."* She added, *"We should have notified you sooner, but Caiaphas' spies have been watching our house for any sign of you."* To his surprise, Nicodemus heard Yeshua say to Martha, *"Your brother will rise again."* (John 11:23) Martha responded immediately, *"I know he will rise again in the resurrection at the last day."* (John 11:24) Yeshua's next words would be the topic of discussion late into the night by all who witnessed the events of the day, *"I am the resurrection and the life. He who believes in me will live, even though he dies; and whoever lives and believes in me will never die. Do you believe this?"* (John 11:25, 26)

There was something familiar in those words to Nicodemus. It had been almost three years earlier when he had approached Yeshua at night. He had rehashed the evening in his mind many times, and now for the first time, he understood. Yeshua had said to Nicodemus that evening, *"For God so loved the world that he gave his one and only Son that whoever believes in him shall not perish but have eternal life."* (John 3:16) Yeshua had been telling Nicodemus long ago that HE was the source of life. In Him was hope beyond the grave. It warmed Nicodemus' heart to hear Martha respond to these words of hope, *"Yes, Lord"*, she told him, *"I believe that you are the Christ, the Son of God, who was to come into the world."* (John 11:27) Yeshua smiled at her, motioned to her home, and began to walk. *"Don't be afraid,"* he said to Martha, *"just believe."*

Yeshua placed a hand on her shoulder and said, *"Go and tell Mary I am here."* She turned immediately and ran down the road to get her sister. Nicodemus and Joseph turned and greeted John, the talmid. John explained to them that by the time they received word of Lazarus' illness, he had already died and that Yeshua knew of his death already in Perea. Within a few moments, Mary came running down the road with Martha trailing behind, obviously winded. The group had barely moved from where Martha had found Yeshua. Mary arrived and fell exhausted at the feet of Yeshua. How many times she had been in this very position! It had been her custom to always sit in the front when Yeshua visited. She hung on his every word. But now, with tears streaming down her cheeks, between gasping for air, she blurted out, *"Lord, if you had been here, my brother would not have died."* (John 11:32) She quickly added, *"I know you would have healed him. I do believe, Lord. I do."* What Nicodemus witnessed next touched him and brought a tear to his own eye. With Mary weeping on her knees, muttering, *"Please Lord. He's my only brother. Please, Lord,"* Yeshua went to one knee next to Mary as Martha came up behind Mary and knelt alongside her. Yeshua beat his breast, looked up to the heavens and said, *"Father? Father?"* as if asking God in heaven to help.

After some time, they rose and began to walk through the streets of Bethany to their home. As they came near the road to the house, Yeshua asked, *"Where have you laid him?"* (John 11:34) Assuming he meant to go to the tomb to mourn, Martha replied, *"Come and see, Lord!"* (John 11:35)

Seeing the tomb in the garden and the many flowers which had been planted by Lazarus' own hand, Yeshua stopped short of the tomb, sat down on a stone and looked down. He was visibly moved. He looked up, and then looked at the tomb with tears streaming down his face. The Talmidim just watched motionless. They had never seen their master so troubled in spirit. The other mourners who had been in the house now came out and walked behind Yeshua and the company with him. Nicodemus could hear people talking under their breath as Yeshua sat on the stone. He didn't like what he was hearing. *"Why didn't he come sooner?"* *"He has healed so many others, why not his friend?"*

Time seemed to stand still. Nicodemus was not even sure how long they stood in the garden mourning the death of Lazarus with the one they all called Messiah and Lord. After a while, Yeshua looked up to heaven and then to the six men who had buried Lazarus, *"Take away the stone!"* (John 11:39) he shouted. *"Remove it now!"* Assuming he wanted to actually see Lazarus, Martha, who was standing next to Yeshua, turned to him and said, *"But Lord, we buried him on Monday. We have sealed the stone, and by this time there is a bad odor, for he has been there four days."* (John 11:39) Yeshua looked at her and clearly no longer weeping, told her,

"Didn't I tell you on the way that if you believed, you would see the glory of God?" (John 11:40) Confused, Martha motioned for the men to do as he said. It took some time for the men to unseal the tomb and roll away the massive stone from the depression carved into the rock. As soon as they had finished, they stepped back exhausted. The smell of decaying flesh wafted from the tomb and overcame several who were near. Everyone retreated behind Yeshua.

The air cleared as Yeshua stepped forward into the sun and looked up to pray, *"Father, I thank you that you have heard me. I knew that you always hear me, but I said this for the benefit of the people standing here, that they may believe that you sent me."* (John 11:41, 42)

Several Pharisees and Sadducees from Jerusalem looked at each other in dismay and shook their heads disapprovingly at these words. But his next words left their mouths agape! Yeshua stepped to the entrance of the tomb, placed his hand on the stone that had encased him and shouted for all to hear: ***"Lazarus, come out!"*** (John 11:43) Rustling could be heard inside the tomb. In a matter of a moment or two, they saw Lazarus move slowly toward the entrance of the tomb. The shroud that had previously covered his whole body was now draped over his shoulder. He was still wrapped in the grave clothes. ('bands' – *"Takhrikhin")* Mary screamed! Martha fell to her knees, as did all the Talmidim and the men who had laid Lazarus in the khukin. Someone shouted, *"Hallelujah!"* Others looked at each other in dismay.

Yeshua motioned to the men, *"Release him from those grave clothes!"* he ordered. The men stepped forward, entered the cave and began to un-wrap Lazarus. One man took off his outer garment and wrapped it around Lazarus as they removed the bands below his waist. Lazarus stepped out of the tomb holding the cloth that had covered his face. His face was beaming. *"He's alive,"* someone shouted from the back, *"how is it possible?"* Mary and Martha rushed forward to embrace their brother. The three stepped forward in front of Yeshua, weeping, laughing and rejoicing. *"My Lord, you are the resurrection and the life!"* Martha repeated Yeshua's words. *"The resurrection and the life,"* she repeated almost laughing. At that all three fell before him and worshiped him.

"Will not perish but have eternal life…will live even though he dies," (John 3:16, 11:25) Nicodemus repeated, combining the words

Yeshua spoke three years earlier to him and His words to Martha along the road. ***"Will not perish but have eternal life…will live even though he dies,"*** (John 3:16, 11:25)

Chapter 20:
Kill

The reunited family spent the remainder of the day at home with a few close friends. After the initial shock of Lazarus walking out of the tomb had worn off a little, many of the Jews who had come from Jerusalem professed their faith in Yeshua. Yet there were a few Pharisees whom Nicodemus had recognized when they arrived earlier in the day, who, despite their shock at the events they witnessed, did not give honor and praise to Yeshua. Instead, they were seen slipping off during the worship and celebration that followed. They talked privately and were the first to leave Bethany.

Mary, Martha and Lazarus had spent many an evening at the feet of Yeshua in this home, but this evening was the sweetest. Sorrow had turned to joy in an instant. And this joy had come by the powerful hand of Yeshua. The humble and faithful friend of Yeshua, the younger brother of Mary and Martha, was his old self: laughing and filled with energy. He was strong and talkative as he ate the food brought by friends. Never before had a man eaten his own funeral food; and Lazarus loved the irony of it.

The resurrection of Lazarus had taken place in the early evening. Nicodemus and Joseph along with their families stayed for the evening but intended to leave the next morning. They spent the evening with Yeshua and his Talmidim, along with Mary, Martha and Lazarus. Mary had surrendered her treasured position at the feet of Yeshua to her brother, who willingly accepted. Food was plentiful, wine flowed, and the evening was filled with singing, prayers of thanksgiving and teaching by Yeshua.

The next morning as Nicodemus and Joseph took their leave, Nicodemus mentioned to John the Talmid that Yeshua and his Talmidim were welcome to use the olive press or Gethsemane (*Gat Shmanim*) on the Mt. of Olives during the upcoming Passover week. *"It may be safer for you and Yeshua given the ongoing rumors of a plot to arrest and kill Yeshua."*

"Yes," John answered, *"we usually stay here in Bethany, but this may be the first place they look for Yeshua."*

"I know the owner very well," Nicodemus responded, *"I'll speak with him as I return to Jerusalem. He usually rents the room at a high price. It is a large underground room and can easily hold several families. I'll pay him in advance so that he holds it open for you to come and go as you feel the need."*

"God bless you my friend," John said.

"May it be a refuge for you and the Talmidim," Nicodemus concluded. *"One more thing, I don't know what it may mean for you, but I saw several Pharisees acting suspiciously yesterday evening before they left."*

"Yes, I saw them too," John answered. *"They have often challenged Yeshua. You may remember at the Feast of Tabernacles when Yeshua was challenged by some Pharisees in the Temple courts?"*

"Yes, that is where I remember seeing one of them before," Nicodemus recalled. *"Certainly, they will report the events of yesterday to Caiaphas. I'll see what I can find out when I pass by the Temple today."*

"Even more reason for us to be careful at Passover. Thank you again." John concluded. They embraced, and Nicodemus and Joseph walked into the house to say their good-byes to Yeshua and the family.

The families of Nicodemus and Joseph decided to stay in the home of Nicodemus in Jerusalem, since it was Friday. They planned to return home to Ein Karem on Sunday morning. Nicodemus and Joseph had been discussing not only the amazing miracle Yeshua had performed in Bethany but how it would be received by the people and the Sanhedrin. It did not take long for the news of Lazarus to spread like wildfire throughout the city. Most of the people received the word with joy and acceptance. But there were those who believed Yeshua had done all these things, even raising Lazarus from the dead, by the power of Satan himself. Debates raged in the temple all day with radical zealots promoting another Maccabean revolt at Passover.

Nicodemus and Joseph entered the temple courts about midday after settling the family at home. There they met Gamaliel, who shared that an emergency meeting of the Sanhedrin had been called for that very afternoon after the evening sacrifice. The men planned to attend so as to update Yeshua and the Talmidim. The meeting was held at the ninth hour (3:00 PM) and as the men entered and took their place, there was loud discussion and frustration expressed. *"What are we accomplishing,"* (John 11:47) some asked rhetorically. *"He performs miracle after miracle and we do nothing!"* another was heard to say.

"The people are all flocking to him, but they don't understand anything!"

"Rome won't stand for this; they will fear a revolt and violence will result!"

These were some of the more reasonable comments Nicodemus heard. The Sadducees were downright angry and spewed vile comments. The resurrection of Lazarus could not be denied. *"How dull and illogical the unbelieving mind is!"* Nicodemus whispered to Joseph.

"True," Joseph responded, *"but don't mistake the motivation. The small amount of power Rome has accorded this body has completely consumed them. Yeshua could walk in here, repeat the same miracles Moses did before Pharaoh, and they would still not believe."*

Just then High Priest and Nasi Joseph Caiaphas stood, pounded his staff on the floor repeatedly and called for silence. His mood was extremely disturbed as he shouted, *"QUIET!"* He had been listening to the various comments of the members near him. *"You know nothing at all!"* (John 11:49) he began. Gamaliel whispered to Nicodemus next to him, *"Typical Sadducee rudeness!"*

Caiaphas continued, *"You do not realize that it is better for you that one man dies for the people than that the whole nation perish."* (Jn. 11:50)

There was silence in the hall, deathly silence. The High Priest was advocating not just the arrest of Yeshua but the death penalty! It was shocking to all in the hall. What had been spoken only in secret among the most radical in Caiaphas' inner circle, he stated openly. Nicodemus and Joseph sat frozen, not only shocked by the audacity of Caiaphas actually stating an opinion that violated every principle of the Sanhedrin, but also illegal by Roman law.

Several Pharisees on the left side of the hall stood and left, shouting toward Caiaphas, *"I will not be part of this!"* Many others followed, which surprised Nicodemus and Joseph. Some of them had been in Bethany the previous day and witnessed Lazarus' resurrection. Gamaliel took note of them and planned to speak with them later.

"I can no longer remain a member of this body," Nicodemus told Joseph, *"let's go."* Joseph and Nicodemus rose to leave. Gamaliel remained seated.

As they walked out, they heard the cat calls: *"Traitor!"* *"Samaritan lover!"* *"Yeshua has a demon!"*

Nicodemus and Joseph decided to return to Bethany in person to warn Yeshua and his Talmidim. They did not want to risk sharing the information they had learned with anyone. Nicodemus spoke with John and shared the threat from Caiaphas. John promised to inform Yeshua who had gone to the Hospice to visit the sick. Nicodemus also offered his large home in Jerusalem for Yeshua's use with his Talmidim should he need it for the Passover meal.

Joseph and Nicodemus retuned to Jerusalem and talked about their plans to resign from the Sanhedrin. They had not attended a regular meeting for months and were no longer comfortable with the hypocrisy, corruption and violence that was now openly supported and encouraged. They would each return to their homes and craft individual letters. They planned to submit them just before Passover.

"This may be the Passover that Yeshua deals with the corrupt Sanhedrin once and for all," Nicodemus shared with Joseph that evening during the Sabbath meal.

"You may be right," Joseph responded, *"but Yeshua is not a soldier! He would not condone violence. I still do not understand how He will declare himself Messiah and King."*

"What do you mean?" Nicodemus asked.

"You have heard him," Joseph answered. *"Remember his words when we were in Caesarea Philippi? Peter made that amazing confession of Yeshua as the Christ. After that he spoke of going to Jerusalem to suffer and die. Remember? I overheard him say something I have not forgotten,* **'For the Son of Man is going to come in his Father's glory.'"** Matthew 16:27

"How do you reconcile those two things, Joseph? He will die and yet come in glory?" Nicodemus asked.

"I don't know," Joseph responded. *"When he speaks of these things, he always does so alone with his Talmidim. Has John said anything to you?"*

"Not a word," Nicodemus said, *"but I've had no reason to ask him."*

"This much I do know," Joseph paused. *"Yeshua is the source of life. We have watched him raise Lazarus and Jairus' daughter. Nothing is beyond him! He can turn death to life!"*

With that the men retired for the evening. On Sabbath they rested and visited the temple for any additional word from the Sanhedrin. They discovered that a specific plot was discussed in the Sanhedrin after they left. Caiaphas and the sons of Annas planned the arrest and execution of Yeshua and his disciples. Caiaphas' outburst was now an action plan.

On Sunday morning, word was sent from Mary and Martha that Yeshua and the Talmidim had again retreated into Perea. They left word that they would return for Passover, but not until the Feast Days had started. Nicodemus and Joseph thought this wise as the will of the people was clearly on Yeshua's side. They would not allow Yeshua to be taken by the Sanhedrin. As long as he stayed among the crowds, Caiaphas was powerless to stop him.

As Nicodemus walked back to Ein Karem with his family, he contemplated how Passover would unfold and specifically how Yeshua would reveal himself as Messiah and take his rightful throne as King of the Jews. How would he remove the Roman rule? Would the Roman soldiers be slain by the angel of death like the Assyrian army during Hezekiah's time? Would a pit open up and swallow the faithless Council and corrupt priests as in Moses' day at Mt. Sinai? What would redemption look like? And what did Yeshua mean by dying in Jerusalem? Was it just a metaphor like so many of his parables? Nicodemus knew he could not be numbered with or connected in any way with the Sanhedrin anymore. His first task would be to craft his letter of resignation. But he would do so and present it as Passover began to protect himself and his family from any potential retaliation of the Council thugs. And he would be there when Yeshua returned for Passover. If he stood by Yeshua as he entered Jerusalem on that day, there could be no safer place.

For the next few months, Nicodemus talked with his father Benjamin and his wife Rachel concerning all that had happened. He kept busy trimming the vines for the spring growth and marketing the bumper crop of olives and wine in his storehouse. There were still many olives to be squeezed into oil from the second and third picking. His Gethsemane (Gat Shmanim) was filled with large jars of virgin olive oil already. Nicodemus loved the work. It reminded him of the many days he spent in the vineyard with John after his parents were killed. His joy had returned since he became a follower of Yeshua. The Law was not just a mental exercise of routines. It became a delight instead of a burden to be born.

Nicodemus' three boys returned to Beth Sepher in Ein Karem. Rabban Terah was still teaching in the synagogue in Ein Karem. He had taught his boys some of the same songs of Scripture that Nicodemus had learned at his feet. After school the boys loved to join their father in the vineyard trimming vines. They had spent many hours there talking about Yeshua's parables. Their favorite was the Good Samaritan, perhaps because their grandfather Benjamin had related the story of how he had been rescued by a Samaritan when their father was just 22. Nicodemus loved to remind his sons of the context of the parable.

"I was once a legalist like that man who approached Yeshua and wanted to justify himself," Nicodemus would tell his sons often, *"but there is no salvation in the law. That is why Yeshua told a parable that illustrates just how impossible it is to be perfectly obedient. It is faith that justifies."*

Benjamin the eldest responded, *"That is why Yeshua has come, isn't it father? To teach us about salvation. To show us how to love our neighbor, even Samaritans, because God loves everyone."*

Samuel, the second born interrupted, *"Did grandfather ever find that Samaritan who helped him, father?"*

"Yes, he did son," Nicodemus answered, *"One day in the marketplace in Jerusalem, he found a Samaritan trying to sell his healing ointments. He wasn't very successful at it. Few would trade with him since he was Samaritan. The man at first did not want to admit what he had done for your grandfather. I think the man was a little afraid since your grandfather is a priest in the Temple."*

"Did he repay the man?" Samuel asked.

"The man would not take money," Nicodemus answered, *"but father arranged for other traders he knew to buy from the man without him ever knowing."*

"When we love our neighbor as ourselves," Samuel responded, *"God blesses us, doesn't he father?"*

"That's right son," Nicodemus beamed at his son's response, *"the law is intended to create community, not divide us as the Pharisees have done."*

Chapter 21:
Hosanna

It was the coldest winter in Ein Karem that Nicodemus could remember. His father had battled a bad cough for most of it but was improving as the weather began to warm. He didn't think he would be able to manage the trip to Jerusalem for Pesach. Many were predicting a tumultuous Passover festival. The followers of Yeshua in Judea—and there were many—expected him to at least take the position of High Priest. Others spoke of revolt and the removal of Roman rule. The radical elements (zealots) hoped to hijack the arrival of Yeshua and throw Pilate out of the holy city entirely, through a revolution like the one Judah Maccabee orchestrated 170 years earlier. Others like Nicodemus and Joseph hoped for a spiritual revolution and looked to the heavens for deliverance from Rome and the Sanhedrin. Several times Joseph had come to visit Nicodemus and his family in the winter. They would sit by the fire in the courtyard of his home with a bottle of wine and a loaf of tasty olive bread. They talked long into the evening about prophecy and the Messiah. As a wealthy landowner, Nicodemus owned a copy of every Hebrew Scripture. One of the Scriptures which especially dominated their discussions was Isaiah 11.

"Isaiah certainly paints an accurate picture of Yeshua," Nicodemus would point out, ***"A Spirit of wisdom, counsel and power,"*** vs. 2 ***"With justice he will give decisions for the poor of the earth."***

"The woman at the well in Sychar is a perfect example of that Scripture, as well as the woman the Pharisees dragged before him in the temple courts. Righteousness and justice is who he is!"

"Later the prophet says: ***'They will neither harm nor destroy on all my holy mountain,'"*** vs. 9 Nicodemus continued, *"I cannot accept that Yeshua will become King of Israel through a violent revolution according to those words. Somehow, he will bring peace without the sword. But how?"*

171

"Micah says the same," Joseph added, *"He speaks of peace without violence"*: ***"He will judge between many peoples and will settle disputes for strong nations far and wide. They will beat their swords into plowshares and their spears into pruning hooks. Nation will not take up sword against nation, nor will they train for war anymore."*** (Micah 4:3 & Isaiah2:4) *"Those words are very specific, and I believe they are literal."*

"Yes, that is not a parable or a metaphor. It means there will be peace, not violence, when Messiah comes," Nicodemus added. *"And if I may say, that is the personality of Yeshua. He is a Rabbi through and through. He is a master teacher, not a soldier. The one zealot among the Talmidim—Simon--seems to have given up his inclination for revolution."*

"You want to know what I think?" Joseph asked. *"I believe we will be shocked to see how he does it. This is not merely a man with a human answer to the problem of sin. This is God's answer. Deliverance will come in a most astounding way. I am sure of it. And when we see it, we must not lose faith."*

"What do you mean, Joseph?" Nicodemus asked.

"Let me answer that with a question. What do you believe is our greatest problem in Israel?" Joseph asked.

"Wow, there are so many: Corruption, Roman rule, poverty in the rural areas, sickness, a lack of spiritual leadership, to name a few." Nicodemus answered.

"If you were able to solve all of those problems in the wink of an eye, would it be paradise?" Joseph asked again.

"Let me think a moment. Well, it would be a start anyway, but I think I see where you are going." Nicodemus continued. *"The real problem is corruption in the human heart. That leads to all the selfishness and sin we see all around us."*

"And what changes hearts?" Joseph continued.

"Hmm,...?" Nicodemus paused.

"Forgiveness, mercy, peace with God!!" Joseph answered his own question. *"I believe that is the great human need that Yeshua*

has come to address. We have seen him do it in part through miracles and teaching. He welcomes rich and poor, Jew and Samaritan, educated and ignorant. He is tearing down dividing walls of hostility. In Galilee, Samaria and Judea, this is what attracts the people. His words are a cool stream in the desert."

"So somehow," Nicodemus responded, *"Yeshua will bring mercy and forgiveness on a grand scale, come Passover?"*

"I humbly pray it is so!" Joseph finished.

"Amen!" Nicodemus added.

By the time the month of Adar rolled around, Benjamin, the father of Nicodemus, was doing much better and had decided that he was going to Jerusalem. *"It may be my last,"* Benjamin told his son, *"but I will not miss Yeshua's arrival. After all, as Messiah he will make all things new and I hope that includes this old body!"*

Nicodemus and his family decided to depart Ein Karem on the 25th. This year the crowds would be especially large. There was a lot of anticipation in advance of Pesach. Nicodemus wanted to gauge the level of hostility in the Sanhedrin in advance of the delivery of his resignation letter. They had decided to do it on lamb selection day, the 10th of Nisan when there would be a lot of distraction in the Temple courts. It may not even be dealt with until well after Passover and that was Joseph and Nicodemus' intention. The Sanhedrin was certain to be distracted by Yeshua and the politics from Roman authorities.

The morning of the 25th was bright, and warmer than usual. The vines were growing well on the hillside. The cold snap from winter had done little damage. Most of Nicodemus' vineyards were on the southern slopes which were always in the sun, even in winter, and seldom were damaged even in the coldest of winters. They almost seemed to do better when spring came after a cold winter. As the family stepped into the cool air of the morning, Nicodemus said a silent prayer that he and his family would fare as well as his vines after Pesach. Despite his growing faith in Yeshua, there seemed to be so many unknowns. *"Lord, I believe,"* he spoke out loud, *"help my unbelief!"*

The journey into Jerusalem was filled with nostalgic moments for Nicodemus. He pointed them out along the way as he always did. His father walked slowly in the same way that the old priest Zechariah did when Nicodemus was just a boy. *"Right here is where Zechariah described how the angel appeared to him in the Temple. Father, remember how you asked Zechariah about the angel? You knew that I wanted to know what it was like to meet an angel, but I was afraid to ask him."*

"I sure do, son," Benjamin answered, *"That was a glorious day!"*

Nicodemus stopped and started to retell the story that his boys had heard countless times. They all sat on the ground as Benjamin found a large stone to rest on. He knew that his son had stopped not just to talk to his sons but to give him a chance to rest.

"A joy and a delight," (Luke 1:14) Nicodemus continued, *"that is how Zechariah described Gabriel's words about John! I did not understand just what that meant until I met Yeshua. The delight of John was Yeshua, pointing to him as… the… Lamb… of God."* A shiver went through Nicodemus. *"The lamb,"* he thought. *"My first daily sacrifice . . . Passover lamb . . . Lamb of God . . . The Lamb has come."* Nicodemus tried to force the image from his mind. *"Simeon had said it, 'The Lamb has come'."*

"What's wrong, father?" his son asked. *"You look like you've seen an angel."*

All the boys chuckled at their brother's joke. But Nicodemus was not laughing. They walked in silence to the next hill where Benjamin sat again at his wife, Rachel's, insistence. *"Take it easy, Ben,"* she said as they sat, *"you've been ill most of the winter. Let's not take any chances or we may have to ask Yeshua to come and heal you!"*

"That would be my pleasure," Benjamin chuckled between breaths.

The family took the same route through the city that Nicodemus had taken so many times before. They had even avoided the gate next to Herod's Palace, now occupied by Roman Procurator Pontius Pilate. They had always done so in honor of Zechariah, who loathed "Herod the Great." Roman soldiers were everywhere, already having been summoned from Caesarea for Passover. Along the way, Rachel, Nicodemus wife, bought food supplies as they passed through the market. Benjamin stopped at the stall of a man selling ointments. It was the Samaritan who had helped him so many years ago on the Jericho Road. Even though Benjamin did not need any ointment, he bought a huge supply as gifts for friends. He always did so when he was in the city. Thanks to Benjamin, the man had a thriving business. The two laughed and embraced. Nicodemus' boys watched with fascination. They were very proud of their grandfather. He had lived their favorite parable of Yeshua, and they smiled and embraced their grandfather as he returned to them.

"Love can change anyone," Benjamin reminded the boys as they approached their home next to the Southern Steps, *"even me!"*

A few years ago, Nicodemus had bought this house that the family had rented for so many years when Benjamin was a priest. Now it served as a home away from home, and Rachel had furnished it nicely. It had been sparse and bare, serving almost as a dormitory for the priests at the temple. Now it had furnishings from Egypt and Arabia, bought in the market. Nicodemus' thriving business had allowed his wife to make the house comfortable for their three boys while they were in the city for the festivals.

The days passed with the boys and Nicodemus spending time in the temple courts, meeting old friends, and attending morning and evening sacrifice. His sons were not nearly as sensitive about the lambs slaughtered each day as Nicodemus had been. In fact, back in Ein Karem, the boys watched with fascination as their mother slaughtered goats and sheep, even a bull. Their father could not stand the sight of blood.

Nicodemus visited with Joseph of Arimathea often. Joseph's house was closer to the Shechem gate where they had entered the city. Just outside that city gate, in a garden, was where Simeon was buried. Joseph's own family tomb was next to Simeon's. The two talked about the rumors surrounding the Sanhedrin and planned how they would present their letters of resignation to the secretary of the Council. They talked to their friends on the Council, but no one was saying anything. There seemed to be a grip of fear and apprehension among the Ruling Council and even among the priests in the temple who were arriving in greater numbers each day. If there was a plot to arrest Yeshua, no one was talking about it. But Joseph and Nicodemus were not surprised by this. Caiaphas could be as cunning and secretive as a snake. Some even called him "Nahas" (snake), but only privately.

In the early evening on the 8th of Nisan, Lazarus arrived at Nicodemus' home with several staff from the hospice. He had come to tell Nicodemus personally that Yeshua had arrived in Jericho and would be coming to Bethany the next morning.

"Yeshua is staying with Zacchaeus," Lazarus told Nicodemus, *"and he plans to walk the Jericho Road on Sabbath."*

"Really?" Nicodemus answered, *"On Sabbath!? What a statement!"*

"Yes, He is Lord of the Sabbath!" Lazarus answered immediately.

"So, the plan then is for Him to enter Jerusalem the next day as we are selecting our lambs for Passover?" Nicodemus asked.

"Fitting, isn't it?" Lazarus continued. He comes as King, Shepherd of the Lord's flock, AND as the Lamb just like the one the Lord provided for Abraham on this very mountain."

Joseph, who was listening to the conversation, asked, *"Lazarus, that lamb was slaughtered! Are you telling us something about Yeshua's intention in Jerusalem? King and Sacrificial Lamb? How is that possible?"*

"I was in the grave for four days and walked out," Lazarus answered confidently. *"How possible was that?"*

The men were left speechless. Lazarus had been known to speak directly and in strange metaphors since he walked out of the tomb. He spoke of Israel as an olive tree with many branches grafted in. He described Jerusalem as raised to the sky and a river of living water flowing out in all directions. Most people dismissed his images as unintelligible descriptions of the world.

On "Lamb Selection Day," the first day of Passover, Nicodemus and Joseph left the city mid-morning and headed for Bethany. They expected to meet Yeshua and his Talmidim and then return to the temple for the day. They left their families at Nicodemus' home not knowing what the Pharisees' plans were. To their surprise, a crowd of more than 100 joined them on the road. Most of them had been witnesses of the resurrection of Lazarus and had spread the word of Yeshua's arrival. As they climbed the Mt. of Olives from the Kidron Valley, the people began to cut down palm and olive branches along the road. Thousands of people had been staying in tents along the road and many of them joined the group ascending the hill toward Bethany. Just short of Bethany, they came to Bethphage, a very small village along the road. It was there that they met Yeshua and his Talmidim along with another large crowd accompanying him from Bethany. They had secured a small donkey colt, placing their outer garments on the colt. Yeshua sat on it and the group proceeded down the slope toward Jerusalem. It was an image of a conquering King, familiar in the ancient world. Nicodemus had only experienced this a few times when the Roman Procurators would enter Jerusalem. He vaguely remembered the time when the 12 king makers from Parthia entered Jerusalem. But that was 33 years ago already. He had watched with fascination as the most powerful men in the world rode camels accompanied by white Arabian steeds. The image of Yeshua on a small donkey certainly was not as visibly impressive, and intentionally so. Yeshua's power was not about intimidation and show. This was a king come to serve his people.

And what a better king He was than the rulers of this world! It was obvious by observing the devotion in the eyes of the people that this was the King of the heart.

The group that had come from Jerusalem now numbered in the hundreds and led the procession down the slope from the Mt. of Olives. Just as the southeastern portion of the City of David came into view, the people began to shout: *"Hosanna!" and "Blessed is the coming kingdom of our father David" Mark 11:9,10* Their voices grew louder as not only Mt. Zion came into view, but began to swell as the Palace of the Maccabees was seen. At this site, the pilgrims began to wave their palm branches and raise their voices as they cried for freedom. Not since Judah Maccabee had such a cry been heard in Israel, and it frightened the Pharisee spies who had joined the group from Jerusalem. Rome would not take kindly to this dramatic cry for freedom and they knew it. But the crowd's voices continued to swell as the Palace of the High Priest, and finally the Palace of Herod, came into view. The cries of *"Hosanna"* continued as people began to lay their outer garments and palm branches along the path in front of Yeshua and the donkey. Gestures of derision were shouted toward Pilate's and Caiaphas' palaces. Some of the Pharisees from the city pushed their way forward and told Yeshua to admonish the people to keep quiet or a riot might start and alert the Romans, who would come and kill with sword and spear. Yeshua dismissed them with *"I tell you if they keep quiet the stones will cry out!"* Luke 19:40

Most of the people leading the procession were pilgrims who had camped outside the city. Nicodemus and those who had come from Jerusalem were completely outnumbered by those who joined the throng along the road. As the road descended, the hill of Olivet obscured the city again. At this the crowd ahead quieted and began to mingle with the crowd behind from Bethany, most of who were witnesses of Lazarus' resurrection. The witnesses pointed to Mary, Martha and Lazarus, who were walking just behind Yeshua on the donkey. *"He was dead and lives by the power of Yeshua's hand!"*

they repeated in loud voices. For a moment, attention was drawn to Lazarus as he was peppered with words of praise between shouts of *"Hallelujah!"* Then the crowd, led by Yeshua, climbed the last steep and rocky incline to a flat piece of bedrock where the entire city of Jerusalem and the temple of the living God instantly burst into view. As Yeshua reached the crest of the small hill, he suddenly broke down in tears, raised his hands toward the city and shouted, *"If you, even you had only known on this day what would bring you peace—but now it is hidden from your eyes. The days...."* (Luke 19:42ff)

His words could not be heard over the shouts of the people as more and more of them reached the top of the hill and spilled in front of Yeshua and down the next hill into the Kidron Valley. More shouts of, *"Hosanna"* and *"Blessed is the king who comes in the name of the Lord"* (Luke 19:38) rang out across the valley.

Nicodemus and Joseph were clearly shocked at this reception of Yeshua. It was undoubtedly a spontaneous outburst from the people. The longing for deliverance and freedom resided deep within the Jewish soul, and the fire seemed to leap from heart to heart, fueled by those who gave testimony to the power, miracles and teaching of Yeshua.

"He healed my son!"

"I was blind and now I see!"

"I was a leper and am now clean!"

"I was a cripple and now look at me dance!"

On and on it went! The procession proceeded slowly, growing in intensity all the way down the road into the Kidron Valley and through the eastern gate toward the Temple.

The entire city was awakened to the procession and people came running from every street. *"Who is he?"* people asked members of the procession. *"Jesus of Nazareth," they answered, "the prophet from Galilee." Matthew 21:10, 11*

But not everyone was rejoicing. Caiaphas and Annas stood in a corner of the temple court as Yeshua entered with the throng of

179

thousands upon thousands. Annas remarked to Caiaphas, **_"Look how the whole world has gone after him!"_** John 12:19

 "Not for long!" replied Caiaphas! *"Not for long!"*

Chapter 22:
Saved

Yeshua did not remain long in the Temple courts. He returned with Mary, Martha and Lazarus, along with his Talmidim, to Bethany. Joseph and Nicodemus returned to their homes and told their families about the day's events along the Bethany Road.

"Intense!" That is how Nicodemus described it. *"Such spontaneous, energetic and intense worship I have never before witnessed. It was befitting a King!"* Joseph was not as enthusiastic, and this surprised Nicodemus.

"What's wrong my friend?" Nicodemus asked him, *"You look almost depressed."*

"We'll talk later Nicodemus," Joseph remarked flatly.

After the boys had gone to bed, Joseph, Nicodemus and their wives retreated to the roof top for a glass of wine and the news that Joseph had yet to reveal.

"Must be pretty serious to interrupt the mood from today," Nicodemus remarked.

"It is," Joseph paused. *"When I was in the temple, one of the temple guards asked to speak with me in private. He had overheard Caiaphas and the Fierce Five discussing Yeshua and the miracle of Lazarus' resurrection. It was heated. They are still planning on the arrest of Yeshua, but not during Passover."*

"That's good news, Joseph. What is the bad news?" Nicodemus asked.

"They are planning to assassinate Lazarus, as a way of intimidating and silencing Yeshua," Joseph stated. *"They want to kidnap Mary and Martha and blackmail Yeshua. They hope to send a signal that will force him to flee Israel. From what the guard said, they fear arresting Yeshua because of the riot that might ensue. So, this is their alternative. Right now, the plan is to do all this sometime this week and then arrest Yeshua if he remains after the feast days."*

"Wow, really?" Nicodemus responded in shock. *"At this point, I doubt that Yeshua will be frightened. Everything points to a dramatic confrontation, perhaps a spiritual cleansing this week."*

"Yes, I know," Joseph said. *"But what if we have the timing wrong? Yes, everything about Pesach is deliverance. And it has long been the traditional belief that Messiah will enter the Temple through the Eastern Gate at Passover, just as Yeshua did today. But doesn't the Feast of Tabernacles fit just as well with the emphasis on deliverance and living water?"*

"Perhaps we should take some precautionary moves just in case. It will take some convincing, but I'll visit Lazarus, Mary, and Martha tomorrow early in the morning and take them to Jericho where they can stay with Zacchaeus for a time. He has so many connections to the east that he could remove them from the country without anyone knowing where they have gone."

"Excellent idea," Joseph responded, *"That will also send a signal to Caiaphas and Annas that we know what they are up to!"*

Rachel, Nicodemus' wife, had been listening quietly to the conversation. She seldom interrupted her husband, preferring to speak with him quietly at home. But she could not help but ask, *"If Caiaphas and Annas can sanction the murder of Lazarus and kidnap two honorable and respected women, aren't our families in danger as well?"*

"I don't think so, Rachel," Nicodemus responded as he took her hand. *"But just in case, I'll appoint one of the servants to accompany you and the boys when you go to the market or to the temple for worship."*

The four of them sang a Psalm, prayed and then retired for the evening.

At dawn, Nicodemus was already on the road to Bethany. He wanted to get past all the pilgrims who were camping on the hills east of Jerusalem before they woke up. By the time the sun was just peeking over the Judean hills to the east, he was already knocking on the door of his friends from Bethany. Lazarus was not shocked at all to hear of the plot to take his life. He seemed to have a strong spirit of discernment about him since the resurrection a few weeks earlier. He liked to say, *"Once you've been to heaven, the ways of man on earth seem clear and simple."* When Nicodemus revealed the plot against Mary and Martha, even Lazarus grew concerned and welcomed Nicodemus' plan to remove them from danger.

"But Yeshua and the Talmidim have been staying here. We can't just leave them without a place to stay." Martha responded.

"Already taken care of Martha," Nicodemus answered, *"I told John, the talmid, that I have a large Gethsemane in the olive grove reserved for them anytime they want to use it. It is below ground, spacious and quite secluded. It will comfortably keep all of them through the feast days. I pointed it out to him as we passed by it yesterday."*

With that, the women packed a few clothes and a few skins of water for the long walk down the Jericho Road to the home of Zacchaeus. The tax collector was enthusiastic to host the women and Lazarus. He gave them one of his rental houses that were now vacant as all Israel was in Jerusalem for Pesach. He encouraged Lazarus to remain in the house since the stories of his resurrection had already spread to Jericho, and it would not be difficult for an assassin from the Sanhedrin to find him. He even posted a man in a shop opposite the home to keep watch for any suspicious activity and report to him immediately.

"If I suspect trouble, I can have all three of you out of the country within 6 hours," Zacchaeus remarked confidently to Nicodemus, *"Don't worry about a thing. I know how to be discreet and I have connections with traders who don't ask questions. Some of them owe me back taxes, and I can call in a favor anytime."*

Nicodemus was anxious to get back to Jerusalem for Pesach, but it was too late in the day to climb back up the hill. He spent the evening with Mary, Martha, Lazarus, and Zacchaeus and enjoyed a wonderful meal while Zacchaeus told the story of hosting Yeshua and the Talmidim just a few days earlier. Already a follower of

Yeshua, Zacchaeus had been honored when Yeshua passed by on his way to Jerusalem and announced for all to hear, *"I must stay at your house today!"* Luke 19:5

"He gave me a chance to publicly redeem my name in the community," Zacchaeus beamed. *"As you know, I am an outcast to the Pharisees in Jericho and they love to deride me in public, present company excluded,"* Zacchaeus nodded and smiled at Nicodemus. *"But since last week, when Yeshua stated,* **"Today salvation has come to this house, because this man too is a son of Abraham. For the Son of Man came to seek and to save what was lost."** (Luke 19:9), *it is like I am reborn. He stood right there,"* Zacchaeus pointed to the head of the table. *"He called me a child of Abraham. Greatest day of my life!"*

"Born again huh?!" Nicodemus smiled, *"I know the feeling!"* The next morning, Nicodemus embraced his friends from Bethany and left for Jerusalem. *"God keep you safe!"* he told Lazarus.

"Not to worry my friend," Lazarus replied with a smile, *"I died once. I'm not afraid. I've seen the other side with these eyes!"* They laughed and embraced again as Nicodemus thanked Zacchaeus once more for this huge favor.

"My pleasure entirely," Zacchaeus responded as Nicodemus left for Jerusalem.

Nicodemus arrived in Bethany exhausted after the long walk from Jericho. The Judean wilderness can be brutal in the summer but in spring time, at Passover, the Jericho road is normally quite pleasant. Nicodemus was also fortunate that a spring shower had passed through the previous evening; it kept down the dust on the road. Still, the rise in elevation took its toll on the middle-aged man.

He checked in at Bethany to see if there was any disturbance at the home of Mary and Martha and found none. As he descended the Mt. of Olives, many of the pilgrims were already lighting fires for the evening meal. He entered the olive grove and met the man who owned the Gethsemane. He mentioned that Yeshua and his disciples had indeed stayed there the previous night. Nicodemus gave the man several denarii and told him to provide bread and wine for the Talmidim when they returned in the evening.

Nicodemus reached his home to the warm welcome of his family and Joseph, who had come to brief him on the events of the last two days. *"You know what we forgot to do before you left?"* Joseph asked Nicodemus as they ascended to the roof for the cool spring breezes off the Mediterranean. *"We never submitted our letters to the Sanhedrin."*

"That's right," answered Nicodemus, *"After the procession of Yeshua into Jerusalem and your news about the plot to kill Lazarus, I entirely forgot."*

"Not to worry," Joseph responded, *"I took your letter along with mine this morning to the Sanhedrin secretary. But let me share what happened at the Temple the last two days. I hardly know where to start. Well, let me start on Monday. Yeshua and the Talmidim arrived very early from Bethany, probably even before you left the city."*

"Yes, Mary said they had left before dawn for the temple," Nicodemus responded.

"Well, remember what Yeshua did three years ago on the eve of Passover?" Joseph asked. *"He did it again, but this time he did not leave. He stayed in the temple courts teaching. And, listen to this: The blind and lame were brought to him, one after another. And He healed them all in the presence of Caiaphas and Annas. I was there with your boys. Your three boys stood up and started shouting in the temple:* **"Hosanna to the Son of David!"** (Matthew 21:15) *All the other children joined in. It was like an unofficial Levitical boys' choir. They sang and sang."*

Nicodemus slumped back in his chair and looked at Rachel. *"They did?"*

"Yes, I could hardly believe it myself." Rachel answered. They both beamed at each other.

"Where are they? Have they gone to bed already?" Nicodemus asked his wife.

"Yes, please don't wake them, my love!" Rachel pleaded.

"Then I am cooking them their favorite breakfast in the morning so I can linger over every word of it from them!" Nicodemus could hardly contain himself. He smiled and laughed and shook his head in amazement. ***"Hosanna to the Son of David?*** *In the Temple? With Caiaphas and Annas watching? My, oh my! What did the high priests do?"*

*"They were livid! They approached Yeshua and asked him **"Do you hear what these children are saying?"*** (Matthew 21:15*) Clearly they expected Yeshua to silence the children. But he didn't. He just said,* **'Yes, have you never read, from the lips of children and infants you have ordained praise?'"** *(Matthew 21:16 & Psalm 8:2)*

"How fitting, the Son of David quotes a Psalm of David, supporting children calling him the Son of David. I love it!" Nicodemus almost could not contain himself.

"That was Monday," Joseph continued. *"Tuesday was even better. I was there the whole day and listened to the interaction of Yeshua with some local Rabbis. They questioned him on his authority. The Pharisees tried to trap him by asking if we should pay taxes to Caesar. But then he turned the tables on a group of Pharisees who were grouped together trying to come up with a question for him. So he asked them,* **'What do you think of the Christ? Whose son is he?'** *They answered,* **'The son of David.'** *Now,"* Joseph paused, *"you are going like this. He asked them,* **'How is it then that David, speaking by the Spirit, calls him Lord? If then David calls him 'Lord' how can he be his son?'"**

"Because Messiah is also the divine Son of God and is beyond time, so he can be both David's son and his Lord. That's simple." Nicodemus responded.

"I know, but they were stuck. If they gave that answer, they knew Yeshua would ask them, 'Then why don't you believe in me?' So they said nothing and walked away."

Joseph and Nicodemus talked long into the evening about everything else Yeshua had taught that day. Nicodemus shared that Lazarus, Mary, and Martha were safe in the hands of Zacchaeus.

On Wednesday morning, Nicodemus was true to his word. He cooked a large breakfast for his boys and listened to them retell the story from Monday morning.

"We heard the people shouting as they were coming to the temple," the eldest, named Benjamin, recalled. *"People were running from every house. We went up onto the rooftop and watched as Yeshua and his Talmidim entered the temple courts while people waved their lulavim. It was an amazing sight. People were running and shouting."*

"Then when we saw Yeshua heal the blind and saw the lame walk and give praise to God," the second born, Jacob, continued, *"we just started singing the same psalms we heard on Sunday."*

"He is Messiah, the son of God, isn't he father?" the youngest asked.

"Yes, he is boys! And he has come to save just like you sang!" Nicodemus answered. *"I am so very proud of you."*

"May I ask you boys, where is the lamb you selected on Sunday?"

"He's on the roof, father." Ben answered. *"We've been taking turns feeding and cleaning up after him. This is our last day with him, isn't it?"*

"That's right boys. I hope you will be able to handle it okay," Nicodemus asked, half hoping there would be a little bit of sorrow over the sacrifice of their Passover lamb. But there wasn't. Nicodemus remembered so clearly not being able to even watch at his first Passover. He had run into the priest's room and talked with Simeon that day. Nostalgia swept over him as he recalled Simeon's story of Simeon's father making his son spank him for his son's rudeness. The image of the lamb's life ebbing away still bothered Nicodemus. He was, forever, Tela.

"No problem, father. We've seen this many times at home when Mom slaughters a goat!" Benjamin just smiled at his father and then chuckled a little. Nicodemus just smiled and shook his head.

Chapter 23:
Horror

On Thursday morning, John, the talmid of Yeshua, came to Nicodemus' house and asked him if Yeshua could use his home for their Passover celebration.

"We found one of your servants bringing water from the well, just as Yeshua instructed us," John stated. *"So we knew it was his will that we use your home. I apologize, I know it is last minute and your family is here."*

"Not at all, John," Nicodemus replied. *"Joseph has a home near the Shechem gate and I know we can easily celebrate the meal with them."*

"We won't be spending the night," John continued. *"Yeshua wants to teach us privately in the nearby olive groves in the evening, and we'll retire for the night at the Gethsemane you have so graciously provided. You are a good friend, and Yeshua told me to extend his thanks."*

"It is my honor and pleasure. All I have is yours. In fact, we will leave some servants here to assist you with the roasting of our lamb," Nicodemus answered.

With that Nicodemus quickly sought out Joseph at the Temple and asked to join his household for Passover. He returned in time to accompany his boys to the Temple for the sacrifice of their lamb. Joseph arranged for the cooking at his home and the cleansing of his home of all leaven at the prescribed hour. Nicodemus ordered the same for his own home. *"Messiah to celebrate Passover in my home,"* he thought, *"I never could have imagined a greater honor. I only wish I could be there."* Nicodemus knew, however, that the celebration of Passover for a Rabbi and his Talmidim was a sacred and private tradition, and it was enough to know that Yeshua would bless his home with his presence.

The evening was filled with joy and laughter. An air of anticipation filled the house as Nicodemus, his father Benjamin, and Joseph discussed how the revelation of Yeshua as Messiah and King of Israel would play out the next day. The theme of deliverance took on new meaning for the men and their families. They sang and recited the traditional Scriptures from Exodus. Nicodemus had even insisted that his boys sing the entire psalm they had sung in the temple courts on Monday. The boys loved singing for their parents and the additional audience added to their joy. They retired in the late evening to the rooftop for one last glass of wine after the traditional meal had been finished. They would sleep well after drinking five glasses of wine. The glasses were small yet of the highest quality from Nicodemus' vineyards.

There was a lot of movement in the streets as the evening wound down. This was quite unusual for Passover Eve. But the whole family slept soundly. The whole house was filled with the joy that comes from faith and hope.

Early the next morning, just after sunrise, a servant from Nicodemus' house arrived in a panic at the home of Joseph.

"We've been looking for you everywhere!" he shouted, *"Yeshua has been arrested!"* He spoke between gasping for air. He went on to explain that he had welcomed Yeshua and the Talmidim just as Nicodemus had instructed him and that they had left for the Gethsemane (Gat Shmanim) on the Mt. of Olives late the previous evening.

"In the middle of the night, the talmid, called John, passed by looking for you. He told us to tell you that Yeshua had been taken by force to the home of Caiaphas. Temple soldiers took him for trial before the Sanhedrin," the servant continued.

"They can't do that," Joseph said to Nicodemus. *"All trials are to be held in the Hall of Hewn Stones in the Temple and never after sunset."*

"I don't think they care about protocol," Nicodemus responded.

"Where is he now?" Joseph asked the servant, *"still with Caiaphas?"*

"On my way here, I heard people saying that he was being taken under heavy guard to Pilate's palace!" the servant replied.

"I don't believe it," Joseph responded in shock. *"Something must have speeded up their intentions. They are risking a riot by the people."*

"Think for a moment, Joseph," Nicodemus said to Joseph, *"This may be Yeshua's plan. He has Caiaphas and Pilate in the same place, the King and the High Priest. I think this may be how he will deliver us. Let us not lose faith now."*

"I don't know, Nicodemus, I have a bad feeling about this!" Joseph responded.

"I'm sorry sir", the servant interrupted. *"I would have come sooner. I didn't know the way to this place. I had to wait for the day staff to arrive who knew where you had gone. What are your orders?"*

"Don't worry," Nicodemus answered, *"you did your best; you may leave."*

With that, the men went inside to inform their families. They warned them to stay inside as the streets would be dangerous.

"Let's go to Pilate's palace and see for ourselves what is going on!" Nicodemus said to Joseph. *"We must see this with our own eyes."*

The two men walked the short distance between Joseph's home and the former palace of Herod the Great, now the residence of Pontius Pilate. They received clarification from eye witnesses along the road who were awakened by the disturbance very early in the morning. A dozen temple guards, almost all members of the Sanhedrin, numerous Rabbis, and Caiaphas himself had bound Yeshua and dragged him through the streets of Jerusalem to Pilate's palace. He had been taken to the Antonio Fortress to stand before Herod Antipas who was in town for Passover. Pilate had tried to shirk his responsibility by sending Yeshua to Herod when it had been revealed to him earlier in the morning that the accused was a Galilean. Several reported to Nicodemus that Yeshua looked bruised and beaten when he passed by. A crowd had followed this parade of shame but most of them were not supporters of Yeshua. Nicodemus' heart began to sink at the prospect that Yeshua had been a victim of the evil plot of the Jewish Ruling Council. For years they had opposed him, vilified him in private and in public forums, intimidated his followers, interrogated those whom he had healed, called him an instrument of Satan, accused him of being insane, frightened the public into silence, and on several occasions tried to stone him. Certainly now Yeshua would stand up to them and put them in their place. Still, he held out hope that the one who weeks earlier had raised Lazarus from the dead would rise and judge his opponents once and for all.

As the two men drew nearer to Pilate's palace, Nicodemus recalled the last time he had been in this very spot and watched as the "King Makers" from Parthia mounted camels, escorted by many blazing white Arabian steeds and 20 Roman soldiers on horses. Later that same day he was told that Herod had dispatched executioners to Bethlehem to rip innocent babies away from their mothers and slaughter them. The Son of David, who had somehow escaped the Roman sword as an infant, was now in this very palace standing before Herod's immoral descendant, Pontius Pilate. He was wicked, ambitious, egotistical and brutal. Pilate was hated by the Jews, especially Galileans. On Passover the previous year, his soldiers had slaughtered a group of zealots from Galilee on the temple grounds and their blood had been mingled with the blood of the animals. (Luke 13:1) The Holy One of Israel was — at this moment — standing before this evil tyrant.

"Let not evil triumph today," Nicodemus said a short prayer as they turned the last corner and the entire palace came into view.

To their horror, their fears were realized. Yeshua stood before them with Roman soldiers on either side. Wearing only his thin one -piece linen garment, it was stained with his own blood from top to bottom. He had been beaten, and severely. Nicodemus could see the blood pooling around his feet. His face was barely recognizable. There was something atop his head.

"What is that?" Nicodemus said to himself. *"A bundle of thorns?"* It had been driven down into his skull, and streams of blood from each thorn streamed down his face.

"Lord, have mercy!" the two men said together. They could not move for a long time until a long transom (patibulum in Latin) was brought and placed on his shoulders and tied there with ropes. It formed a cruciform when attached to the vertical beam.

Suddenly the two men could hear the chants of the crowd. The shock had made them deaf to all sounds around them for a moment. Then they heard the awful words, "CRUCIFY HIM! CRUCIFY HIM!"

Yeshua was poked and prodded forward by long rods held by soldiers who did not want to stain their hands with Jewish blood. A column of soldiers on either side created a barrier between Yeshua and the people as they made their way through the narrow streets between Pilate's palace and the Shechem gate. A centurion led the way.

"How is this possible?" Nicodemus turned to Joseph.

"I don't believe it!" Joseph responded

They followed behind the crowd, heartbroken by the sight of Yeshua, who stumbled through the street carrying the instrument of death for which the Romans were famous. Nicodemus looked down, almost unable to take a step. As he glanced down at the paving stones at his feet, there it was: The imprint of the foot of Yeshua in his own blood! He broke down and began to weep uncontrollably.

The remainder of the "death walk" was just a blur. Somehow the two men made it outside the Shechem gate to the place where many rebels, traitors and murderers had been crucified before. The place was right next to the road, not more than 100 meters from the Shechem gate, in keeping with the intent of this barbaric death sentence: intimidation. As people passed by, they received the message. Oppose Rome and this is your fate! And it had been effective for the most part. It had even tempted the man in the highest spiritual position in Israel to

204

sell his soul to Satan. High Priest Joseph Caiaphas had cooperated with the oppressors of Israel to kill Messiah!

Neither Nicodemus nor Joseph could walk any further than the Shechem gate. It was then that Nicodemus noticed the other two who were sentenced to die along with Yeshua. They writhed and squirmed on the ground like trapped animals, screaming for mercy. It was horrific to watch. Fifty feet in front of them they watched the evil proceedings: the pounding of nails into flesh, the wailing of women. When they drove the nails into the hands of Yeshua, he did not make a sound. He did not struggle. Nicodemus watched as Yeshua actually offered his hand to the Centurion, whose duty it was to drive home the nails. Nicodemus found himself walking forward, drawn to this other worldly attraction of Yeshua being nailed to a cross and WILLINGLY. The soldiers lifted the transom with Yeshua's wrists nailed to each end. They dropped it into place with a thud, affixing the crossbeam to the post (Gibbet in Latin). Yeshua slumped and pushed up on the foot rest (supperdaneum in Latin) to relieve the pressure of the nails on his wrists. Still not a word from Yeshua despite the obvious agony and torture of this ordeal.

The centurion stepped forward, positioned the feet of Yeshua so that he could drive home a single nail through both feet. The two criminals had screamed and twisted when he had done the same to them, trying to avoid the obvious agony. But Yeshua did not! He actually placed his feet on the foot rest in the position for the centurion to do his work. The centurion was amazed, looked down to compose himself, and then looked up to pound the final nail.

"What is he doing!?" Joseph said under his breath to Nicodemus.

"He was led like a lamb to the slaughter, and as a sheep before her shearers is silent, so, (Joseph paused in stunned silence) *he did not...open his mouth!"* (Isaiah 53:7) *"Isaiah's perfect description of Messiah, and... this!"* Nicodemus gestured toward Yeshua.

"The Lamb has come," Nicodemus said under his breath. *"The Lamb has come."* The last words Simeon had whispered in Zechariah's ear.

"What did you say?" Joseph asked.

But there was no time to answer. Suddenly walking past them, there were Annas and Caiaphas! They laughed derisively at the scene before them. No one said a word to them as the crowd parted and they approached Yeshua on the cross. Pilate had posted a sign at the top of the crossbeam: *"Yeshua the Nazarene, King of the Jews!"* Caiaphas took exception and was shouting something to the centurion. But the Roman was having none of it. He drew his sword and the High Priests backed away.

"Let's go, we need to be there!" Joseph said to Nicodemus after a long time. The two men stepped out of the shadows and stepped into the bright sunshine. Suddenly the fog of shock and emotion slipped away as the morning sun warmed his face. Nicodemus recalled his first conversation with Jesus. ***"Whoever lives by the truth comes into the light, so that it may be seen plainly that what he has done has been done through God."*** John 3:21

Ahead Nicodemus could see John the talmid, holding a woman who had slumped against him. It was the mother of Yeshua, and she looked absolutely broken. *"A mother should not have to watch her son die, and in such a horrible way,"* Nicodemus thought immediately. Yeshua was looking toward the heavens and all heard him say, ***"Father, forgive them for they do not know what they are doing!"*** (Luke 23:34) Nicodemus could not believe his ears.

"He is asking the Father to forgive them?" Nicodemus asked Joseph.

"Even now," Joseph looked up into the face of Yeshua, *"He is a friend to sinners!"*

His words sparked more derision from Caiaphas and the sons of Annas. *"Forgiveness? We don't need forgiveness!"* one of the sons of Annas shouted.

"King of Israel, you have saved others, save yourself now if you are the Christ! Come down from the cross and we will believe in you!" (Matt. 27:42) another shouted.

The evil and heartless comments became contagious as Pharisees, Rabbis and the elders mocked and insulted Yeshua.

Surprisingly, the centurion who had witnessed all this turned, drew his sword and pointed it at Caiaphas and shouted, *"Stop! Isn't this enough!?"* He spoke perfect Aramaic and with a slight Galilean accent. It shocked the High Priest. He opened his mouth to respond but the centurion took a step toward him. *"Don't test me Nasi!"* the centurion warned Caiaphas, *"you may have Pilate's ear, but I have his sword!"*

Caiaphas retreated and watched from a distance. Rome had been his instrument of evil and he dared not provoke them.

Yeshua spoke several more times from the cross. He entrusted his mother to the care of John, his beloved talmid. He promised paradise to one of the men crucified with him.

"Every single word from his mouth has been about others," Joseph remarked to Joseph as noon approached. *"How do you go through this and only mention the needs of others?"*

"The Lamb has come!" Nicodemus responded. *"I can't explain it, but I am more convinced than ever that he knows what he is doing. I just don't know why."*

As soon as the words were out of his mouth, the sun that had been shining brightly suddenly stopped shining. There was not a cloud in the sky, yet it was completely dark. Stars suddenly began to shine. It not only surprised and shocked the Jews present, but especially the superstitious Romans. The dozen who had been in charge of this execution for the past three hours lit their torches in an

attempt to drive away the darkness and the presumed evil that accompanied it. But they could not hide their fear, drawing their swords and guarding the scene as if some dark force was about to vindicate the slaughter of the innocent. Only Mary and John were allowed near the cross. Everyone else stepped back as the contingent of soldiers moved forward with swords and torches. Fear gripped many and they retreated back into the city. Most of the members of the Sanhedrin left the scene, convinced they were done with Yeshua. Nicodemus and Joseph remained.

After three long hours of darkness, suddenly Yeshua lifted his head and looked to the heavens with an expression of shock on his face. He shouted to the heavens in Aramaic, *"Eloi, Eloi, lama sabachthani?" (My God, my God, why have you forsaken me?!"* (Matthew 27:46) The look of dread and shock left him as quickly as it came, and he shouted again in Aramaic, *"It is finished!"* (John 19:30)

It had been six long hours. Joseph and Nicodemus were emotionally exhausted. Just then they heard the three trumpet blasts coming from the Temple. It was the time for the evening sacrifice. Instinctively all who remained at the cross of Yeshua turned and faced the temple, all except Nicodemus. He looked into the eyes of Yeshua. Nicodemus remembered his first evening sacrifice. In the midst of the horrific sight in front of him, he allowed his mind to recall standing with this father Benjamin, as he watched the lamb turn its head and expose his neck to the priest.

Just then Yeshua did the same and said in a loud voice as the three trumpet blasts could still be heard echoing across Jerusalem, *"Father into your hands I commit my spirit."* (Luke 23:46)

Nicodemus watched as Yeshua closed his eyes and his head slumped. Nicodemus' heart broke. He did not understand. In the last six hours he had come to see that this was the will of Yeshua. He had willingly died just like the lamb. He had somehow connected the picture of the Passover lamb with Yeshua in his mind, but his heart still hurt. He remembered Simeon's story about sin and forgiveness. *"Sin brings pain!"* Those were Simeon's last words to Nicodemus. He felt the sting of sin more than he ever thought possible as he looked up at the lifeless body of his Messiah!

Instantly the sun began to shine brightly again and a rumble could be heard coming from the east. The ground began to shake, violently throwing everyone to the ground. The centurion had been thrown to the ground next to Nicodemus. He stood and helped Nicodemus to his feet. The two just looked at each other, trying to stabilize themselves on the still trembling ground. They looked at Yeshua, at each other, then at the ground. There was a look of amazement and sadness in the eyes of the Roman. Nicodemus didn't know what to make of it.

"I knew this man," the Roman said to him. *"A long time ago he helped me.* **Surely he was a righteous man, and the Son of God."** (Matthew 27:54 & Luke 23:47) *"Let me know if you need any help with his burial."* The Roman soldiers, gripped by fear, began to break the legs of those crucified but at the insistence of the centurion they did not break Yeshua's legs.

They stood there looking at Yeshua for a long time. The sun was now shining brightly and was positioned immediately behind the cross of Yeshua as Nicodemus looked up at him. The sun seemed to be scattered in every direction from the body of Yeshua. The image was emblazoned in the mind of Nicodemus as he stood motionless before him. **"I am the light of the world. Whoever follows me will never walk in darkness."** (John 8:12) Nicodemus recalled the words of Yeshua from the Temple courts.

Finally, Joseph said to Nicodemus, *"We need to bury him, and before Sabbath in a few hours. Let me go to Pilate and ask for his body."* Joseph hurried off and disappeared into the Shechem gate. While he was gone, Nicodemus spoke to the women who were there and told them that he and Joseph would see to the burial. Mary and Mary the wife of Cleopas thanked him.

"We never imagined this is how it would end," the wife of Cleopas said to Nicodemus through her tears. Mary the mother of Yeshua looked up at Nicodemus. She was clearly grieving, so it surprised Nicodemus when she said to him, *"I know you. You have been following Yeshua for some time, haven't you? You are not like the others."*

"Yes," Nicodemus responded. *"From the Passover when he cleansed the Temple three years ago. I came at night to speak with Yeshua. My name is Nicodemus."*

"I've seen you in Galilee too," she responded.

Nicodemus was struck how sensitive and interested she was in him. *"Yes, I made several trips there with my family."* He paused and then said, *"I want you to know I did not consent to this."* Nicodemus felt he needed to explain that he was not part of the plot to kill her son. But her response surprised him.

"The Sanhedrin did not do this," she explained, her voice rising as she pointed to Yeshua on the cross. Remember his words, ***"I lay down my life for the sheep...No one takes it from me but I lay it down of my own accord."*** (John 10:15, 18)

"But why?" Nicodemus asked as sensitively as he could.

"Nicodemus," there was strength in her voice, *"Because he is the Lamb!"*

Nicodemus was speechless. He gave her a half smile and just nodded as he looked up at Yeshua. ***"Like a lamb to the slaughter."*** (Isaiah 53:7) the words of Isaiah rang in his mind.

Nicodemus returned within the hour carrying a heavy load. The centurion was true to his word. He had dismissed all but two of the other soldiers after they had disposed of the other two crucified men. They helped with the tools necessary to remove the long iron nails from Yeshua's hands and feet. On the way back from the city Joseph had bought a linen cloth as well as myrrh and aloes for anointing Yeshua's body for burial. The soldiers did the most difficult work, extracting the nail from his feet. Then they were able to lower the cross beam with ropes and remove the nails from his hands while he was on the ground. The ground around the cross was soaked in Yeshua's blood and all of them were covered in his blood by the time the gruesome job was finished. The Roman soldiers brought water to wash the body at the Centurion's request. Once the body was washed, they carried Yeshua using Nicodemus' outer garment. They carried his body, assisted by the centurion, to a nearby stone tomb that belonged to Joseph. It was immediately adjacent to where Simeon had been laid to rest. Inside the tomb, they washed the body again and laid Yeshua on the linen cloth in one of the "kukhin". The two men then wrapped his body in strips of cloth in keeping with Jewish tradition, anointing his body with the ointment as they applied the strips of cloth. Before covering Yeshua with the same linen cloth, Nicodemus placed a separate cloth on his face.

They completed the burial well before sunset. The women who were at the cross were also there standing outside the tomb while Nicodemus and Joseph completed the burial. They were Mary, the mother of Yeshua, along with John the talmid, John's grandmother who was Mary the wife of Cleopas and Mary Magdalene. The men and the Romans together rolled the heavy stone in front of the tomb. The tomb would be sealed after Sabbath. There was not time now for details. The women promised to return at dawn on Sunday with more spices and to make final the burial of Yeshua.

Finally taking a breath, Nicodemus and Joseph walked back with the Roman soldiers into the city. All were covered in the blood of Yeshua. They parted ways just inside the Shechem gate, as the Romans continued on to the Antonio Fortress. The Centurion turned and gave them a short wave. Nicodemus and Joseph reached Joseph's home just before the sun had set. But Nicodemus climbed the outside stairs to the roof top. He wanted to watch the sun go down on this day. He stood motionless; facing the western sun as it slowly touched the horizon. In the foreground was the Golgotha, stained with the blood of Yeshua! He slowly repeated the words of Yeshua, *"I am the light of the world. Whoever believes in me will never walk in darkness."* (John 8:12)

Stepping Into the Light
Bible Study

Outline of Sessions

Introduction "Stepping into the Light" is a book of Biblical historical fiction. Much of the contents however is based on incidents recorded in the Bible. This study offers a look at some of those incidents. The studies are not long and can be covered by a home group Bible study and should last only one hour. It is recommended that all participants will have read the chapters referenced before the study. Quotations are taken from "The Life and Times of Jesus the Messiah" written by Alfred Edersheim. Bible references are quoted from the NIV 1984 edition. A short review of the chapters covered introduces each study. At the end of each study is a list which specifies if the incident is factual, fictional or an embellishment of an historical or Biblical fact.

1. Chapters 1, 2   **Disappointment & Ein Karem**

2. Chapters 3, 4   **Pesach & Nunc Dimittis**

3. Chapters 5-7   **Slaughter, The Law, The Baptist**

4. Chapters 8, 9   **Essenes, Samaritan**

5. Chapters 10, 11   **Contrasts and Contradictions, A Den of Thieves**

Lesson #1: Nicodemus at Golgotha and Ein Karem
Chapter #1. Disappointment,
#2. Ein Karem

"The Dead Christ" by Gustave Doré

Review

Nicodemus is mentioned only three times in Scripture and all in the book of John. The author places him in the same home town as Zechariah and Elizabeth: Ein Karem. We do not know where Nicodemus grew up. This book presents a plausible description of how he grew up and how he may have come to believe in Yeshua as the Messiah.

After chapter one, which introduces Nicodemus at the cross of Yeshua, the story flashes back 33 years to a time just before Passover in 6 B.C. Zechariah and Elizabeth have a 6 month old baby called John who will become known as "The Baptist." Nicodemus is presented as 10 years older than John and has a personal relationship with Zechariah. Nicodemus' father is presented as a wealthy priest and a landowner who farms grapes and olives. Zechariah, Nicodemus and his father Benjamin walk from Ein Karem to the Temple in Jerusalem. Even though it is only 7 miles today, the area was hilly and covered by olive groves in the first century. They are on their way to Jerusalem for the celebration of Passover. Even though Nicodemus is only 10, his father intends to transfer him for his primary school education to a Rabbi in Jerusalem. On the way Zechariah recounts for the 10 year old Nicodemus his encounter with the angel Gabriel in the Temple more than a year earlier.

Once in Jerusalem, Nicodemus is confronted with the twice daily morning and evening sacrifice of a lamb. The description is an accurate description of the morning and evening sacrifice. Nicodemus is presented as a sensitive boy, nicknamed "Tela" meaning "wounded lamb" in Aramaic. He is deeply religious, an excellent student of Scripture and has memorized much of the Torah already under his rabbi in Ein Karem.

On Sunday, Nicodemus and his father select their lamb, as prescribed by Jewish law, five days before Passover.

Study

Read Luke 1:5-25 The appearance of Gabriel to Zechariah

1. Gabriel reveals how special John will be in vs. 16, 17
List the ramifications of John's birth and note how each is significant

a.

_____

b.

_____

c.

_____

d.

_____

e.

_____

2. Faith trusts in God's promises
a. What is the biological difficulty for Zechariah in Gabriel's message?

b. How did the Lord's chastisement fit Zechariah's failing?

Application: The wondrous miracle of conception and birth can be perceived as just normal and natural. The Bible describes each of us as *"knit together in our mother's womb."* Ps. 139:13, 14 How does this truth elevate the value of each and every life?

Read Luke 1:57-80 John is born
1. Who is the first to insist that the newborn baby is to be called John?

What does this indicate about Elizabeth?

2. In Zechariah's song, which words indicate that he remembers Gabriel's words?

Read Numbers 28:2-5 Exodus 29:38-46 Morning and Evening Sacrifice
1. Note the type of lamb sacrificed. Of what does this remind you?

How is this sacrifice described as significant?

Some historians indicate that the priesthood had altered the time of the evening sacrifice to much earlier than at twilight as God directed. They seemed to do this for their own convenience particularly on Passover weekend when there were so many Passover lambs to be slaughtered at the Temple. If the evening sacrifice was shifted to 3:00 PM as some indicate, why is this significant?

217

Facts

1. Zechariah and Elizabeth did live in Ein Karem.

2. Beth Sepher was the name of primary education for children in 1st Century Israel. It was normally conducted by the Rabbi in each town and was held at the local synagogue.

3. The rotation of priests serving in divisions for one week every six months is historical.

4. All families were to have a male representative in Jerusalem for Passover.

5. John was raised as a Nazarite with a strict dietary and lifestyle restrictions. Luke 1:15

6. Zechariah's description of his vision of Gabriel in the Temple is accurate and recorded in Luke 1:5ff

7. The geography around Ein Karem was noted for its olive groves and grape vineyards. The area today is developed as a suburb of Jerusalem. The town center was noted to have a flowing spring.

8. Bet Midrash was the equivalent of secondary school for a Jewish child in the 1st Century.

9. The physical location of Herod the Great's Palace is accurate and it was an eye sore to many devout Jews at the time.

10. The reference on p. 11 to Antipater and the appointment of his two sons in Galilee and Judea is accurate. Also the reference to Herod the Great's history in Galilee and Judea is also true. The reference to the Parthian influence in the region is an often overlooked fact in the conflict between Rome and Parthia. The paranoia of Herod and the slaughter of many of the sons of his wives is well documented.

11. The Psalms of Ascent is true. Psalm 121 was just one. P. 13

12. The reference to the northern gate of Damascus--or Shechem to the Jews--is true. It is still present today but it is built on top of the 1st Century gate.

13. The description of the Roman presence and the Antonio Fortress and the southern tower used as an observation platform is also true. P. 14. Also the description of the number of men on duty in the Antonio Fortress is accurate.

14. The description of the morning and evening sacrifice is given in Numbers 28:2-5 and is faithfully described. The adjusted time for the evening sacrifice from "evening" or "between the two evenings" to 3:00 PM by the Pharisees in Jesus' day is supported by Alfred Edersheim in his book "The Temple: Its Ministry and Services as they were at the time of Christ." P. 143

15. The Altar of Burnt Offering is accurately described as well as the procedure of the sacrifice.

Fiction

1. Nicodemus is nicknamed "Tela" by his father, a word which does in fact mean "wounded lamb" in Aramaic. However, this nickname is an invention by the author.

2. We do not know the name of Nicodemus father or if he was from the tribe of Levi or served as a priest.

3. The Rabbi in Ein Karem is unknown. The author calls him Terah.

4. It is unknown if John the Baptist and Nicodemus knew each other.

Embellishment

1. The mention of Gamaliel in Jerusalem as a respected leader of the School of Hillel cannot be firmly established in this specific time frame although he was a member of the Sanhedrin and later becomes the teacher of the Apostle Paul.

2. Songs were often used as memory devices for Scripture and it was common for significant portions of Scripture to be sung.

Lesson #2: Nicodemus at Passover
Chapters #3. Pesach
#4. Nunc Dimittis

"The Firstborn Slain" by Gustave Doré

Review

Zechariah and Benjamin (Nicodemus' father) have come to Jerusalem to serve as priests for the highest of holy festivals: Pesach (Passover)! Priests were divided into one of 24 divisions called "cohanim." Each division served in rotation during the year but all were encouraged to serve at Passover when every Jewish family was to have at last one male representative in Jerusalem. Most historians assume that the population of Jerusalem swelled to more than one million during Passover and as many as 250,000 lambs were sacrificed at the Temple...

Passover in Yeshua's day was not celebrated as the Israelites did on that first Passover in Egypt. It was celebrated while reclining and the focus was on redemption. There was joy as the Jewish celebration recalled God's deliverance more than 900 years earlier. It was matched with expectation at the promised Messiah to come.

Zechariah and Simeon are presented as knowing each other, which is quite likely. This is the author's conclusion as they are both elderly priests, Simeon living in or spending a great deal of time at the Temple.

On the Sunday before Passover each family would select their lamb from their own flock or would buy one from an approved vendor. After the 25th day of Adar (the last month in the Jewish Calendar) before Nisan (the first month), all vendors in the countryside were closed and one could only buy a lamb in Temple Courts. These lambs were sold at a premium and corruption was known to be common.

Nicodemus is presented as caring for the family lamb and becomes very attached to it over the next five days.

The author depicts the birth of Yeshua (Jesus) as taking place just before Passover. The appearance of His star is mentioned as well as the order of Augustus which brings the Holy Family from Nazareth to Bethlehem. They then would have traveled to Jerusalem for Mary's purification and Yeshua's circumcision on the 8th day. Passover would seem fitting for the events of the birth of Yeshua as the Jews believed Messiah would arrive at Passover.

Study
Read Exodus 12:1-14 The first Passover
Note how the Lord consecrates his people even by the Calendar.

1. Note some of the details regarding lamb selection and the meal. There are at least 10

Where are the corresponding spiritual elements?
Lamb selection day-

Age and condition –

Blood –

Leaven –

Read Exodus 13:1, 2 The first born
How is this command connected to Passover?

How is this fulfilled in Yeshua?

Read Luke 2:21-40

1. What are the three reasons why Mary and Joseph come to the Temple?

a._____

b._____

c. _____

From Alfred Edersheim Vol. 1, p. 196 On the offering of Mary and Joseph:

There was also a special 'superintendent of turtle-doves and pigeons,' required for certain purifications, and the holder of that office is mentioned with praise in the Mishnah. Much, indeed, depended upon his uprightness. For, at any rate as regarded those who brought the poor's offering, the purchasers of pigeons or turtle-doves would, as a rule, have to deal with him. In the Court of the Women there were thirteen trumpet-shaped chests for pecuniary contributions, called 'trumpets.' Into the third of these they who brought the poor's offering, like the Virgin-Mother, were to drop the price of the sacrifices which were needed for their purification. As we infer, the superintending priest must have been stationed here, alike to inform the offerer of the price of the turtle-doves, and to see that all was in order.

Facts

1. The celebration of Sabbath is accurately described. P. 20, 21

2. Often families would celebrate Passover together. In fact, it was required that one lamb should feed 10 adults and participants should strive to have no left-overs. Remaining parts of the lamb were to be burned the next morning. Imagine the smell of the remains of Passover lambs in Jerusalem on the morning Yeshua is crucified.

3. The two major Schools were in fact called Hillel and Shammai. Shammai were known for their strict adherence to Sabbath laws particularly. The School of Hillel took a more liberal approach to the Law in general especially Sabbath laws. Hillel, the founder, was known to still be alive and living in Jerusalem at this time, although he was more than 100.

4. Simeon's receiving of the Holy Family in the Temple courts is accurately described. P. 32

Fiction

1. A young Nicodemus meeting Simeon is completely unknown and is added by the author to inject another reference to the symbol of the "lamb of God" appearing in the Temple at Passover. It also allows the reader to consider the idea of a Messiah who sacrifices himself and that this concept may have been understood by some in Judea and Galilee.

Embellishment

1. The priest Simeon would have been at the Temple at this time but his relationship to the priest Zechariah is unknown. It is likely given their comparable ages. There were rooms for priests to change and prepare for service in the temple. The author added the Hebrew alphabet as a way to designate the various "lockers" and expression of seniority.

2. Was the star which directed the Magi seen in Jerusalem? Most likely but it is not mentioned in Scripture if it was noted by

residents there. The author places the birth of Yeshua at Passover in the spring which seems more likely.

3. The slaughter of the Passover lamb in the Temple was the practice of the day but it was not required in Scripture. The disciples of Yeshua most likely slaughtered the lamb for their meal and roasted it whole over a fire. There is no mention of the disciples taking the Passover lamb to the Temple for slaughter.

Lesson #3: Nicodemus Meets the Magi
Chapters #5. Slaughter
#6. The Law
#7. The Baptist

"The Wise Men Guided by the Star" by Gustave Dore

Review

As Chapter 5 opens, Nicodemus recalls the death of Simeon the priest. Nicodemus has begun his studies under a Rabbi in the Temple. Background is shared on the importance of a religious education and the unique technique of learning at some of the ancient Jewish sites.

The arrival of the Magi is introduced, and the author gives historical background on the history of Magi and their influence as king-makers from Parthia. The fear that grips Herod the Great and the city becomes obvious when one understands the Roman/Parthian conflict on Jewish soil. This combined with Herod's well-known paranoia explains just how disturbing the Magi's arrival really is. Nicodemus observes all of this and the reader already knows how Herod will respond with the slaughter of the infants of Bethlehem.

Chapter 6 gives some background on the religious context of the day, the Sanhedrin, and how the Law began to replace God's covenant of grace among the Judean ruling class and religious groups.

The technique of religious debate called "Remez" is introduced which will provide insight into Yeshua's public and private debates.

On a learning trip to Jericho, the author introduces the historical incident of Herod's slaughter of the 40 zealot priests in the theater in Jericho. After Herod's death, a period of political turmoil follows and during this time Nicodemus returns to Ein Karem.

The death of Zechariah and Elizabeth is of course a fictional addition here and is used by the author to focus on John the Baptist and his preparation in the desert of Judea. His exposure and the possibility of his residency with the Essenes is a matter of some dispute based on the differing perspectives of John and the Essenes.

Study
Read Matthew 2:1-12 The Magi arrive in Jerusalem

Notice the very informal inquiry of these Magi. Vs. 2

1. The NIV doesn't arrange well the prepositional phrase "in the east."

-Was the star in the eastern sky or were the magi viewing the star while they were in the east?

2. Why is it ironic that **Matthew** mentions their intent to "worship him?"

3. Vs. 3 mentions that Herod and Jerusalem's reaction to this inquiry regarding the birth of the King of the Jews was *"disturbed."* In reality that was an understatement!

Alfred Edersheim Vol. 1 p. 204 On the Magi

In their simplicity of heart, the Magi addressed themselves in the first place to the official head of the nation. The rumor of such an inquiry, and by such persons, would rapidly spread throughout the city. But it produced on King Herod, and in the capital, a far different impression from the feeling of the Magi. Unscrupulously cruel as Herod had always proved, even the slightest suspicion of danger to his rule - the bare possibility of the Advent of One, Who had such claims upon the allegiance of Israel, and Who, if acknowledged, would evoke the most intense movement on their part - must have struck terror to his heart. Not that he could believe the tidings, though a dread of their possibilitymight creep over a nature such as Herod's; but the bare thought of a Pretender, with such claims, would fill him with suspicion, apprehension, and impotent rage. Nor is it difficult to understand, that the whole city should, although on different grounds, have shared the 'trouble' of the king.

What might some of the specific causes of disturbance among the people of the city be?

4. Vs. 7 indicates there may have been a second conversation between Herod and the Magi. Why didn't Herod simply send a cohort of soldiers to accompany the Magi?

Read Ezekiel 34:1-16 Bad Shepherds
In Chapter 6 the author uses the Jewish teaching and debate technique called "Remez" to introduce the spiritual state of Judea in particular. Nicodemus seems to have escaped the corruption that was rampant among the Pharisees.

1. In Ezekiel 34, the Lord describes the failings of the spiritual leadership of the day.
What were the bad shepherds doing and not doing, which he describes?

2. The Lord responds how the Messiah will deal with this corruption:

-Vs. 10

-Vs. 11

-Vs. 13

-Vs. 14

-Vs. 15

-Vs. 16

Facts
1. Herod's slaughter of the Innocents is correctly described. Historians believe however that the death toll of infants was limited to about 20 given the limited population of Bethlehem at the time.
2. The reaction of conservative Jews to Roman and Greek influence was through education in the Law of Moses.
3. A debate technique that would later in time be referred to as "Remez" was employed often by Jewish teachers of the law. It involved the oblique reference to a Scripture in the midst of a discussion. It was the student's duty to determine the meaning by the context of the reference. It assumed a thorough knowledge of Scripture. It is more completely described by Ray Vander Laan in

his series "That the World May Know" and his book "The Life and Ministry of Jesus the Messiah."

4. Herod's slaughter of those who removed the golden eagle from the Temple entrance is described as well as his wish to be mourned at this death that resulted in the arrest of prominent citizens of Jerusalem to be slaughtered in the Hippodrome. These are historical facts.

Fiction

1. There is no historical basis to believe that Nicodemus was to be asked by Gamaliel to be his disciple.

2. It is unknown how Zechariah and Elizabeth died. The author adds this to facilitate John's departure for the Judean wilderness.

Embellishment

1. Nicodemus was known to be a wealthy man, but the source of his wealth is unknown. The author makes his father a wealthy landowner and trader in wine and olive oil for the Temple.

2. The arrival of the Magi is described as a powerful entourage of Parthian priests. The background of the Magi is mysterious. Alfred Edersheim believes they were descendants of a secret caste of astronomers and theologians from Daniel's time in the Medo-Persian Empire who eventually became powerful as they were recognized as the ones who anointed the most powerful kings in the world. He makes his case in "The Life and Times of Jesus the Messiah" Vol. 1 pp 202-213 Their appearance linked to the recent history with the Parthians would certainly have troubled Herod and all of Jerusalem.

Lesson #4: Nicodemus and the Samaritan
Chapters #8. Essenes
#9. Samaritans

"Arrival of the Good Samaritan at the Inn" *by Gustave Doré*

Review

There is a short reference in Luke 1:80 which would seem to indicate that John lived and was prepared for his role as forerunner of Jesus in the desert of Judea. It says, *"And the child grew and became strong in spirit and he lived in the desert until he appeared publicly in Israel."*

The author places John in Ein Karem which is well established as the home of Zechariah and Elizabeth. He attends Beth Sepher (Jewish primary education) under the instruction of the local Rabbi. This would have been the most logical and realistic experience of John. However at 12, the author has John taken by Nicodemus' father to an Essene community in the Qumran area. This is mere opinion and may or may not have happened. John's lifestyle was similar to the Essenes but he became a public prophet and preacher while the Essenes were recluse and separated themselves from society and particularly the corrupt Temple worship.

The process of Nicodemus joining the Sanhedrin is an accurate historic description. The wealthy Jewish families in Jerusalem did hold the power of nominating individuals to the Council of 71. Often those same families had been the benefactors that supported bright students in their studies. Some of those same students eventually became members of the Sanhedrin. The President or "Nasi" would then present the nominee to the Council for approval. Two religious schools existed at this time also: The Shammai and Hillel, named for their founders. The Shammai were the more strict followers of the Torah, particularly Sabbath law.

The expression "S'mikhah" is also introduced and will prove relevant in the ministry of Yeshua. The word means "having authority" and refers to those Rabbis who had the right to "interpret Scripture." Only a few of the most respected Rabbis had "authority." Others could only repeat accepted interpretations and rulings.

Benjamin is attacked on his way back from Qumran, where he leaves young John. He is ascending the Jericho road and is befriended by a Samaritan after the attack. This incident injects Yeshua's parable of the Good Samaritan into real life. Nicodemus, meanwhile, is to meet with those who would propose his name for the Sanhedrin including the famous teacher, Gamaliel and Joseph of Arimathea. As they enter the Temple grounds, the three pass by a 12 year old speaking with some of the learned teachers. This is the second time Nicodemus crosses paths with Yeshua. The boy Yeshua is discussing the relationship of faith and obedience with the teachers. "Just believe" will be a phrase that is repeated throughout the story as Nicodemus interacts with Yeshua and The Baptist.

Nicodemus goes to look for his overdue father and meets Mary and Joseph on the Jericho Road. They are hurrying back to Jerusalem to look for their lost son. Nicodemus finds his father at an Inn further down the Jericho Road. This spot in the road was commemorated by the church down through the ages. In the 6th Century a Byzantine monastery was built. At the same site, a mosaic museum was built in 2009 which you can visit today.

Interestingly Benjamin had an interaction with Mary and Joseph who had cared for him the previous evening. Chapter 9 closes with the wedding of Nicodemus and Rachel, his betrothed. The description of a typical Jewish wedding of the day is culturally accurate. It was common for a wedding ceremony to be a reminder and reflection of God's relationship with his people.

Study
Read Luke 10:25-37 Parable of the Good Samaritan

Note the significant context of this parable. Vs. 25-29

1. Vs 29 is key for it is the motivation that sparks Yeshua's response.

Note some of the significant elements of "being a neighbor" that Yeshua describes specifically for this "expert in the law."

2. What does this tell us about the spiritual perspective in Jesus day? ...especially how the Law was interpreted in the relationship between Jews and Samaritans?

Samaritans described by Alfred Edersheim. The Life and Times of Jesus the Messiah Vol 1, p. 395-398. Note the significant issues between Judea and Samaria!

The shorter road from Judæa to Galilee led through Samaria; and this, if we may credit Josephus, was generally taken by the Galileans on their way to the capital. On the other hand, the Judæans seem chiefly to have made a détour through Peræa, in order to avoid hostile and impure Samaria.

...The first foreign colonists of Samaria brought their peculiarforms of idolatry with them. But the Providential judgments, bywhich they were visited, led to the introduction of a spurious Judaism, consisting of a mixture of their former superstitions withJewish doctrines and rites.   Although this state of matters resembled that which had obtained in the original kingdom of Israel, perhaps just because of this, Ezra and Nehemiah, when reconstructing the Jewish commonwealth, insisted on a strict separation between those who had returned from Babylon and theSamaritans.

...The religious separation became final when (at a date which cannot be precisely fixed) the Samaritans built a rival temple on

Mount Gerizim, and Manasseh, the brother of Jaddua, the Jewish High-Priest, having refused to annul his marriage with the daughter of Sanballat, was forced to flee, and became the High-Priest of the new Sanctuary.

... In the troublous times of Antiochus IV. Epiphanes, the Samaritans escaped the fate of the Jews by repudiating all connection with Israel, and dedicating their temple to Jupiter. In the contest between Syria and the Maccabees which followed, the Samaritans, as might be expected, took the part of the former.

3. What message is Jesus sending by making the *"one who had mercy"* a Samaritan?

Marriage as a Reflection of God and Man (if time, read and discuss the following)

Jeremiah 31:1-33	**I was a husband to them**
Ezekiel 16:32-34	**The Broken Marriage**
Hosea 9:1	**Unfaithful Israel is a harlot**
Ephesians 5:25-33	**Christ's love mirrored John**
3:29	**The friend of the bridegroom**
Revelation 21:2	**The Bride adorned**

Facts

1. The Essene community did in fact exist and has been noted by historian Josephus. The remains of one of their communities have been excavated at the Qumran caves where the Dead Sea Scrolls were discovered.

2. "Having authority" is described as the right to interpret Scripture referred to with the Hebrew word "S'mikhah." The reference has deep roots in the Old Testament and was connected to the laying on of hands and was practiced by Isaac with Jacob, Moses with the 70 elders and Moses with Joshua. In Yeshua's day, a teacher who

had "S'mikhah" was allowed to make new interpretations of Scripture while other Rabbis could only repeat accepted rulings. This provides insight into Matthew 7:28 and Matthew 21:23-27 where Jesus is referred to as having authority or having his authority questioned. Ray Vander Laan speaks about this right of "having authority" in his series "That the World May Know".

3. Jewish hatred and revulsion at the thought of associating with Samaritans is accepted as historic fact. This historical context only magnifies Yeshua's parable of the Good Samaritan which Nicodemus' father lives out in the book.

Fiction

1. It is unknown if Nicodemus was married but as it was accepted tradition for the Sanhedrin members to be married, it would seem logical that he was.

2. It is unlikely that Nicodemus met Mary and Joseph on the Jericho road.

Embellishment

1. It is not known if John the Baptist spent time with the Essene community. His Nazarite lifestyle of simplicity and self-denial has some parallels to the Essenes however the Essenes were separatists from the religious community. John's ministry was the very public preparation for the Messiah and here is where John and the Essenes differ. The author has John spend some of his early time with the Essenes but leaves when the Lord begins to prepare him for his time of ministry.

Lesson #5: Nicodemus and the Temple Cleansing
Chapters #10. Contrasts and Contradictions
#11. A Den of Thieves

"The Buyers and Sellers Driven Out of the Temple" by Gustave Doré

Review

Chapter 10 is an historical interlude which gives an accurate description of the political climate in the early first century in Judea and Galilee. The transition from Herodian rule in Judea to the system of Procurators is outlined. The depravity of Herod the Great's son Antipas is clearly described. The High Priest becomes a puppet of Rome, appointed by Rome and filled with vice and corruption. Immorality becomes the order of the day.

Chapter 11 begins with Nicodemus content to be a farmer in Ein Karem. He builds several olive presses (gat shmanim or Gethsemane). Joseph of Arimathea visits and invites him to become a "Pharisee from love", one of the various sub-sects within Phariseaism. He accepts and over a meal they discuss the new High Priest: Joseph Caiaphas. The make-up of the Sanhedrin is described; Pharisees made up the majority with Sadducees, the vocal and derisive minority. Caiaphas interestingly was a Sadducee.

John the Baptist has raised eyebrows in the Sanhedrin and his condemnation of political and religious indiscretions has not endeared him to those in high positions. Joseph and Nicodemus discuss visiting the Baptist to see if he is Nicodemus childhood friend.

On Preparation Day before Passover, as Gentile Proselytes are trying to pray in their court, Nicodemus and Gamaliel observe the chaos of animals filling the Gentile court while priests try to sweep the court of any leaven.

Into this chaotic scene the prophet from Galilee, Yeshua, enters and forcibly removes animals, money changers and attendants. The henchmen of Annas confront him over his authority but he quickly dismisses their foolish objection.

239

Study
Context

Describe in one sentence the geopolitical and religious circumstance regarding...

1. The High Priesthood

_____

2. The Roman rule

_____

3. Corruption

_____

4. Morality

_____

Read John 2:12-22 Yeshua cleanses the Temple

The timing of this event is not agreed upon by all Biblical scholars. Some believe that there was only one cleansing by Yeshua and that it took place on Monday of Holy Week. They believe John has placed it here thematically and not chronologically. Others believe Jesus cleansed the Temple twice, once at the outset of his ministry and again at the end. The author believes the latter.

1. Why were the animals in the Temple courts?

2. On the presence of the money-changers and their offenses

A. E. Vol. 1 p. 367-372

A month before the feast (on the 15th Adar) bridges and roads were put in repair, and sepulchres whitened, to prevent accidental pollution to the pilgrims. Then, some would select this out of the three great annual feasts for the tithing of their flocks and herds, which, in such case, had to be done two weeks before the Passover;

...This Temple-tribute had to be paid in exact half-shekels of the Sanctuary, or ordinary Galilean shekels. When it is remembered that, besides strictly Palestinian silver and especially copper coin, Persian, Tyrian, Syrian, Egyptian, Grecian, and Roman money circulated in the country, it will be understood what work these 'money-changers' must have had. From the 15th to the 25th Adar they had stalls in every country-town. On the latter date, which must therefore be considered as marking the first arrivals of festive pilgrims in the city, the stalls in the country were closed, and the money-changers henceforth sat within the precincts of the Temple.

...We can picture to ourselves the scene around the table of an Eastern money-changer – the weighing of the coins, deductions for loss of weight, arguing, disputing, bargaining - and we can realize the terrible truthfulness of our Lord's charge that they had made the Father's House a mart and place of traffic. But even so, the business of the Temple money-changers would not be exhausted. Through their hands would pass the immense votive offerings of foreign Jews, or of proselytes, to the Temple; indeed, they probably transacted all business matters connected with the Sanctuary.

...there can be little doubt, that this market was what in Rabbinic writings is styled 'the Bazaars of the sons of Annas' (Chanuyoth beney Chanan), the sons of that High-Priest Annas, who is so infamous in New Testament history.

...Of the avarice and corruption of this High-Priestly family, alike Josephus and the Rabbis give a most terrible picture. Josephus describes Annas (or Ananus), the son of the Annas of the New Testament, as 'a great hoarder up of money,' very rich, and as despoiling by open violence the common priests of their official revenues.

...It would be easy to add from Rabbinic sources repulsive details of their luxuriousness, wastefulness, gluttony, and general dissoluteness. No wonder that, in the figurative language of the Talmud, the Temple is represented as crying out against them: 'Gohence, ye sons of Eli, ye defile the Temple of Jehovah!'

Yeshua demonstrates the moral equivalent of "righteous anger!" We can conclude that anger is not always sinful and here it most certainly is not. What makes this circumstance unique from a moral perspective?

3. The disciples remember this incident after Yeshua's resurrection. This is mentioned in vs 17, 22. What are the two specific aspects they remember about this event?

4. Remembering the context of Passover Preparation Day, connect the Messianic aspect of Passover with Yeshua's reaction to what he observes in the Temple. Discuss.

Facts
1. The paradox that was Jerusalem is described in Chapter 10. All of this is historical fact, from the influence of Hellenism, Roman domination and manipulation of the Sanhedrin. The political world shifts from the Herodian rule to Rome appointed Procurators in Judea while Antipas, son of Herod the Great remains in control of Galilee for the next 43 years.
2. Gethsemane is often referred to as The Garden of Gethsemane but Scripture never refers to it in those terms. A Gethsemane is an anglicizing of the Hebrew expression for "olive press": "Gat Shmanim" These were not always owned by every grower of olives. A Gethsemane protected from the elements on the Mt. of Olives may well have been where the disciples and Yeshua spent Holy Week.
3. The official meeting place of the Sanhedrin was a room on the

northern side of the Temple court called "The Hall of Hewn Stones." It was a windowless room where all official meetings of the Council of 71 were to take place.

4. Most historians feel the Sanhedrin or Council had a membership of 71. The President or Nasi presided and had great power. The "av bet din" or vice president ruled in his absence. Joseph Caiaphas had just been appointed as High Priest and Nasi. Caiaphas was also a Sadducee. The ruthlessness and corruption of Caiaphas and Annas is well documented.

Fiction

1. Nicodemus investigation of John the Baptist is added for dramatic effect, to heighten the curiosity of Nicodemus, and to connect to his conversation with Zechariah at the outset of the book.

Embellishment

1. It is not known when Joseph of Arimathea and Nicodemus came to know each other. The author brings the two together under the umbrella as Pharisees in this chapter. We first met him in Chapter 8 when Nicodemus is introduced to him by Gamaliel. These two must have been kindred spirits as they are the only two we know for sure were followers of Yeshua while still in the Sanhedrin.

2. Yeshua's presence at Passover is well documented. Whether this cleansing of the Temple took place at the outset of his ministry or during Holy Week is a matter of much discussion. It is not known beyond a shadow of a doubt that there were two cleansings by Yeshua or just one. Much of the discussion revolves around whether one takes John's Gospel to be chronological or topical, especially his early chapters.

Lesson #6: Nicodemus Meets the Baptist and Yeshua
Chapters #12. A Voice
#13. Born Again

"John the Baptist Preaching in the Wilderness" by Gustave Doré

Review

After the cleansing of the Temple, Yeshua remains in Jerusalem for Passover and performs many miraculous signs according to John 2:23. The miracles create quite a stir and get the attention of all in Jerusalem.

Nicodemus leaves Jerusalem in search of the Baptist. He finally finds him along the Jordan at the springs of Aenon on the border with Galilee. This is historically true according to John 3:23 although this is not where Yeshua is baptized by John. This took place earlier at Bethany on the other side of the Jordan.

Nicodemus discovers the Baptist is in fact his childhood friend John. John tells him that he has spent ten years in the desert of Judea before the Lord called him. John also reveals that John and Andrew were his disciples but have been sent back to Galilee to await the Messiah's call. This could have been exactly what did happen as we find Andrew fishing in Galilee with Peter in Luke 5 and John has been arrested by then.

John introduces Nicodemus to a man named James who will connect him with Yeshua's disciple John. This is the same John who is now a follower of Yeshua.

As Chapter 13 begins Nicodemus and James have returned to Jerusalem and meet John who will introduce Nicodemus to Yeshua the next evening just before Sabbath. He returns to the family home and discusses his upcoming visit with Yeshua, with his father, and Joseph of Arimathea.

The next evening Nicodemus, watched by followers of Yeshua, is taken by John from the Temple to the home of John where Yeshua is sharing a Sabbath meal with others.

A typical Jewish home of the day would have had an outside stairs to the roof where families would eat and relax in the cool of the evening.

The conversation between Yeshua and Nicodemus is recorded—at least in part—in John 3:1-22. The possible thoughts of Nicodemus during this conversation are described as the chapter closes.

Study
Read Matthew 3:1-12 John the Baptist
A. E. Vol. 1 p. 391,393 On John and where he baptized.

Never before had such deep earnestness and reality been witnessed, such devotedness, such humility and self-abnegation, and all in that great cause which set every Jewish heart on fire. And then, in the high-day of his power, when all men had gathered around him and hung on his lips; when all wondered whether he would announce himself as the Christ, or, at least, as His Forerunner, or as one of the great Prophets; when a word from him would have kindled that multitude into a frenzy of enthusiasm -he had disclaimed everything for himself, and pointed to Another! ...John baptized at Ænon (the springs), near to Salim. The latter site has not been identified. But the oldest tradition, which places it a few miles to the south of Bethshean (Scythopolis), on the border of Samaria and Galilee, the next event was John's imprisonment by Herod. This strange suggestion is made by Godet has this in its favour, that it locates the scene of John's last public work close to the seat of Herod Antipas, into whose power the Baptist was so soon to be delivered. But already there were causes at work to remove both Jesus and His Forerunner from their present spheres of activity. As regards Christ, we have the express statement, that the machinations of the Pharisaic party in Jerusalem led Him to withdraw into Galilee.

1. John's message and ministry is prophesied in Isaiah 40:3 How does repentance in John's Baptism connect with Gabriel's words to his father Zechariah that John will *"make ready a people prepared for the Lord."* Luke 1:17

There is much discussion out there about John's Baptism and Christian Baptism. How are they similar? Different?

Read John 3:1-21

1. Why does Nicodemus seem nervous and tentative?

2. What is the nature of his opening statement?

The author sees this conversation as a struggle between the earthly and spiritual planes. Comment.

3. Characterize Nicodemus response to Yeshua's challenge that he must be "born again?"

4. In many ways Jewish teachers had turned God's saving activity into a series of laws and regulations as if man entered the kingdom by proving himself worthy. Jesus next statement undercuts this corruption of God's Word. How? Vs. 5-8

5. Imagine a learned Pharisee and member of the Sanhedrin asking "How?" It is the equivalent of a PhD. saying "I don't understand!" in regard to the simplest of truths in his own field. Yeshua responds to this curious, humble man, willing to say, "How". He concludes by personalizing the Gospel and challenging Nicodemus at the same time. In what state do you think this left Nicodemus?

6. What is ironic about Yeshua's use of "light" as an illustration?

7. Any final thoughts on the ebb and flow of this conversation?

Facts
1. John did baptize at the Springs of Aenon

Fiction
1. Nicodemus visits John the Baptist near the springs of Aenon. We do know from Scripture that Priests and Levites did investigate John the Baptist (John1:19ff) but this was earlier while John was still located in Bethany beyond Jordan. He has now shifted to the Springs of Aenon near the border with Galilee. But Nicodemus' visit is an addition to add to Nicodemus search for truth.

Embellishment
1. Nicodemus meets with Yeshua in Jerusalem. This is fact. How he came to meet him is unknown. The author adds that he came by referral through one of John the Baptist's disciples called James who connects him to a former disciple called John who is now a disciple of Yeshua.

The conversation follows the text from John 3 with some additional thoughts running through the mind of Nicodemus. The depth of Yeshua's spiritual teaching compared to the legalistic mindset of Nicodemus is highlighted.

Lesson #7: Nicodemus at Sychar and with Jairus
Chapters #14. Living Water
#15. Doubt
#16. Believe

"Jesus Raising Up the Daughter of Jairus" by Gustave Doré

Review

As Chapter 14 begins Nicodemus is walking back to his home in Jerusalem. His father and Joseph are awaiting him, and he discusses his conversation with Yeshua. Nicodemus reflects on the similarity between Jn 3:16 and Genesis 15. Joseph and Nicodemus decide to trail Yeshua and his disciples. They finally find them outside Sychar in the middle of Samaria near Shechem. They are barely within hearing distance as Yeshua and a woman talk at the ancient well of Jacob. Again, Nicodemus hears Yeshua elevate the conversation from the mundane to the divine.

It is unclear whether Samaritans still worshiped on Mt. Gerizim but most likely not. Some historians claim that the Romans had rebuilt it as a worship site of a pagan deity. It is here, in Samaria, that Yeshua says plainly, "I am the Messiah."

In Chapter 15 the woman reacts to Yeshua's words, *"I who speak to you am he!"* John 4:26 She races back to town, leaving her containers and her donkey. Then the disciples return and as the crowd approaches led by the woman, Yeshua proclaims, *"Open your eyes and look at the fields. They are ripe for harvest."* John 4:35 Yeshua spends the next two days in Sychar teaching and healing Samaritans. What a cross cultural experience for the mostly Galilean disciples! This is recorded in John 4:40.

Joseph and Nicodemus walk back to Jerusalem and the farther they are removed from Yeshua; the more Nicodemus begins to doubt.

Chapter 16 begins several months later with news that the Baptist has been arrested and put in the prison in Machaerus. Through Gamaliel's influence, Nicodemus and Joseph are appointed by Caiaphas to confirm the Baptist's arrest and to investigate the Galilean Yeshua by speaking to Jairus the Capernaum synagogue Rabbi.

They arrive in Machaerus, have audience with Antipas who is in the palace and spend time with the Baptist. Again, Nicodemus is encouraged to "just believe" and come into the light.

The Biblical event of the raising of the daughter of Jairus follows as the reader experiences it through the eyes of Jairus' guests: Nicodemus and Joseph of Arimathea. It is an emotionally moving and highly charged experience for both and confirms Joseph's faith that Yeshua is indeed Messiah!

Study
Read John 4:1-43 The Woman at the well at Sychar
A. E. Vol. 1 p. 405,406 At the well of Jacob

And it was, as we judge, the evening of a day in early summer, when Jesus, accompanied by the small band which formed His disciples, emerged into the rich Plain of Samaria. Far as the eye could sweep, 'the fields' were 'already white unto the harvest.'

...Probably John remained with the Master. They would scarcely have left Him alone, especially in that place; and the whole narrative reads like that of one who had been present at what passed.

1. Vs. 4 indicates something has been leading Yeshua to this place. It is not merely logistical as they had been in Galilee and returned there afterward. Discuss the probability that the covenant connection to this well and the Father's desire to complete it in Yeshua explains the strange wording that Yeshua *"had to go through Samaria."*

2. In the conversation between Yeshua and the woman note the number of noted differences between the two.
        a. Cultural
        b. Drawing implements
        c. Type of water
        d. Personal life
        e. Worship locations
        f. Identity of Yeshua
Which one is the most dramatic for you?

3. The next two days must have been an epiphany time for the disciples

How did the response of these Samaritans to Yeshua differ from those in Galilee and Judea? Why such a different response?

Read Luke 8:40-56 Raising of the daughter of Jairus

1. Yeshua is on his way to the home of Jairus when word comes that his daughter has died. Again, Nicodemus hears the words, ***"Don't be afraid, just believe..."*** Luke 8:50 from Yeshua's lips. This time it is said in the face of death. Discuss the saying, "Faith walks the path when nothing else can pass."

2. The story is told very matter-of-factly. It is anything but this. It was an astoundingly personal miracle. Many of us have experienced the untimely death of someone taken very young. Describe the impact on the various individuals present: parents, the girl, the disciples, the mockers.

Facts

1. After the conversation between Nicodemus and Yeshua, Yeshua and his disciples do indeed leave for the Judean countryside as noted in John 3:22
2. The well at Sychar is indeed the well Jacob dug for his herds and the location exists to this day.
3. Shechem is a place of significant history for which the Jews even named one of the gates that lead north to this first capital of Israel. The roads that passed by are accurately described.

4. There were two wells near Sychar. The well on the north side was used by most as it was closer to the city. This provides some insight into the social standing of this woman.

5. Yeshua does in fact remain in Sychar for several days performing miracles and teaching. This is recorded in John 3:39-42.

6. The arrest of John the Baptist is faithfully described in Chapter 16. John the Baptist spends his final days at the Machaerus prison. The remote nature of this palace of Antipas and the geography is faithfully described.

7. The raising of the daughter of Jairus is described faithfully as it took place and is recorded in Luke 8:40-56

Fiction

1. It is unknown how Nicodemus reacted to the very challenging conversation he had with Yeshua. Yeshua's closing comments about light, it is assumed, bothered Nicodemus. The author carries this concept of coming into the light into future conversations. Since we know that it is only by exposure to the Word and Yeshua that change comes, the author runs with this concept and makes this the driving force in Nicodemus future experiences.

2. It is unknown if Nicodemus responds immediately to his conversation. The author sends him to follow Yeshua and they finally find him near Shechem.

3. Yeshua most likely did not interact with Nicodemus at this well. There is no indication that Nicodemus was there from Scripture. This is the author's addition.

4. We are not told if anyone except for John the Baptist's disciples visited John in Machaerus.

5. Nicodemus visit to Jairus is not included in Scripture if it indeed took place

Embellishment

1. The woman's statement about the proper place to worship is usually interpreted as a intentional distraction from Yeshua's probing statement about her "husbands." The author however believes her response is rather a genuine interest in seeking the proper place to obtain the water he describes.

2. Nicodemus hesitancy to respond to the miraculous events in Sychar is intentional by the author. The deep-rooted legalism and instruction Nicodemus has had over many years does not loosen its grip immediately. Eventually it will be Yeshua's connection to the Feast of Tabernacles that will finally penetrate his heart.

3. It is unknown where Zacchaeus first met Yeshua. He may have heard of and listened to Yeshua before the incident described in Luke 19. The author leans in this direction and even makes Zacchaeus a follower whom Nicodemus and Joseph meet in Jericho on their way to visit John the Baptist.

Lesson #8: Nicodemus at Tabernacles
Chapter #17. Sukkot

Review

Nicodemus and Joseph return to Jerusalem and discuss the events of the last week and how they will report to Caiaphas. On the way back to Jerusalem they stop and visit with Mary, Martha and Lazarus in Bethany.

Nicodemus returns to Ein Karem to prepare the harvest which will coincide with the fall festival of Sukkot or Tabernacles.

The seven-day festival commemorates the 40 years in the desert when God's people lived in tents. The tradition of the "lulavim" is described. Each day the people would carry a citron and a cluster of olive, palm and myrtle branches to the temple while priests carried the wine and water as drink offerings. The water was brought from the Pool of Siloam as it was "living water."

The significant events in history that took place on Tabernacles were: 1. Solomon's Temple dedication 2. The Maccabean Revolt 160 years earlier. This heightened the celebration and deepened its meaning to the people.

The four huge Menorah in the Court of Women would be lit on the last day of Tabernacles at nightfall. On this last day of the Feast, there was an intensity seldom seen in the Temple, even on Passover. A procession led by the High Priest carried the living water from the Pool into the Temple. To song and recitation of Psalms, the water would be poured into the silver flutes on the Great Altar.

As the water is poured, there is a time of quiet during which Yeshua stands and declares words fitting for the occasion and his person: *"If anyone is thirsty, let him come to me and drink. Whoever believes in me, as the Scripture has said, streamsof living water will flow within him."* John 7:37

The author adds a touch of emotion by placing the woman and the Samaritans from Sychar to this scene who then declare Yeshua to be Messiah. This is entirely plausible as Yeshua had been teaching them for two days and directed them to Jerusalem as the place to worship rightly. What an event of celebration this must have been to witness!

Study
Read Leviticus 23:33-44 The Festival of Tabernacles
1. The Offerings and Priests
A. E. Vol. 2 p. 156

The celebration of the Feast corresponded to its great meaning. Not only did all the priestly families minister during that week, but it has been calculated that no fewer than 446 Priests, with, of course, a corresponding number of Levites, were required for its sacrificial worship. In general, the services were the same every day, except that the number of bullocks offered decreased daily.

The "lulavim"
A.E. Vol. 2 p. 157

Let us suppose ourselves in the number of worshippers, who on 'the last, the Great Day of the Feast,' are leaving their 'booths' at daybreak to take part in the service. The pilgrims are all in festive array. In his right hand each carries what is called the Lulabh, which, although properly meaning 'a branch,' or 'palm-branch,' consisted of a myrtle and willow-branch tied together with a palm-branch between them. This was supposed to be in fulfilment of the command, Lev. xxiii. 40. 'The fruit (A.V. 'boughs') of the goodly trees,' mentioned in the same verse of Scripture, was supposed to be the Ethrog, the so-called Paradise-apple (according to Ber. R. 15, the fruit of the forbidden tree), a species of citron.

3. The Procession
A.E. Vol. 2 p. 158-9

When the Temple-procession had reached the Pool of Siloam, the Priest filled his golden pitcher from its waters. Then they went back to the Temple, so timing it, that they should arrive just as they were laying the pieces of the sacrifice on the great Altar of Burnt-offering, towards the close of the ordinary Morning-

Sacrifice service. A threefold blast of the Priests' trumpet welcomed the arrival of the Priest, as he entered through the 'Water-gate,' which obtained its name from this ceremony, and passed straight into the Court of the Priests. Here he was joined by another Priest, who carried the wine for the drink-offering. The two Priests ascended 'the rise' of the altar, and turned to the left. There were two silver funnels here, with narrow openings, leading down to the base of the altar. Into that at the east, which was somewhat wider, the wine was poured, and, at the same time, the water into the western and narrower opening, the people shouting to the Priest to raise his hand, so as to make sure that he poured the water into the funnel. For, although it was held, that the water-pouring was an ordinance instituted by Moses, 'a Halakhah of Moses from Sinai,' this was another of the points disputed by the Sadducees. And, indeed, to give practical effect to their views, the High-Priest Alexander Jannæus had on one occasion poured the water on the ground, when he was nearly murdered, and in the riot, that ensued, six thousand persons were killed in the Temple.

Immediately after 'the pouring of water,' the great 'Hallel,' consisting of Psalms cxiii. To cxviii. (inclusive), was chanted antiphonally, or rather, with responses, to the accompaniment of the flute. As the Levites intoned the first line of each Psalm, the people repeated it; while to each of the other lines they responded by Hallelu Yah ('Praise ye the Lord'). But in Psalm cxviii. The people not only repeated the first line, 'O give thanks to the Lord,' but also these, 'O then, work now salvation, Jehovah,' 'O Lord, send now prosperity;' and again, at the close of the Psalm, 'O give thanks to the Lord.' As they repeated these lines, they shook towards the altar the Lulabh Except on a Sabbath, and on the first day of the Feast. On these occasions it had been provided the day before. which they held in their hands - as if with this token of the past to express the reality and cause of their praise, and to remind God of His promises. It is this moment which should be chiefly kept in view.

4. Discuss the depth of this Festival.

Read John 7:37-44 Yeshua at the Feast of Tabernacles
Note the specific timing of Yeshua's words given the people's attention on sin, redemption and the living water.
1. Just before Yeshua's words, the Assembly had chanted responsively Psalm 113-118. Note the key closing words intoned by the Levites in Psalm 118:22-29. Discuss.
These verses point to the Messiah. In a few words describe each reference

Vs. 22_____

Vs. 25_____

Vs. 27_____

2. In Yeshua's words we see a very early reference to the Pentecost outpouring. Describe.

3. What are the various reactions to Yeshua's words?

Facts
1. The Feast of Tabernacles with its significant connection to living water and the "lulavim" is accurately depicted in Chapter 17. The historical significance of this event directed the people's attention back in time to both their time in the wilderness as well as the events that led to the construction of the four great Menorah in the Court of Women.
2. It is at this Feast that Yeshua makes a bold statement in John 7:37-44 referring to himself as the source of "living water."

Fiction

1. The presence of the Samaritans is not in Scripture and is the author's addition. They are added to enhance the tension among the Chief Priests and Sanhedrin. Certainly, it is plausible for them to follow Yeshua's direction to worship in Jerusalem and not at Gerizim.

2. It is this Feast combined with Yeshua's claim to be the source of living water that finally convinces Nicodemus that Yeshua is the long-awaited Messiah.

Embellishment

1. The drama that is involved in the celebration and Yeshua's presence while not specifically noted would seem to be the natural. The addition of the Samaritans from Sychar only enhances the drama.

Lesson #9: Nicodemus and the Woman Caught in Adultery
Chapter #18. Dust

"Jesus and the Woman Taken in Adultery" by Gustave Doré

Review

As Chapter 18 opens, the men—Nicodemus, Joseph of Arimathea, Benjamin and Gamaliel—are discussing the stunning words of Yeshua in the Temple on Sukkot. The bold convincing words of Yeshua connecting himself to Tabernacles convinced Nicodemus. How fitting that the Word in flesh proclaiming in word that he is the living water finally changes Nicodemus heart from skeptic to believer. In humility he confesses this before the other men.

At the convening of the Jewish Council, we see the second Biblical reference to the person: Nicodemus. Jn. 7:51 Caiaphas reveals his plot to arrest Yeshua as the temple guards confess their reluctance to follow through with their orders. This is accurately described in Jn. 7:45ff

Chaos follows and leads to the next incident described: the woman caught in adultery described in John 8:2ff. The event actually took place at dawn the next morning, but the author pushes them together for emphasis.

The motivation of the Pharisees and Teachers of the Law is highly suspect. Their interest in justice is just a façade as they have neglected to secure any witness and have not brought the alleged guilty man. These two facts are blatantly disregarded by Yeshua's opponents and signal their hypocrisy. The incident has been manufactured with the real intent of trapping Yeshua.

Yeshua offers no reply to the charge against this woman; instead he kneels and draws in the dust on the pavement stones left by the worshipers at Tabernacles.

The author presents a plausible explanation for this gesture on the ground by Yeshua. He sees an application of the Jewish teacher's technique of "Remez." This would have been known to the Teachers of the Law; it also explains the dramatic departure of the eldest first who would have understood exactly what Yeshua was doing. The author sees a reference to Jeremiah 17:13 where the prophet warns those who have rejected the Lord as the spring of living water. This may have been Yeshua's reference to the just concluded Festival incident.

Yeshua confronts the hypocrisy of these men with His words recorded in John 8:7. Yeshua then shows grace and forgiveness to the woman—which only the Lord himself can do. The author presents the woman as a pawn in this scheme.

Study

Read Jeremiah 17:5-18 Cursed is the one who trusts in man, blessed is the one who trusts in the Lord

1. A well-known section of Jeremiah and memorized by Teachers of the Law.

Parallel words in Psalm 1. Read for emphasis.

Vs. 5 Unbelief is characterized as the shifting of confidence from the Lord to oneself.

How was this evident among the enemies of Yeshua?

Vs. 6 Reference to the poisonous fruit of the Agar tree. It looks appealing outwardly but is both empty and filled with fibrous poison.

Vs. 7 Contrasted is the Acacia tree known as "The Bedouin's friend." It has a long tap root so it can withstand drought. It provides shade and highly nutritious food for camels and goats.

Note all the applicable references to the motivation of those standing before Yeshua: corrupt, selfish, known to God.

Vs. 13 The plausible reference of Yeshua with just a gesture. "written in the dust" opposite of "written in the Book of Life"

What aspect of Yeshua's response is particularly appealing to you?

Read John 8:1-11 The woman caught in adultery
Vs. 1-4 What is missing?

Vs. 6 John exposes their motivation
Explain the nature of the trap.

Vs. 7, 8 Twice Yeshua stoops to draw in the dust, pointing to his action as his response to their question.

Vs. 9 *"Older ones first"* - Most likely the teachers of the Law. They would have been more knowledgeable. Highly likely they are responding to the combination of Yeshua's words and actions. It is clear they drew a conclusion from Yeshua's response.

VS. 11 Explain Yeshua's release of the woman from condemnation.

Facts

1. The meeting of the Sanhedrin seems to be implied as a response to the words of Yeshua at the Feast of Tabernacles. This is mentioned in John 7:45-52. In this meeting we see the second mention of Nicodemus in Scripture as he stands to object to the condemnation of Yeshua without a hearing. This demonstrates some willingness on Nicodemus part to stand and be counted for Yeshua.

2. The order to arrest Yeshua is mentioned also in John 7. This would have had to have come from Caiaphas. This is a startling development in the opposition to Yeshua in the Council, which up until this event has been unofficial.

Fiction

1. It is unknown if Nicodemus was present for this event. However, he was present at the meeting the previous day and seems logical that he would have been there the next day.

Embellishment

1. Nicodemus finally connects Yeshua to the prophesies that he knows so well from Jeremiah 2:13 and Isaiah 29:14, 19. He is embarrassed at how foolish he feels not having seen the obvious nature of Yeshua as fulfilling Scripture before his very eyes.

2. The arrest of the woman "caught in adultery" follows immediately. While her presentation to Yeshua is recorded in John 8:1ff, many manuscripts do not record this incident. As it is included as John 8:1-11, and we have no doubt it did indeed happen, the incident states it took place the next morning after the conclusion of the Feast of Tabernacles.

3. It is the author's feeling that the reason Yeshua "drew in the dust" is an act of "REMEZ" and connected to Jeremiah 17:13 and links Yeshua's reference to himself as the source of "living water" rejected by these same teachers of the law and Pharisees (most likely all Sanhedrin members or their operatives). This

interpretation is mentioned by Ray Vander Laan in his teaching series "That the World May Know." It seems sensible as it connects the tradition of "REMEZ" in discussions between a learned Rabbi and his students as well as the events of the previous day. It also explains why the older men are the first to leave after Yeshua's challenge in John 8:7. They would have been the most experienced at the technique and meaning behind Yeshua's actions.

Lesson #10: Nicodemus and Lazarus
Chapter #19. Lazarus
#20. Kill

"Resurrection of Lazarus" by Gustave Doré

Review

As Chapter 19 opens Nicodemus is reflecting on the incident in the temple and how Yeshua had restored the dignity of the woman and very deftly corrected and admonished his enemies. The new-found faith of Nicodemus motivates him to spend time following Yeshua everywhere. He even brings his family along. He reasoned that his sons were learning more about God by listening to Yeshua than they would in the best Beth Sepher.

A few months before Passover, Yeshua takes his Talmidim into Perea alone. Nicodemus stops at the home of Mary, Martha and Lazarus. Lazarus is ill so Mary and Martha send for Yeshua. Late that evening Lazarus worsens and dies. The death of Lazarus devastates the sisters. They regret not sending for Yeshua sooner.

Joseph is asked to speak at the funeral the next day and he focuses on Psalm 34:18,19. Lazarus is laid in the family burial tomb, having earlier been carved by Lazarus own hands. He was wrapped in strips of cloth, a burial shroud and a cloth covering his face. The next three days are the toughest for the sisters. Many come from Jerusalem to comfort them.

Word reaches the house that Yeshua is on the way. He meets Martha first on the road and encourages her. John 11:25, 26. Nicodemus sees the similarity in Yeshua's words to how Yeshua spoke to him in John 3:16. Martha runs to tell Mary and they both return and fall at his feet. Yeshua asks them where Lazarus has been laid. They enter the garden familiar to Yeshua as he has spent many a restful hour with the family here. He is overcome with grief and weeps.

Yeshua prays to His father and asks the men to remove the stone. He calls Lazarus to come out. To the shock of all, Lazarus moves slowly out of the niche and to the entrance. Quickly the men, who laid him in the tomb, unbind him. The family rejoices beyond measure. Laughter, song, and praise continue into the night.

Chapter 20 begins with Nicodemus noticing that a number of Yeshua's opponents, who witnessed Lazarus resurrection, have left for the city. A meeting of the Sanhedrin follows, and Caiaphas utters the prophetic words of John 11:50 and an open plot to kill Yeshua comes into the open.

Nicodemus returns home and contemplates how Yeshua will reveal himself as Messiah at the upcoming Passover.

Study
Read John 11:1-57 The Raising of Lazarus

1. Vs. 4 Shows Yeshua knows our days

2. Vs. 15 The reasons behind Yeshua allowing Lazarus to die. One person's misfortune may present a benefit to another.

3. Vs. 25, 26 A key verse in Yeshua's lesson for the sisters Yeshua = Life and Resurrection.

What does this sentence mean?

4. Vs. 35 Shortest verse in Scripture that aptly identifies Yeshua as our brother. Not sobbing but quiet tears.

5. Vs. 43, 44 A more dramatic scene I cannot imagine

6. Vs. 45 Will later be reported by some to the Sanhedrin

7. Vs. 48 The pompous, self-serving, prideful, motivation of Yeshua's opponents.

A.E. Vol. II p. 308 The Raising of Lazarus

The raising of Lazarus marks the highest point (not in the Manifestation, but) in the ministry of our Lord; it is the climax in a history where all is miraculous - the Person, the Life, the Words, the Work. As regards Himself, we have here the fullest evidence alike of His Divinity and Humanity; as regards those who witnessed it, the highest manifestation of faith and of unbelief. Here, on this height, the two ways finally meet and part. And from this high point - not only from the resolution of the Sanhedrists, butfrom the raising of Lazarus - we have our first clear outlook on the Death and Resurrection of Christ, of which the raising of Lazarus was the typical prelude. From this height, also, have we an outlook upon the gathering of the Church at His empty Tomb, where the precious words spoken at the grave of Lazarus received their full meaning - till Death shall be no more.

8. There are many great and powerful lessons on the divinity and humanity of Yeshua in this account. Is there one word, verse or truth that stands out for you?

Facts

1. The death and resurrection of Lazarus is recorded in John 11:1-57

2. The resurrection of Lazarus is told in the Chapter 19 with great accuracy and very little embellishment. It is simply told from the viewpoint of one who could have been there.

3. The burial of Lazarus is not recorded but we do know that tradition held that Jewish burials were to be conducted the same day as the death. (A.E. Vol. #2 p. 311) The tomb was most likely just as described as well as the burial cloths. It was also traditional for men to conduct the burial with woman approaching the tomb separately.

4. As Lazarus exits the tomb, Yeshua tells those in charge *"Take off the grave clothes and let him go."* John 11:44 This indicates that Lazarus must have been bound in the traditional way at death, with strips of cloth in addition to a long shroud.

5. John 11:46, 47 mentions the presence of some who report this miracle to the Sanhedrin Pharisees and a meeting is called to discuss the "problem of Yeshua." It is at this meeting that Caiaphas utters those famous prophetic words of Jn. 11:50

Fiction
1. Nicodemus may have witnessed the resurrection of Lazarus, but his presence is not recorded in Scripture.
2. We don't know how much the followers of Yeshua discussed how he would announce his Messianic plans. In fact, most of the disciples seemed oblivious to the reality of Yeshua's suffering and death even though he spoke of it with increasing regularity during the last months before Passover. There may have been others who discussed these things on the scholarly level as there are plenty of references to the suffering and death of Yeshua in the Old Testament and certainly learned followers of Yeshua such as Nicodemus and Joseph would have known these references very well. How much they thought and discussed these issues is completely unknown.

Embellishment
1. The reference on p. 155 to Yeshua using the son of Nicodemus for his teaching on becoming like children is enhancement although the incident did take place, most likely not with the son of Nicodemus. It is recorded in Matthew 18:2-4
2. Joseph of Arimathea's devotion based on Psalm 34 is fiction but it is based on the tradition in Jewish funerals for there to be such an address.
3. The meeting of the Sanhedrin was most likely extremely tense and chaotic. The author enhances the meeting with a confrontation between the Sanhedrin haters of Yeshua and Nicodemus and Joseph.
4. Passover was believed, at the time, to be the time when Messiah would reveal himself. There had been false Christs who had appeared and disappointed. This desire and tradition for a Messiah was well known to the Romans and special divisions were brought into Jerusalem just for Passover. The author has Joseph and Nicodemus discuss Yeshua's death briefly.

Lesson #11: Nicodemus on Palm Sunday
Chapter #21 Hosanna

"Entry of Jesus Into Jerusalem" *by Gustave Doré*

Review

As Passover approached, the Roman presence in Jerusalem increased, heightening the longing of the people for freedom. The history of the Maccabean Revolt under Judah Maccabee contributed to the kind of freedom the people desired.

Joseph and Nicodemus discuss the real freedom God's people needed and Scripture prophesied. The qualities of peace not revolution are cited in Micah and Isaiah. This discussion is given voice to how great a revelation we have in the New Testament that now is assumed in the Church. But in Israel at the time of Yeshua, it was hidden. There could have been those who longed for spiritual deliverance, mercy and forgiveness in the coming of Messiah. We certainly see this elevated in the songs of Mary, Elizabeth, Zechariah and Simeon.

As Nicodemus walks to Jerusalem on the 25th of Adar (the last month of the Jewish calendar) with his family, he reminisces about those same walks as a boy in the company of Zechariah.

On the 8th of Nisan Lazarus arrives at Nicodemus' home to report that Yeshua is in Jericho at the home of Zacchaeus.

The author places Nicodemus and Joseph on the road from Bethany to welcome Yeshua. Many who had camped in the Kidron Valley join them as they meet Yeshua at Bethphage. The initial descent from the Mt of Olives by the assembly with Yeshua leading the procession on a donkey is met with shouts of praise. Olivet blocks the view of Jerusalem for a time and the crowd notices Lazarus in the group that his followed Yeshua from Bethany. At the crest of the hill Yeshua begins to sob as he is the first to catch a view of the Holy City. The crowd swells with more words of praise for Yeshua as the city of Jerusalem and key residences and palaces come into view one by one.

The throng of people and the commotion is noticed by Annas who remarks *"Look how the whole world has gone after him."* John 12:19

Study

Read John 12:12-19 Triumphal Entry/Palm Sunday/Lamb Selection Day

1. Compare the aspects of the people's shouts with their expectations

2. John mentions the missed emphasis by the disciples Vs. 16

3. Those that witnessed Lazarus resurrection were in the crowd. This confirms that therewere believers and followers of Yeshua present besides the disciples

Read Matthew 21:1-11 Triumphal Entry

1. Matthew adds the story of the colt and the prophesy from Zechariah 9:9

2. He also mentions in detail how the people honored Yeshua as King. Vs. 5

Read Mark 11:1-10 The Triumphal Entry

Mark gives the briefest account of the Entry into Jerusalem

Read Luke 19:28-44 Triumphal Entry

1. Pharisees who were enemies of Yeshua are also mentioned as present. They tell Yeshua to caution the crowd. What historical basis do they use as an excuse?

274

Reflect on the statement: "Praise often defies fear and logic!"

2. Only Luke mentions Yeshua pausing to weep over the city. This type of weeping means "to sob audibly!" As Luke concludes the triumphal entry here, no mention is made of anyone noticing or responding. Certainly this would have been noticed as all focus was on Yeshua!
Given that this day was "Lamb Selection Day" for Passover, how might this have heightened the sadness of Yeshua over the city?

Facts
1. The nature of the promised Messiah should have been obvious to the spiritual leaders of Gods people. Instead it is clouded by the Roman occupation, the focus on the law in the educational system, the Maccabean Revolt of the 2nd Century B.C., the corruption of the Sanhedrin along with the priesthood. The author portrays this in the conversation between Joseph and Nicodemus. Their conversation focuses on the prophesies of Isaiah and Micah.
2. The increase of a Roman presence leading up to Passover is well documented by historians.
3. Jesus arrives in Jerusalem on a Sunday, the 10th of Nisan which would have also been the day that every Jewish family was to select a lamb and bring it into the house.
4. The depiction of Yeshua's arrival in Jerusalem on what we call Palm Sunday is documented realistically and accurately. It would have been natural for the many people from outside Jerusalem, who are camped in the Kidron Valley for Passover week, to welcome Yeshua. Many of these may have even been his supporters from Galilee. Scripture does mention that many who had witnessed the resurrection of Lazarus came out of the city to join the throng. (John 12:12, 17, 18)

5. The procession into Jerusalem is often depicted as one stream of people leaving Bethany like the start of a parade. However, this was most likely not the case as we know a crowd followed him from Bethany along with the disciples and another crowd came out to meet him somewhere around Bethphage where Yeshua obtains the colt to ride on. Alfred Edersheim describes the scene well as the two crowds join together as one. A.E. Vol. 2 pp. 366

6. As the procession descends from the Mt. of Olives, the geography is significant as the various portions of the city come into view one by one. First the Palace of the Maccabees, then the High Priests Palace, various gardens, the house of Herod and finally the Temple itself. Each most likely brought a response from the huge crowd of people. Alfred Edersheim describes the scene well. A.E. Vol 2 pp. 367

Fiction

1. Lazarus arrival in Jerusalem is not mentioned in Scripture.

2. Lazarus presence at the entrance of Yeshua is not mentioned in Scripture.

Embellishment

1. The shouting and praising Yeshua for his miracles is not specifically mentioned in Scripture but it would seem quite natural that many who came for Passover had heard Yeshua before and been healed.

Lesson #12: Nicodemus at the Crucifixion
Chapters #22. Saved
#23. Horror

"The Erection of the Cross" *by Gustave Doré*

Review

As Chapter 22 begins, Palm Sunday has concluded, and Joseph has discovered a plot in the Sanhedrin. It is reported in Scripture that the Sanhedrin had decided to kill Yeshua but not during the feast days out of fear for how the people would respond. John 12:9-11 also reveals that Lazarus was also included in the same plot. The author adds the plan to kidnap Mary and Martha hoping to intimidate Yeshua and drive him out of Israel. The author adds to this that Nicodemus plans to remove Mary, Martha and Lazarus from Bethany and engage Zacchaeus in Jericho to hide them. When they arrive, Zacchaeus recounts for the four of them how Yeshua had visited him just days before. He is quite willing to assist and even help them to escape Judea entirely on a trade route if necessary.

Nicodemus returns for Passover in Jerusalem. Joseph tells him of the events of Monday and Tuesday. The author adds the sons of Nicodemus to the children who sang Hosanna to Yeshua in the Temple. This is recorded in Matthew 21:15

Chapter 23 begins with John the disciple approaching Nicodemus for the use of his house for Yeshua and the disciples on Thursday evening for Passover. The Bible does not specify where Yeshua and the disciples celebrated Passover, but the author coordinates a servant of Nicodemus as the one mentioned in Luke 22:7-13 whom Peter meets carrying a water jar. The author adds John to the scene. Nicodemus' family changes plans and joins the family of Joseph for Passover. Joseph's house is near the Shechem gate. It is a joyous celebration, filled with the anticipation of what Passover might bring.

Word comes early the next morning that Yeshua was arrested near the Gethsemane where they were staying. Word on the street reveals that Yeshua was taken to Pilate's Palace early that morning. Nicodemus and Joseph quickly move to the home of Pilate, anticipating that Yeshua will now reveal himself as Messiah in a powerful way. They discover that Yeshua has been condemned to death by crucifixion. They follow the crowd shocked and despondent. From a distance just outside the Shechem gate, they watch the events unfold. Yeshua willingly extends his hands and feet for the Roman soldier.

The High Priest Caiaphas arrives and objects to the sign Pilate has posted above Yeshua on the cross. The centurion who speaks Aramaic with a Galilean accent confronts him. During the first hour of the crucifixion, Nicodemus notices that Yeshua speaks only about the needs of others: those who crucified him, his mother, and the man crucified next to him.

Darkness covers the land at noon for three hours and brings terror to the superstitious Roman soldiers. Many depart the scene for the more lighted areas of Jerusalem inside the gate.

At the ninth hour or 3:00 PM, the trumpet sounds from the Temple and all go quiet and face the Temple for the moment of the evening sacrifice. Just as the trumpet finishes Yeshua shouts from the cross: *"It is finished!"* John 19:30

Nicodemus and Joseph decide to remove the body of Yeshua who has died. Joseph hurries to seek permission from Pilate to bury Yeshua. Nicodemus converses with Mary and comforts the mother of Yeshua.

Nicodemus brings 75 pounds of ointments and the two, with the help of the Centurion and several soldiers, remove Yeshua from the cross, wash his body and carry him to Joseph's family tomb nearby.

Having closed the tomb, Joseph and Nicodemus along with the Roman centurion return to the city. The confessing Centurion is an interesting addition at the grave by the author. Joseph and Nicodemus return to Joseph's home and the Centurion returns to the Antonio Fortress. The book closes with Nicodemus standing on the rooftop looking out past the Shechem gate and Golgotha. As the setting sun enlightens the gruesome scene, it also warms the face of Nicodemus. He recalls the words of Yeshua, *"I am the light of the world. Whoever believes in me will never walk in darkness."* John 8:12

The ending intentionally takes place on Good Friday evening, leaving the reader to think deeply about what has just taken place and its impact on Nicodemus.

Study
Read Matthew 27:32-61 The crucifixion of Jesus Christ
1. Vs. 32-38 The Roman role in the crucifixion

2. Vs. 39-44 The Roman intention in crucifixion was not only punishment but intimidation of those contemplating revolt. These verses present the level of disdain that many religious officials had for Yeshua. Passers-by, priests, rabbis and elders mock Yeshua.

3. Vs. 45 The great 3 hours of Darkness
   Seems to be something symbolic. What might be the meaning of this?

4. Vs. 46 Matthew only includes Yeshua's 4th word from the cross. This word gives insight into the real burden Yeshua bore.

5. List the events that coincide with Yeshua's death
   a. _____

   b. _____

   c. _____

   d. _____

   e. _____

6. Matthew mentions three who were there for the burial: Joseph, Mary Magdalene, the other Mary (perhaps mother of James and Joses who was the wife of Cleopas)

Read Mark 15:21-47 The Crucifixion
1. Vs. 25 Mark adds the specific time when the crucifixion began

2. Vs. 34 Repeats only Yeshua's fourth word

3. Vs. 40 Mark adds Salome (sister of the Virgin Mary) as present. Salome was the wife of Zebedee and mother of James and John

Read Luke 23:26-56 The Crucifixion
1. Vs. 28-31 Luke adds Yeshua's words to the wailing women
What is the prophetic historical reference by Yeshua?

2 Vs. 40 Luke adds the change of heart by one criminal and Yeshua's second word to Him

3. Vs. 46 At his death Luke adds Yeshua's 7th word

Read John 19:16-42 The Crucifixion
John adds the Aramaic name for the place of crucifixion: Golgotha
1. Vs. 21 John adds the complaint of Caiaphas to Pilate

2. Vs. 22 John adds the prophecy of Psalm 22:18 concerning Yeshua's garments.
John adds those at the cross—as he was there: Virgin Mary, Salome, Mary wife of Cleopas, Mary Magdalene

3. Vs. 26, 27 John adds the third word from the cross to Mary

4. Vs. 28-30 John also adds the 5th and 6th words of Yeshua.

Vs. 28_____

Vs. 30_____

5. Vs. 36, 37 John adds also the prophecies of the piercing and no bone being broken.

Exodus 12:46   Zechariah 12:10

6. John also mentions Nicodemus presence at the cross.

Discuss the images at the cross and their meaningfulness.

a. Rejection
b. Willingness
c. Passover
d. King of the Jews
e. Blood and water
f. Gentile confession
g. Resurrection
h. Paradise
i. Forgiveness
j. Darkness
k. Light

Facts
1. It is true that a plot to execute Yeshua had been devised but it is not always mentioned that the execution of Lazarus was also planned. This is mentioned in John 12:9-11
2. Mention is made that the first three words from Yeshua at the cross all deal with the circumstances of others: those who crucified him, his mother, and the malefactor.

3. So many things took place at 3:00 PM as Yeshua breathes his last, cries out with a loud voice: "It is finished." The darkness ceased and suddenly there was sunshine! The trumpet sounded from the Temple signifying the evening sacrifice! There was a great earthquake! Saints were resurrected! Yeshua dies! The Centurion declares him to be the Son of God!

Fiction
1. While a plot against Lazarus is factual, the author adds the kidnapping of Mary and Martha with the intent to intimidate Yeshua and drive him out of Judea. The latter plan is not mentioned in Scripture and no historian mentions anything of the kind. The author adds the escape plan hatched by Nicodemus to hide the three in Jericho in one of the rental homes of Zacchaeus.
2. There is no evidence to suggest that the Roman soldiers helped with the burial of Yeshua but certainly they were the ones who knew how to extract the long iron nails from the hands and feet so it is possible they remained to finish this gruesome task with Joseph and Nicodemus.

Embellishment
1. In Matthew 21:15 it mentions that children sang praises to Yeshua in the Temple courts. The author adds the sons of Nicodemus as those who sang.
2. Luke 22:7-13 mentions that Yeshua sent Peter and John into the city to find a man carrying a water jar and ask him for a place where they can prepare a room for them to celebrate Passover and make everything ready. Tradition has held that this was the home of John Mark but the author inserts the servant of Nicodemus as the one who meets Peter and John and Yeshua and his disciples ask for Nicodemus home. Nicodemus readily agrees and moves in with Joseph of Arimathea for Passover.
3. A number of events that took place on Passover evening are not noted, including Jesus in Prayer at Gethsemane, Judas betrayal, trial before Caiaphas, Pilate, Herod and the scourging of Yeshua.

We meet him as Nicodemus and Joseph awake the morning after Passover and discover Yeshua has been arrested and is about to be taken for crucifixion. This scenario removes Nicodemus and Joseph from the illegal trail of the Sanhedrin condemning Yeshua for blasphemy.

4. A confrontation between the Centurion and Caiaphas who objects to the inscription above the head of Yeshua is added. Implied is that this centurion might actually be from Galilee and is the same centurion who built the synagogue in Capernaum. He is given a Galilean accent and speaks Aramaic in accosting Caiaphas. It is interesting to consider that the many (often 480 soldiers) Roman soldiers called in as reinforcements for Passover might have included this Centurion from Capernaum.

5. The darkness that covered the whole land for three hours must have created a lot of fear among the witnesses of the crucifixion. The author plays on this, has many flee into the city and emphasizes the superstition of the Romans.

6. The author adds a conversation between Nicodemus and the Virgin Mary and Mary the wife of Cleopas.

7. We know that Nicodemus and Joseph of Arimathea buried the body of Yeshua and some of the women were also present. It was normal practice for women to come to the tomb separately from the men, who performed this grim task. Luke 23:55, 56 indicates that the women followed but does not specify that they assisted with the burial, only that they witnessed the body of Yeshua in the tomb.

8. We don't, of course, know what Nicodemus and Joseph do after this as they are never mentioned again specifically in Scripture. The author has them return to Joseph's nearby home and contemplate the events that they have just witnessed. It must have been a terribly traumatic experience that could send someone into shock. The book concludes with Nicodemus on the rooftop of Joseph's home, facing the glow of the setting sun, contemplating what has been the theme of his life: The Light!

Made in the USA
Monee, IL
01 February 2022

99849127R00154